THE LONG
TOMORROW

OTHER CAEZIK NOTABLES TITLES
www.CaezikSF.com

Friday by Robert A. Heinlein

Midnight at the Well of Souls by Jack L. Chalker

The Long Tomorrow by Leigh Brackett

Double Star by Robert A. Heinlein

Bolo: Annals of the Dinochrome Brigade by Keith Laumer

The Warlock in Spite of Himself by Christopher Stasheff

Dark Universe by Daniel F. Galouye

Norstrilia by Cordwainer Smith

THE LONG TOMORROW

LEIGH BRACKETT

NOTABLES

ARC MANOR
ROCKVILLE, MARYLAND

＊

SHAHID MAHMUD
PUBLISHER

www.CaezikSF.com

This is a work of fiction.

Cover art by Christina P. Myrvold; artstation.com/christin

ISBN: 978-1-64710-031-5

First CAEZIK Notables Edition.
2023
2 3 4 5 6 7 8 9 10

CA≡ZIK
NOTABLES

An imprint of Arc Manor LLC

www.CaezikSF.com

Contents

INTRODUCTION

WRITER OF WONDERS
by Howard Andrew Jones

It was a young woman who introduced me to Leigh Brackett. I don't remember the date, but it must have been in the late 1970s that my teenaged sister, my elder by nine years, loaned me Leigh Brackett's Skaith books. Neither of us knew about Brackett's long history in the genre, or her years of writing Western screenplays, or even that she had sometimes drafted episodes of one of the detective shows we watched with our father, *The Rockford Files.* In those days I don't recall anyone talking much about Brackett having written the first draft of *The Empire Strikes Back*, either. Certainly neither of us talked about it.

All my sister Allison knew was that the Eric John Stark series was pretty swell, and all I knew was that she and I had similar taste and I trusted her judgment. So soon I was pouring over the books and wandering Skaith with a grizzled loner from beyond the stars, searching a dying planet for his foster father with the aid of some colorful locals, not the least of which were some oversized telepathic hounds. It was grand stuff.

According to her husband, the science-fiction-great Edmond Hamilton, Leigh Brackett grew up a sunburned tomboy with a vivid imagination, one given to playing pirates on the beach near her grandfather's home until she was gifted a copy of Edgar Rice Burroughs *The Gods of Mars.*

It is hard not to overstate the influence once cast by Burroughs over two or three generations of readers and future writers. He may not be mostly forgotten, like his influential contemporaries A. Merritt and Lord Dunsany, but he's chiefly remembered now as the creator of Tarzan. When Brackett was young, and for many decades thereafter, Burroughs was much more than that. Among science fiction fans, his creations towered over the imaginary landscape like a juggernaut, rather like *Star Wars*, the Marvel cinematic universe, and *Game of Thrones* all rolled up into one.

Certainly his Mars burned an indelible imprint upon the imagination of Leigh Brackett, who was soon writing her own version of a dying, desert planet fourth from Sol with lost tombs, ancient, decadent canal cities, and jaded wanderers from Terra. To Burroughs's swashbuckling warrior cultures Brackett added grim back alleys and a hard-boiled economy, using precise language that could soar to poetic heights. In her fiction of a Mars and Venus that never were, as well as her short stories and novellas in deeper space, she gave us rogues and outlaws who would have been right at home in today's science-fiction-adventure extravaganzas. Brackett was a trailblazer.

Regrettably, the real planet Mars has neither a breathable atmosphere nor an ancient culture of canal cities, and when that truth became known by scientists and science fiction readers, Leigh Brackett was forced by the market to cease writing tales set in her wonderful, fading Mars and jungle-rich Venus. However, she didn't completely abandon Eric John Stark, but sent him on to a planet beyond our solar system for three book-length adventures, which is how I first met him—and experienced the power of Brackett's prose.

I discovered my love of reading through science fiction, and for years it was as a science fiction reader that I loved Leigh Brackett. Some have looked down their noses at her for being an adventure writer—something I think would have amused her, for she always said she loved swashbuckling stuff and was bored to tears by domestic drama—but these seem to be the kind of critics who don't realize it's not so much a genre that marks fiction as good or bad, but the crafting of the prose. And as her husband said, upon reading her magazine fiction before their marriage, "this gal can *write!*"

He was neither the first nor the last to note that. Howard Hawks famously requested that Brackett "guy" be brought in to help the writing of the screen adaption of Raymond Chandler's *The Big Sleep*, mostly on the strength of Brackett's dialogue in her first detective novel, *No Good from a Corpse*. It was a partnership that was to endure over the course of many years, and launch her onto a career path that would see her working on famed movies with other luminaries like John Wayne and Robert Altman.

For all her successes in Hollywood, Brackett rarely had a secure position in the studios. She continually ran up against writer's strikes, dissolving production companies, or other entanglements, which is why she was always ready to try her hand at other kinds of writing, like her Western novel *Follow the Free Wind* (centered upon the real-life Jim Beckwourth,

Indian trader and scout), additional detective novels, science fiction short stories, television scripts, and *The Long Tomorrow*.

The 1950s are remembered for many things, not the least of which was the omnipresent Cold War and its threat of nuclear war via fission bomb, which could destroy cities and incinerate thousands of human beings at or near a drop zone—in addition to bathing an area in radiation.

Brackett and her husband, Edmond Hamilton, lived for most of their married lives in Kinsman, Ohio, a community surrounded by Amish farmland. At some point in the late 1940s or early 1950s, she thought that if there was one group likely to survive a fission bomb war, it was the Amish. Thus was born the seed of *The Long Tomorrow*, widely credited as one of the very first pastoral apocalypse novels, wherein the survivors of a nuclear war have settled in the countryside to live as our forefathers had. Brackett's people have taken up Amish and Mennonite ways of life and worship, and shun both scientific progress and big settlements (under the book's Thirtieth Amendment, no cities can be built that house more than one thousand people).

Our guide to this culture is young Len Colter, aided and egged on by his older cousin Esau, who is more desperate even than Len to seek hidden knowledge and uncover lost wisdom. Before long, they choose to leave the world they know in search of fabled Bartorstown, a city where men still revere learning and understand the secrets of the past.

More than fifty years after its writing, *The Long Tomorrow* still evades easy categorization. It begins almost like a boy's-own adventure story, but while Len grows and has experience as he journeys, they aren't swashbuckling adventures a la Rafael Sabatini so much as painful experiences that enable him to come to grips with his life's path. It might seem that the book will grow into a kind of buddy novel, but over the course of the story both Len and the reader better understand Esau has always been a selfish ass, one incapable of true growth.

This tale, however, is not a black-and-white depiction of the evils of a pretechnological society versus one that is more advanced. Although we see the savage fear and hate of Len's people toward progress and change, we also see their kindness, most especially in Len's wonderful father, which is among the most sympathetic portrayals of a patriarch in science fiction literature.

Leigh Brackett didn't leave much comment about the book or what she wanted readers to take away from it. Initially, I was disappointed it wasn't the kind of adventure story I'd expected after I'd fallen in love with her other fiction. But on revisiting the book I found it to be a window into discussion about the nature of humanity and the perils of the different kind of societies we build, as well as the ways we find faith. Some of Brackett's characters may preach, but she does not, to the extent that it's not entirely clear what her own stance is—merely that she might want us to do some thinking about our own viewpoint.

While the book is strangely resonant in some ways, it can't help but be dated in others—the high technology hidden in Bartorstown no longer seems sophisticated to those of us who routinely carry powerful computers in our pockets, and there are virtually no female characters with much agency or personality. But then we shouldn't fault Brackett for not better imagining technological breakthroughs, nor for following the mold of many science fiction writers of her generation—where men were the ones having adventures. In any case, few characters in this book are important beyond Len, male or female, for during this time period it was society rather than individuals that was her particular focus.

Rather than saying much more, I think it's time for me to step aside and let you draw your own conclusions as you revisit this work, or maybe even read it for the first time. I think you'll find much to love. But then, as a wise man said, this gal can write!

THE LONG TOMORROW

"No city, no town, no community of more than one thousand people or two hundred buildings to the square mile shall be built or permitted to exist anywhere in the United States of America."

—*CONSTITUTION OF THE UNITED STATES, Thirtieth Amendment*

BOOK ONE

ONE

Len Colter sat in the shade under the wall of the horse barn, eating pone and sweet butter and contemplating a sin. He was fourteen years old, and he had lived all of them on the farm at Piper's Run, where opportunities for real sinning were comfortably few. But now Piper's Run was more than thirty miles away, and he was having a look at the world, bright with distractions and gaudy with possibilities. He was at the Canfield Fair. And for the first time in his life Len Colter was faced with a major decision.

He was finding it difficult.

"Pa will beat the daylights out of me," he said, "if he finds out."

Cousin Esau said, "You scared?" He had turned fifteen just three weeks ago, which meant that he would not have to go to school any more with the children. He was still a long way from being counted among the men, but it was a big step and Len was impressed by it. Esau was taller than Len, and he had dark eyes that glittered and shone all the time like the eyes of an unbroken colt, looking everywhere for something and never quite finding it, perhaps because he did not know yet what it was. His hands were restless and very clever.

"Well?" demanded Esau. "Are you?"

Len would have liked to lie, but he knew that Esau would not be fooled for a minute. He squirmed a little, ate the last bite of pone, sucked the butter off his fingers, and said, "Yes."

"Huh," said Esau. "I thought you were getting grown-up. You should have still stayed home with the babies this year. Afraid of a licking!"

"I've had lickings before," said Len, "and if you think Pa can't lay 'em on, you try it some time. And I ain't even cried the last two years now. Well, not much, anyway." He brooded, his knees hunched up and his hands crossed on top of them, and his chin on his hands. He was a thin, healthy, rather solemn-faced boy. He wore homespun trousers and sturdy hand-pegged boots, covered thick in dust, and a shirt of coarse-loomed cotton with a narrow neckband and no collar. His hair was a light brown, cut off square above the shoulders and again above the eyes, and on his head he wore a brown flat-crowned hat with a wide brim.

Len's people were New Mennonites, and they wore brown hats to distinguish themselves from the original Old Mennonites, who wore black ones. Back in the Twentieth Century, only two generations before, there had been just the Old Mennonites and Amish, and only a few tens of thousands of them, and they had been regarded as quaint and queer because they held to the old simple handcraft ways and would have no part of cities or machines. But when the cities ended, and men found that in the changed world these of all folk were best fitted to survive, the Mennonites had swiftly multiplied into the millions they now counted.

"No," said Len slowly, "it's not the licking I'm scared of. It's Pa. You know how he feels about these preachin's. He forbid me. And Uncle David forbid you. You know how they feel. I don't think I want Pa mad at me, not that mad."

"He can't do no more than lick you," Esau said.

Len shook his head. "I don't know."

"Well, all right. Don't go, then."

"You going, for sure?"

"For sure. But I don't need you."

Esau leaned back against the wall and appeared to have forgotten Len, who moved the toes of his boots back and forth to make two stubby fans in the dust and continued to brood. The warm air was heavy with the smell of feed and animals, laced through with wood smoke and the fragrance of cooking. There were voices in the air, too, many voices, all blended together into a humming noise. You could think it was like a swarm of bees, or a wind rising and falling in the jack pines, but it was more than that. It was the world talking.

Esau said, "They fall down on the ground and scream and roll."

Len breathed deep, and his insides quivered. The fairgrounds stretched away into immensity on all sides, crammed with wagons and carts and sheds and stock and people, and this was the last day. One more night lying under the wagon, wrapped up tight against the September chill, watching the fires burn red and mysterious and wondering about the strangers who slept around them. Tomorrow the wagon would rattle away, back to Piper's Run, and he would not see such a thing again for another year. Perhaps never. In the midst of life we are in death. Or he might break a leg next year, or Pa might make him stay home like Brother James had had to this time, to see to Granma and the stock.

"Women, too," said Esau.

Len hugged his knees tighter. "How do you know? You never been."

"I heard."

"Women," whispered Len. He shut his eyes, and behind the lids there were pictures of wild preachings such as a New Mennonite never heard, of great smoking fires and vague frenzies and a figure, much resembling Ma in her bonnet and voluminous homespun skirts, lying on the ground and kicking like Baby Esther having a tantrum. Temptation came upon him, and he was lost.

He stood up, looking down at Esau. He said, "I'll go."

"Ah," said Esau. He got up too. He held out his hand, and Len shook it. They nodded at each other and grinned. Len's heart was pounding and he had a guilty feeling as though Pa stood right behind him listening to every word, but there was an exhilaration in this, too. There was a denial of authority, an assertion of self, a sense of being. He felt suddenly that he had grown several inches and broadened out, and that Esau's eyes showed a new respect.

"When do we go?" he asked.

"After dark, late. You be ready. I'll let you know."

The wagons of the Colter brothers were drawn up side by side, so that would not be hard. Len nodded.

"I'll pretend like I'm asleep, but I won't be."

"Better not," said Esau. His grip tightened, enough to squeeze Len's knuckles together so he'd remember. "Just don't let on about this, Lennie."

"Ow," said Len, and stuck his lip out angrily. "What do you think I am, a baby?"

Esau grinned, lapsing into the easy comradeship that is becoming between men. "'Course not. That's settled, then. Let's go look over the horses again. I might want to give my dad some advice about that black mare he's thinking of trading for."

They walked together along the side of the horse barn. It was the biggest barn Len had ever seen, four or five times as long as the one at home. The old siding had been patched a good bit, and it was all weathered now to an even gray, but here and there where the original wood was projected you could still see a smudge of red paint. Len looked at it, and then he paused and looked around the fairground, screwing up his eyes so that everything danced and quivered.

"What you doing now?" demanded Esau impatiently.

"Trying to see."

"Well, you can't see with your eyes shut. Anyway, what do you mean, trying to see?"

"How the buildings looked when they were all painted like Gran said. Remember? When she was a little girl."

"Yeah," said Esau. "Some red, some white. They must have been something." He squinted his eyes up too. The sheds and the buildings blurred, but remained unpainted.

"Anyway," said Len stoutly, giving up, "I bet they never had a fair as big as this one before, ever."

"What are you talking about?" Esau said. "Why, Gran said there was a million people here, and a million of those automobiles or cars or whatever you called them, all lined up in rows as far as you could see, with the sun just blazing on the shiny parts. A million of 'em!"

"Aw," said Len, "there couldn't be. Where'd they all have room to camp?"

"Dummy, they didn't have to camp. Gran said they came here from Piper's Run in less than an hour, and they went back the same day."

"I know that's what Gran said," Len remarked thoughtfully. "But do you really believe it?"

"Sure I believe it!" Esau's dark eyes snapped. "I wish I'd lived in those days. I'd have done things."

"Like what?"

"Like driving one of those cars, *fast*. Like even flying, maybe."

"Esau!" said Len, deeply shocked. "Better not let your pa hear you say that."

Esau flushed a little and muttered that he was not afraid, but he glanced around uneasily. They turned the corner of the barn. On the gable end, up above the door, there were four numbers made out of pieces of wood and nailed on. Len looked up at them. A one, a nine with a chunk gone out of the tail, a five, with the little front part missing, and a two. Esau said that was the year the barn was built, and that would be before even Gran was born. It made Len think of the meetinghouse in Piper's Run—Gran still called it a church—that had a date on it too, hidden way down behind the lilac bushes. That one said 1842—before, Len thought, almost anybody was born. He shook his head, overcome with a sense of the ancientness of the world.

They went in and looked at the horses, talking wisely of withers and cannon bones but keeping out of the way of the men who stood in small groups in front of this stall and that, with slow words and very quick eyes. They were almost all New Mennonites, differing from Len and Esau only in size and in the splendid beards that fanned across their chests, though their upper lips were clean shaven. A few, however, wore full whiskers and slouch hats of various sorts, and their clothes were cut to no particular pattern. Len stared at these furtively, with an intense curiosity. These men, or others like them—perhaps even still other kinds of men that he had not seen yet—were the ones who met secretly in fields and woods and preached and yelled and rolled on the ground. He could hear Pa's voice saying, "A man's religion, his sect, is his own affair. But those people have no religion or sect. They're a mob, with a mob's fear and cruelty, and with half-crazy, cunning men stirring them up against others." And then getting close-lipped and grim when Len questioned further and saying, "You're forbidden to go, that's all. No God-fearing person takes part in such wickedness." He understood now, and no wonder Pa hadn't wanted to talk about those women rolling on the ground and probably showing their drawers and everything. Len shivered with excitement and wished it would come night.

Esau decided that although the black mare in question was a trifle ewe-necked she looked as though she would handle well in harness, though his own choice would have been the fine bay stallion at the top of the row. And wouldn't he just take a cart flying! But you had to think of the women, who needed something safe and gentle. Len agreed, and they wandered out again, and Esau said, "Let's see what they're doing about those cows."

They meant Pa and Uncle David, and Len discovered that he would rather not see Pa just now. So he suggested going down to the traders' wagons instead. Cows you could and did see all the time. But traders' wagons were another matter. Three, four times in a summer, maybe, you saw one in Piper's Run, and here there were nineteen of them all together in one place at the same time.

"Besides," said Len with pure and simple greed, "you never can tell. Mr. Hostetter might give us some more of those sugar nuts."

"Fat chance," said Esau. But he went.

The traders' wagons were all drawn up in a line, their tongues outward and their backs in against a long shed. They were enormous wagons, with canvas tilts and all sorts of things hung to their ribs inside, so they were like dim, odorous caves on wheels.

Len looked at them, wide-eyed. To him they were not wagons, they were adventurous ships that had voyaged here from afar. He had listened to the traders' casual talk, and it had given him a vague vision of the whole wide and cityless land, the green, slow, comfortable agrarian land, in which only a very few old folk could remember the awesome cities that had dominated the world before the Destruction. His mind held a blurred jumble of the faraway places of which the traders spoke: the little shipping settlements and fishing hamlets along the Atlantic, the lumber camps of the Appalachians, these endless New Mennonite farm lands of the Midwest, the southern hunters and hill farmers, the great rivers westward with their barges and boats, the plains beyond and the horsemen and ranches and herds of wild cattle, the lofty mountains and the land and sea still farther west. A land as wide now as it had been centuries before, and through its dusty roads and sleepy villages these great trader wagons rolled, and rested, and rolled again.

Mr. Hostetter's wagon was the fifth one down, and Len knew it very well, because Mr. Hostetter brought it to Piper's Run every spring on his way north and again every fall on his way south, and he had been doing that for more years than Len could personally remember. Other traders dropped through haphazardly, but Mr. Hostetter seemed like one of their own, though he had come from somewhere in Pennsylvania. He wore the same flat brown hat and the same beard, and went to meeting when he happened to be there on the Sabbath, and he had rather disappointed Len by telling him that where he came from was no different from where Len came from except that there were mountains around it, which did not seem right for a place with a magical name like Pennsylvania.

"If," said Len, harking back to the sugar nuts, "we offered to feed and water his team—" One could not beg, but the laborer is worthy of his hire.

Esau shrugged. "We can try."

The long shed, open on its front but closed in back to afford protection from rain, was partitioned off into stalls, one for each wagon. There wasn't much left in them now, after two and a half days, but women were still bargaining over copper kettles, and knives from the village forges of the East, or bolts of cotton cloth brought up from the South, or clocks from New England. The bulk cane sugar, Len knew, had gone early, but he was hoping that Mr. Hostetter had held onto a few small treasures for the sake of old friends.

"Huh," said Esau. "Look at that."

Mr. Hostetter's stall was empty and deserted.

"Sold out."

Len stared at the stall, frowning. Then he said, "His team still have to eat, don't they? And maybe we can help load stuff in the wagon. Let's go out back."

They went through the doorway at the rear of the stall, ducking around under the tailboard of the wagon and on past its side. The great wheels with the six-inch iron tires stood higher than Len did, and the canvas tilt loomed up like a cloud overhead, with EDW. HOSTETTER, GENERAL MERCHANDISE painted on it in neat letters faded to gray by the sun and rain.

"He's here," said Len. "I can hear him talking."

Esau nodded. They went past the front wheel. Mr. Hostetter was just opposite, on the other side of the wagon.

"You're crazy," said Mr. Hostetter. "I'm telling you—"

The voice of another man interrupted. "Don't worry so much, Ed. It's all right. I've got to—"

The man broke off short as Len and Esau came around the front of the wagon. He was facing them across Mr. Hostetter's shoulder, a tall lean young fellow with long ginger hair and a full beard, dressed in plain leather. He was a trader from somewhere down South, and Len had seen him before in the shed. The name on his wagon tilt was William Soames.

"Company," he said to Mr. Hostetter. He did not seem to mind, but Mr. Hostetter turned around. He was a big man, large-jointed and awkward, very brown in the skin and blue in the eyes, and with two wide streaks of gray in his sandy beard, one on each side of his mouth. His movements were always slow and his smile was always friendly. But now he turned around fast, and he was not smiling at all, and Len stopped as though something had hit him. He stared at Mr. Hostetter as at a stranger, and Mr. Hostetter looked at him with a queer kind of a hot, blank glare. And Esau muttered, "I guess they're busy, Len. We better go."

"What do you want?" said Hostetter.

"Nothing," said Len. "We just thought maybe …." He let his voice trail off.

"Maybe what?"

"We could feed your horses," said Len, feebly.

Esau caught him by the arm. "He wanted more of those sugar nuts," he said to Hostetter. "You know how kids are. Come on, Len."

Soames laughed. "Don't reckon he's got any more. But how would some pecans do? Mighty fine!"

He reached into his pocket and pulled out four or five nuts. He put them in Len's hand. Len said, "Thank you," looking from him to Mr. Hostetter, who said quietly, "My team's all taken care of. Run along now, boys."

"Yes, sir," said Len, and ran. Esau loped at his heels. When they were around the corner of the shed they stopped and shared out the pecans.

"What was the matter with *him*?" he asked, meaning Hostetter. He was as astonished as though old Shep back at the farm had turned and snarled at him.

"Aw," said Esau, cracking the thin brown shells, "he and the foreigner were rowing over some trading deal, that's all." He was mad at Hostetter, so he gave Len a good hard shove. "You and your sugar nuts! Come on, it's almost time for supper. Or have you forgotten we're going somewhere tonight?"

"No," said Len, and something pricked with a delightful pain inside his belly. "I ain't forgotten."

TWO

That nervous pricking in his middle was all that kept Len awake at first, after he had rolled up for the night under the family wagon. The outside air was chilly, the blanket was warm, he was comfortably full of supper, and it had been a long day. His eyelids would droop and things would get dim and far away, all washed over with a pleasant darkness. Then *pung*! would go that particular nerve, warning him, and he would tense up again, remembering Esau and the preaching.

After a while he began to hear things. Ma and Pa snored in the wagon overhead, and the fairgrounds were dark except for burned-out coals of the fires. They should have been quiet. But they were not. Horses moved and harnesses jingled. He heard a light cart go with a creak and a rattle, and way off somewhere a heavy wagon groaned on its way, the team snorting as they pulled. The strange people, the non-Mennonites like the gingery trader in his buckskin clothes, had all left just after sundown, heading for the preaching place. But these were other people going, people who did not want to be seen. Len stopped being sleepy. He listened to the unseen hoofs and the stealthy wheels, and he began to wish that he had not agreed to go.

He sat up cross-legged under the wagon bed, the blanket pulled around his shoulders. Esau had not come yet. Len stared across at Uncle David's wagon, hoping maybe Esau had gone to sleep himself. It was a long way, and cold and dark, and they would get caught sure. Besides that, he had felt guilty all through supper, not wanting to look straight at Pa. It was the first time he had, deliberately and of choice, disobeyed his father, and he knew the guilt must show all over his face. But Pa hadn't noticed it, and somehow that made Len feel worse instead of better. It meant Pa trusted him so much that he never bothered to look for it.

There was a stir in the shadows under Uncle David's wagon, and it was Esau, coming quietly on all fours.

I'll tell him, thought Len. I'll say I won't go.

Esau crept closer. He grinned, and his eyes shone bright in the glow of the banked-up fire. He put his head close to Len's and whispered, "They're all asleep. Roll your blanket up like you were still in it, just in case."

I won't go, thought Len. But the words never came out of his mouth. He rolled up his blanket and slid away after Esau, into the night. And right away, as soon as he was out of sight of the wagon, he was glad. The darkness was full of motion, of a going and a secret excitement, and he was going too. The taste of wickedness was sweet in his mouth, and the stars had never looked so bright.

They went carefully until they came to an open lane, and then they began to run. A high-wheeled cart raced by them, the horse stepping high and fast, and Esau panted, "Come on, come on!" He laughed, and Len laughed, running. In a few minutes they were out of the fairgrounds and on the main road, deep in dust from three rainless weeks. Dust hung in the air, roiled up by the passing wheels and roiled again before it could settle. A team of horses loomed up in it, huge and ghostly, shaking foam off their bits. They were pulling a wagon with an open tilt, and the man who drove them looked like a blacksmith, with thick arms and a short blond beard. There was a stout red-cheeked woman beside him. She had a rag tied over her head instead of a bonnet and her skirts blew out on the wind. From under the tied-up edge of the tilt there looked a row of little heads, all yellow as corn silk. Esau ran fast beside the wagon, shouting, with Len pounding along behind him. The man pulled down his horses and squinted at them. The woman looked too, and they both laughed.

"Lookit 'em," the man said. "Little flat-hats. Where you goin' without your mama, little flat-hats?"

"We're going to the preaching," Esau said, mad about the flat-hat and madder still about the little, but not mad enough to lose the chance of a lift. "May we ride with you?"

"Why not?" said the man, and laughed again. He said some stuff about Gentiles and Samaritans that Len did not quite understand, and some more about listening to a Word, and then he told them to get in, that they were late already. The horses had not stopped all this time, and Len and Esau were floundering in the roadside briers, keeping up. They scrambled in over the tailboard and lay gasping on the straw that was there, and the man yelled to the horses and they were off again, banging and bumping and the dust flying up through the cracks in the floor boards. The straw was dusty. There was a big dog in it, and seven kids, all staring at Len and Esau with round-eyed hostility. They stared back, and then the oldest boy pointed and said, "Looka the funny hats." They all laughed. Esau asked, "What's it to you?" and the boy said, "This's our wagon, that's what's it to me, and if you don't like it you can get out." They went on making fun of their clothes, and Len glowered, thinking that they didn't have much room to talk. They were all seven barefoot and had no hats at all, though they looked thrifty enough, and clean. He didn't say anything back, though, and neither did Esau. Three or four miles was a long way to walk at night.

The dog was friendly. He licked their faces all over and sat on them impartially, all the way to the preaching ground. And Len wondered if the woman on the wagon seat would get down on the ground and roll, and if the man would roll with her. He thought how silly they would look, and giggled, and suddenly he was not mad at the yellow-haired kids any more.

The wagon came in finally among many others in a very large open field that sloped down toward a little river, running maybe twenty feet wide now with the dry weather, and low between its banks. Len thought there must be as many people as there had been at the fair, only they were all crowded together, the rigs jammed in a rough circle at the back and everybody gathered in the center, sitting on the ground. One flat-bed wagon, with the horses unhitched, was pulled close to the riverbank. Everybody was facing it, and a man was standing on it, in the light of a huge bonfire. He was a young man, tall and big-chested. His black beard came down almost to his waist, shiny as a crow's breast in the spring, and he kept shaking it as he moved around, tossing his head and shouting. His voice was high and piercing, and it did not come in a continuous flow of words. It came in short sharp pieces that stabbed the air, each one, clear to the farthest rows before the next one was flung out. It was a minute before Len realized the man was preaching. He was used to a different way of it in Sabbath meeting, when Pa or Uncle David or anybody could get up and speak to God, or about Him. They always did it quietly, with their hands folded.

He had been staring out over the side of the wagon. Now, before the wheels had fairly stopped turning, Esau punched him and said, "Come on." He jumped out over the tailboard. Len followed him. The man called something after them about the Word, and all seven of the kids made faces. Len said politely, "Thank you for the ride." Then he ran after Esau.

From here the preaching man looked small and far away, and Len couldn't hear much of what he said. Esau whispered, "I think we can get right up close, but don't make any noise." Len nodded. They scuttled around behind the parked rigs, and Len noticed that there were others who seemed to want to remain out of sight. They hung back on the edges of the crowd, in among the wagons, and Len could see them only as dark shapes silhouetted against the firelight. Some of them had taken their hats off, but the cut of their clothes and hair still gave them away. They were of Len's own people. He knew how they felt. He had a shyness himself about being seen.

As he and Esau worked their way down toward the river, the voice of the preaching man grew louder. There was something strident about it, and stirring, like the scream of an angry stallion. His words came clearer.

"—went a-whoring after strange gods. You know that, my friends. Your own parents have told you, your own old grannies and your aged grandpas have confessed it, how that the hearts of the people were full of wickedness, and blasphemies, and lust—"

Len's skin prickled with excitement. He followed Esau in and out through a confusion of wheels and horses' legs, holding his breath. And finally they were where they could see out from the shelter of a good black shadow between the wheels of a cart, and the preacher was only a few yards away.

"They lusted, my brethren. They lusted after everything strange, and new, and unnatural. And Satan saw that they did and he blinded their eyes, the heavenly eyes of the soul, so that they were like foolish children, crying after the luxuries and the soul-rotting pleasures. And they forgot God."

A moaning and a rocking swept over the people who sat on the ground. Len caught hold of a wheel spoke in each hand and thrust his face between them.

The preaching man sprang to the very edge of the wagon. The night wind shook out his beard and his long black hair, and behind him the fire burned and shot up smoke and sparks, and the preaching man's eyes burned too, huge and black. He flung his arm out straight, pointing at the people, and said in a curious harsh whisper that carried like a cry, "*They forgot God!*"

Again the rocking and the moaning. It was louder this time. Len's heart had begun to pound.

"Yes, my brethren. They forgot. But did God forget? No, I tell you, He did not forget! He watched them. He saw their iniquities. He saw how the Devil had hold on them, and He saw that they liked it—yes, my friends, they liked old Satan the Betrayer, and they would not leave his ways for the ways of God. And why? Because Satan's ways were easy and smooth, and there was always some new luxury just around the next bend in the downward path."

Len became conscious of Esau, crouched beside him in the dust. He was staring at the preaching man, and his eyes glittered. His mouth was open wide. Len's pulses hammered. The voice of the preaching man seemed to flick him like a whip on nerves he had never known he had before. He forgot about Esau. He hung to his wheelspokes and thought hungrily, Go on, go on!

"And so what did God do, when He saw that His children had turned from Him? You know what He did, my brethren! You know!"

Moan and rock, and the moaning became a low strange howl.

"He said, 'They have sinned! They have sinned against My laws, and against My prophets, who warned them even in old Jerusalem against the luxuries of Egypt and of Babylon! And they have exalted themselves in their pride. They have climbed up into the heavens which are My throne, and they have rent open the earth which is My footstool, and they have loosed the sacred fire which lies at the very heart of things, and which only I, the Lord Jehovah, should dare to touch.' And God said, 'Even so, I am merciful. Let them be cleansed of their sin.'"

The howling rose louder, and all across the open field there was a tossing of arms and a writhing of heads.

"Let them be cleansed!" cried the preaching man. His body was strained up, quivering, and the sparks shot up past him. "God said it, and they were cleansed, my brethren! With their own sins they were chastised. They were burned with the fires of their own making, yea, and the proud towers vanished in the blazing of the wrath of God! And with fire and famine and thirst and fear they were driven from their cities, from the places of iniquity and lust, even our own fathers and our fathers' fathers, who had sinned, and the places of iniquity were made not, even as Sodom and Gomorrah."

Somewhere across the crowd a woman screamed and fell backward, beating her head against the earth. Len never noticed.

The voice of the preaching man sank down again to that harsh far-carrying whisper.

"And so we were spared of God's mercy, to find His way and follow it."

"Hallelujah," screamed the crowd. "Hallelujah!"

The preaching man held up his hands. The crowd quieted. Len held his breath, waiting. His eyes were fixed on the black burning eyes of the man on the wagon. He saw them narrow down, until they looked like the eyes of a cat just ready to spring, only they were the wrong color.

"But," said the preaching man, "Satan is still with us."

The rows of people jerked forward with a feral yelp, held down and under by the hands of the preacher.

"He wants us back. He remembers what it was like, the Devil does, when he had all those soft fair women to serve him, and all the rich men, and the cities all shining with lights to be his shrines! He remembers, and he wants them back! So he sends his emissaries among us—oh, you wouldn't know them from your own God-fearing folk, my brethren, with their meek ways and sober garments! But they go about secretly proselyting, tempting our boys and young men, dangling the forbidden serpent's fruit in front of them, and on the brow of every one of them is the mark of the beast—the mark of Bartorstown!"

Len pricked his ears up higher at that. He had heard the name of Bartorstown just once before, from Granma, and he remembered it because of the way Pa had shut her up. The crowd yowled, and some of them got up on their feet. Esau pressed up closer against Len, and he was quivering all over. "Ain't this something?" he whispered. "Ain't this something!"

The preaching man looked all around. He didn't quiet the people this time, he let them quiet down of themselves, out of their eagerness to hear what he had to say next. And Len sensed something new in the air. He did not know what it was, but it excited him so he wanted to scream and leap up and down, and at the same time it made him uneasy. It was something these people understood, they and the preaching man together.

"Now," said the man on the wagon, quietly, "there are some sects, all God-fearing folk, I'm not saying they don't try, that think it's enough to say to one of these emissaries of Satan, 'Go, leave our community, and don't come back.' Now maybe they just don't understand that what they're really saying is, 'Go, and corrupt somebody else, we'll keep our own house clean'!" A sharp downward wave of his hands stifled a cry from the people as though he had shoved a cork in their mouths. "No, my friends. That is not our way. We think of our neighbor as ourself. We honor the government law that says there shall be no more cities. And we honor the Word of God, who saith that if our right eye offend us we must pluck it out, and if our right hand offend us we must cut it off, and that the righteous can have no part with evil men, no, not if they be our own brothers or fathers or sons!"

A noise went up from the people now that turned Len hot all over and closed up his throat and made his eyeballs prick. Somebody threw wood on the bonfire. It roared up a torrent of sparks and a yellow glaring of flame, and there were people rolling on the ground now, men and women both, clawing up the dirt with their fingers and screaming. Their eyes were all white, and it was not funny. And over the crowd and the firelight went the voice of the preaching man, howling shrill and mighty like a great animal in the night.

"If there be evil among you, cast it forth!"

A lank boy with the beard just sprouting on his chin leaped up. He pointed. He cried out, "I accuse him!" and the froth ran wet in the corners of his mouth.

There was a sudden violent surge in one place. A man had sprung up and tried to run, and others caught him. Their shoulders heaved and their legs danced, and the people around them hunkered out of the way, pushing and tugging at them. They dragged the man back finally, and Len got a clear look at him. It was the ginger-haired trader William Soames. But his face was different now, pale and still and awful.

The preaching man yelled something about root and branch. He was crouched on the edge of the wagon now, his hands high in the air. They began to strip the trader. They tore the stout leather shirt off his back and they ripped the buckskin breeches from his legs, exposing him white and stark. He wore soft boots on his feet and one of these came off, and the other they forgot and left on him. Then they drew back away from him, so that he was all alone in the middle of an open space. Somebody threw a stone.

It hit Soames on the mouth. He reeled over a little and put up his arms, but another stone came, and another, and sticks and clods of earth, and his white skin was all blotched and streaked. He turned this way and that, falling, stumbling, doubling up, trying to find a way out, trying to ward off the blows. His mouth was open and his teeth showed with the blood running over them and down into his beard, but Len couldn't hear whether he cried out or not because of the noise the crowd was making, a gasping screeching greedy obscene gabble, and the stones kept hitting him. Then the whole mob began to move toward the river, driving him. He came close past the cart, past the shadow where Len was watching through the spokes, and Len saw clearly into his eyes. The men came after him, their boots striking heavy on the dusty ground, and the women came too, with their hair flying and the stones in their hands. Soames fell down the bank into the shallow river. The men and women went after him and covered him the way flies cover a piece of offal after a butchering, and their hands rose and fell.

Len turned his head and looked at Esau. He was crying, and his face was white. Esau had his arms folded tight across his middle, and his body was bent over them. His eyes were huge and staring. Suddenly he turned and rushed away on all fours under the cart. Len bolted after him, scrambling, crabwise, with the air dark and whirling around him. All he could think about was the pecans Soames had given him. He turned sick and stopped to vomit, with a terrible icy coldness on him. The crowd still screamed by the riverbank. When he straightened up, Esau was gone in the shadows.

In a panic he fled between the carts and the wagons. He kept saying, "Esau! Esau!" but there was no answer, or if there was he couldn't hear it for the voice of murder in his ears. He shot out blindly into an open space, and there was a tall looming figure there that stretched out long arms and caught him.

"Len," it said. "Len Colter."

It was Mr. Hostetter. Len felt his knees give. It got very black and quiet, and he heard Esau's voice, and then Mr. Hostetter's, but far and tiny, like voices carried by the wind on a heavy day. Then he was in a wagon, huge and full of unfamiliar smells, and Mr. Hostetter was boosting Esau in after him. Esau looked like a ghost. Len said, "You said it would be fun." And Esau said, "I didn't know they ever—" He hiccuped and sat down beside Len, his head on his knees.

"Stay put," said Mr. Hostetter. "I have to get something."

He went away. Len raised up and watched, his eyes drawn toward the fire glare and the wailing, sobbing, shrieking mob that wavered to and fro crying that they were saved. Glory, glory, hallelujah, the wages of sin are death, hallelujah!

Mr. Hostetter ran across the open space to another trader's wagon, parked beside a clump of trees. Len couldn't see the name on the canvas, but he was sure it was Soames' wagon. Esau watched too. The preaching man was going at it again, waving his arms high in the air.

Mr. Hostetter jumped out of the other wagon and ran back. He was carrying a small chest, maybe a foot long, under one arm. He climbed up onto the seat, and Len scuttled forward inside the wagon. "Please," he said. "Can I sit beside you?"

Hostetter handed him the box. "Stow this inside. All right, climb up. Where's Esau?"

Len looked back. Esau was curled up on the floor, lying with his face down on a bundle of homespun. He called him, but Esau did not answer. "Passed out," said Hostetter. He uncurled his whip with a crack and shouted to the horses. The six great bays leaned like one horse into the breastbands and the wagon rolled. It rolled faster and faster, and the firelight was left behind, and the voice of the crowd. There was the dark road and the dark tree beside it, the smell of dust, and the peaceful fields. The horses slowed to an easier gait. Mr. Hostetter put his arm around Len, and Len clung to him.

"Why did they do it?" he asked.

"Because they're afraid."

"Of what?"

"Of yesterday," said Mr. Hostetter. "Of tomorrow." Suddenly, with astounding fury, he cursed them. Len stared at him, openmouthed. Hostetter shut his jaws tight in the middle of a word and shook his head. Len could feel him tremble all over. When he spoke again his voice was normal, or almost.

"Stick with your own people, Len. You won't find any better."

Len murmured, "Yes, sir." Nobody spoke after that. The wagon rocked along and the motion made Len drowsy, not a good drowsiness of sleep, but the sickish kind that comes with exhaustion. Esau was very quiet in the back. Finally the team slowed to a walk, and Len saw that they were back in the fairgrounds.

"Where's your wagon?" asked Hostetter, and Len told him. When they came in sight of it, the fire was built up again and Pa and Uncle David were standing beside it. They looked grim and angry, and when the boys got down they did not say a word, except to thank Hostetter for bringing them back. Len looked at Pa. He wanted to get down on his knees and say, "Father, I have sinned." But all he could do was to stand there and begin to sob and shake again.

"What happened?" asked Pa.

Hostetter told him, in four words. "There was a stoning."

Pa looked at Esau and Uncle David, and then he looked at Len and sighed. "Only once in a long time do they really do such a thing, but this had to be the time. The boys were forbidden, but they would go, and so they had to see it." He said to Len, "Hush, boy. Hush now, it's all over." He pushed him, not ungently, toward the wagon. "Go on, Lennie, you get into your blanket and go to sleep."

Len crept under the wagon and rolled the blanket around him and lay there. A weak, dark feeling came over him, and the world began to slip away, carrying with it the memory of Soames' dying face. Through the canvas he heard Mr. Hostetter saying, "I tried to warn the man this afternoon that the fanatics were whispering about him. I followed him there tonight, to get him to come away. But I was too late, there was nothing I could do."

Uncle David asked, "Was he guilty?"

"Of proselyting? You know better than that. The men of Bartorstown don't proselyte."

"Then he was from Bartorstown?"

"Soames came from Virginia. I knew him as a trader, and a fellow man."

"Guilty or not," Pa said heavily, "it's an unchristian thing. And blasphemous. But as long as there are crazed or crafty leaders to play on old fears, a mob like that will turn cruel."

"All of us," answered Hostetter, "have our old fears."

He climbed up on the seat again and drove away. But Len never heard the end of his going.

THREE

Three weeks had gone by, lacking a day or two, and in Piper's Run it was October, and a Sabbath afternoon. Len sat alone on the side stoop.

After a while the door behind him opened, and he knew from the scuffling footsteps and the thump of the cane that it was Gran coming out. She clamped one bony amazingly strong hand on his wrist and clambered down two steps and then sat, folding up stiffly like a dry twig when you bend it.

"Thank you, thank you," said Gran, and began arranging her several layers of skirts around her ankles.

"Do you want a rug for under you?" asked Len. "Or do you want your shawl?"

"No, it's warm in the sun."

Len sat down again, beside her. With his brows pulled together and his mouth pulled down, he looked nearly as old as Gran and much more solemn. She peered at him closely, and he began to feel uncomfortable, knowing that he had been sought out.

"You're mighty broody these days, Lennie."

"I guess so."

"You ain't sulking, are you? I hate a sulker."

"No, Gran. I'm not sulking."

"Your pa was right to punish you. You disobeyed him, and you know

now he forbid you for your own good."

Len nodded. "I know."

Pa had not delivered the expected beating. In fact, he had been gentler than Len would have dreamed possible. He had spoken very seriously about what Len had done and what he had seen, and he had finished with the statement that Len was not to go to the fair next year at all, and perhaps not the year after, unless he had been able to prove by then that he could be trusted. Len considered that Pa had been mighty decent. Uncle David had licked Esau to the last inch of his skin. And since at this moment Len did not feel that he ever wanted to see the fair again, being denied it was no hardship.

He said so, and Gran smiled her toothless ancient smile and patted his knee. "You'll feel different a year from now. That's when it'll hurt."

"Maybe."

"Well, if you're not sulking, there's something else the matter with you. What is it?"

"Nothing."

"Lennie, I've had a lot to do with boys, and I know no natural healthy boy should mope around like you do. And on a day like this, even if it is the Sabbath." She looked up at the deep blue sky and sniffed the golden air, and then she looked at the woods that encircled the farmstead, seeing them not as groups of individual trees but as a glorious blur of colors she had almost forgotten the names for. She sighed, half in pleasure, half in regret.

"Seems like this is the only time you see real colors any more, when the trees turn in the fall. The world used to be full of colors. You wouldn't believe it, Lennie, but I had a dress once, as red as that tree."

"It must have been pretty." He tried to picture Gran as a little girl in a red dress and failed, partly because he could not imagine her as anything but an old woman, and partly because he had never seen anybody dressed in red.

"It was beautiful," said Gran slowly, and sighed again.

They sat together on the step, and did not speak, and looked at nothing. And all at once Gran said, "I know what ails you. You're still thinking about the stoning."

Len began to shake a little. He did not want to, but he couldn't make it stop. He blurted out, "Oh, Gran, it was—He still had one boot on. He was all naked except for this one boot, and he looked so funny. And they kept on throwing stones—"

If he shut his eyes, he could see again how the blood and the dirt ran together on the man's white skin, and how the hands of the people rose and fell.

"Why did they do it, Gran? Why?"

"Better ask your pa."

"He said they were afraid, and that fear makes stupid people do wicked things, and that I should pray for them." Len ran the back of his hand violently across his nose. "I wouldn't pray a word for them, except that somebody would throw stones at them."

"You've only seen one bad thing," said Gran, shaking her head with the close white cap slowly from side to side, her eyes half shut and looking inward. "If you'd seen the things I saw, you'd know what fear can do. And I was younger than you, Lennie."

"It was awful bad, wasn't it, Gran?"

"I'm an old woman, an old old woman, and I still dream—There were fires in the sky, red fires, there and there and there." Her gaunt hand pointed out three places in a semicircle westward, and from south to north. "They were cities burning. The cities I used to go to with my mother. And the people from them came, and the soldiers came, and there were shelters in every field, and people crowded into the barns and the houses anywhere they could, and all our stock was butchered to feed them, forty head of fine dairy cows. Those were bad, bad times. It's a mercy anybody lived through them."

"Is that why they killed the man?" asked Len. "Because they're afraid he might bring all that back again—the cities, and all?"

"Isn't that what they said at the preaching?" said Gran, knowing full well, since she had been to preachings herself many decades ago when the terror brought the great boiling up of faith that birthed new sects and strengthened the old ones.

"Yes. They said he tempted the boys with some kind of fruit, I guess they meant from the Tree of Knowledge like it says in the Bible. And they said he came from a place called Bartorstown. What is Bartorstown, Gran?"

"You ask your pa," she said, and began to fuss with her apron. "Where'd I put that handkerchief? I know I had it—"

"I did ask him. He said there wasn't any such place."

"Hmph," said Gran.

"He said only children and fanatics believed in it."

"Well, I ain't going to tell you any different, so don't try to make me."

"I won't, Gran. But was there ever, maybe a long time ago?"

Gran found her handkerchief. She wiped her face and her eyes with it, and snuffled, and put it away, and Len waited.

"When I was a little girl," said Gran, "we had this war."

Len nodded. Mr. Nordholt, the schoolmaster, had told them a good bit about it, and it had got connected in his mind with the Book of Revelations, grand and frightening.

"It came on for a long time, I guess," Gran continued. "I remember on the teevee they talked about it a lot, and they showed pictures of the bombs that made clouds just like a tremendous mushroom, and each one could wipe out a city, all by itself. Oh yes, Lennie, there was a rain of fire from heaven and many were consumed in it! The Lord gave it to the enemy for a day to be His flail."

"But we won."

"Oh, yes, in the end we won."

"Did they build Bartorstown then?"

"Before the war. The gover'ment built it. That was when the gover'ment was still in Washington, and it was a lot different than it is now. Bigger, somehow. I don't know, a little girl doesn't care much about those things. But they built a lot of secret places, and Bartorstown was the most secret of all, way out West somewhere."

"If it was so secret, how did you know about it?"

"They told about it on the teevee. Oh, they didn't tell where it was or what it was for, and they said it might be only a rumor. But I remember the name."

"Then," said Len softly, "it was real!"

"But that's not saying it is now. That was a long time ago. It's maybe just the memory of it hung on, like your pa said, with children and fanatics." She added tartly under her breath that she wasn't either one of those, herself. Then she said, "You leave it alone, Lennie. Don't have any truck with the Devil, and he won't have any with you. You don't want happening to you what happened to that man at the preaching."

Lennie turned hot and cold all over again. But curiosity made him ask in spite of that, "Is Bartorstown such a terrible place?"

"It is," said Gran with sour wisdom, "if everybody thinks it is. Oh, I know! All my life I've had to watch my tongue. I can remember the world the way it was before. I was only a little girl, but I was old enough for that, almost as old as you. And I can remember very well how we got to be Mennonites, that never were Mennonites before. Sometimes I wish—" She broke off, and looked again at the flaming trees. "I did love that red dress."

Another silence.

"Gran."

"Well, what is it?"

"What were the cities like, really?"

"Better ask your pa."

"You know what he always says. Besides, he never saw them. You did, Gran. You can remember."

"The Lord in His infinite wisdom destroyed them. It's not up to you to question. Nor me."

"I'm not questioning—I'm only asking. What were they like?"

"They were big. A hundred Piper's Runs wouldn't have made up a half of even a small city. They had all hard pavements, with walks at the side for the people, and big wide roads in the middle for the cars, and there were great big buildings that went way up in the air. They were noisy, and the air smelled different, and there were always a lot of people hurrying back and forth. I always liked to go to the city. Nobody thought they were wicked then."

Len's eyes were large and round.

"They had big movie theaters, huge, with plush seats, and supermarkets twice as big as that barn, with every kind of food in them, all in bright shiny packages—the things you could buy any day in the week that you've never even heard of, Lennie! White sugar, we thought nothing of it. And spices, and fresh vegetables all winter, frozen into little bricks. And the things there were in the stores! Oh, so many things, I couldn't begin to tell you, clothes and toys and 'lectric washers and books and radios and teevee sets—"

She rocked back and forth a little, and her old eyes flashed.

"Christmas time," she said. "Oh, at Christmas time with the windows all decorated and the lights and the carols! All colors and brightness and people laughing. It wasn't wicked. It was wonderful."

Len's jaw dropped. He sat that way, with his mouth open, and a heavy step vibrated along the floor from inside, and he tried to tell Gran to hush, but she had forgotten he was there.

"Cowboys on the teevee," she mumbled, reaching far back across the troubled decades. "Music, and ladies in beautiful dresses that left their shoulders all bare. I thought I would look like that when I got big. Picture books, and Mr. Bloomer's drugstore with the ice cream and the chocolate rabbits at Easter—"

Pa came out the door. Len got up and went down to the bottom of the steps. Pa looked at him, and Len crumbled inside, thinking that life had been nothing but trouble for the last three weeks.

"Water," said Gran, "that ran out of shiny faucets when you turned them. And a bathroom right in the house, and 'lectric light—"

Pa said to Len, "Did you get her talking?"

"No, honest," said Len. "She started off herself, about a red dress."

"Easy," said Gran. "All easy, and bright, and comfortable. That was the world. And then it was gone. So fast."

Pa said, "Mother."

She glanced up at him, sidelong, and her eyes were like two faded sparks, snapping and flaring. She said, "Flat-hat."

"Now, Mother—"

"I wish I had it back," said Gran. "I wish I had a red dress, and a teevee, and a nice white porcelain toilet, and all the other things. It was a good world! I wish it hadn't ended."

"But it did end," said Pa. "And you are a foolish old woman to question the goodness of God." He was talking less to her than to Len, and he was very angry. "Did any of those things help you to survive? Did they help the people of the cities? Did they?"

Gran turned her face away and would not answer.

Pa came down and stood in front of her. "You understand me, Mother. Answer me. Did they?"

Tears came into Gran's eyes, and the fire died out of them. "I'm an old woman," she said. "It isn't right for you to yell at me that way."

"Mother. Did those things help one single person to survive?"

She let her head fall forward and moved it slowly from side to side.

"No," said Pa, "and I know because you told me how no food came in any more to the markets, and nothing would work on the farms because there was no power any more, and no fuel. And only those who had always lived without all the luxuries, and done for themselves with their own hands, and had no truck with the cities, came through without hurt and led us all in the path of peace and plenty and humility before God. And you dare to scoff at the Mennonites! Chocolate rabbits," said Pa, and stamped his boots on the earth. "Chocolate rabbits! No wonder the world fell."

He swung around to include Len in the circle of his wrath. "Haven't you got any thankfulness in your hearts, either of you? Can't you be grateful for a good harvest, and good health, and a warm house, and plenty to eat? What more does God have to give you to make you happy?"

The door opened again. Ma Colter's face appeared, round and pink and full of reproof, framed in a tight white cap. "Elijah! Are you raising your voice to your mother, and on the Sabbath day?"

"I had provocation," said Pa, and stood breathing hard through his nose for a minute or two. Then, more quietly, he said to Len, "Go to the barn."

Len's heart sank down into his knees. He began to shuffle away across the yard. Ma came clear out the door, onto the stoop.

"Elijah, the Sabbath day is no time—"

"It's for the good of the boy's soul," said Pa, in the voice that meant no more argument. "Just leave this to me, please."

Ma shook her head, but she went back inside. Pa walked behind Len toward the open barn doors. Gran sat where she was on the steps.

"I don't care," she whispered. "Those things were good." After a minute she repeated fiercely, "Good, good, *good!*" Tears ran slowly down her cheeks and dropped onto the bosom of her drab homespun dress.

Inside the barn, warm and shadowy and sweet with the stored hay, Pa took the length of harness strap down from its nail on the wall, and Len took off his jacket. He waited, but Pa stood there looking at him and frowning, drawing the supple leather through his fingers. Finally he said, "No, that's not the way," and hung the strap back on the wall.

"Aren't you going to lick me?" Len whispered.

"Not for your grandmother's foolishness. She's very old, Len, and the very old are like children. Also, she lived through terrible years and worked hard and uncomplainingly for a long lifetime—perhaps I shouldn't blame her too much for thinking of the easeful things she had in her childhood. And I suppose it's not in the nature of a human boy not to listen to it."

He turned away, walking up and down by the stanchions, and when he stopped he kept his face turned from Len.

He said, "You saw a man die. That's your trouble, isn't it, and the cause of all these questions?"

"Yes, Pa. I just can't forget it."

"Don't forget it," said Pa with sudden forcefulness. "Since you saw it, remember it always. That man chose a certain path, and it led him to a certain end. The way of the transgressor has always been hard, Len. It'll never be easy."

"I know," said Len. "But just because he came from a place called Bartorstown—"

"Bartorstown is more than a place. I don't know whether it exists or not, in the way that Piper's Run exists, and if it does, I don't know whether any of the things they say about it are true. Whether they are or not doesn't matter. Men believe them. Bartorstown is a way of thought, Len. The trader was stoned to death because he chose that way."

"The preaching man said he wanted to bring the cities back. Is Bartorstown a city, Pa? Do they have things there like Gran had when she was little?"

Pa turned and put his hands on Len's shoulders. "Many and many is the time, Len, that my father beat me, here in this very place, for asking questions like that. He was a good man, but he was like your uncle David, quicker with the strap than he was with his tongue. I heard all the stories, from Mother and from all the people of the generation before her who were still alive then and remembered even better than she did. And I used to think how fine all the luxuries must have been, and I wondered why they were so sinful. And Father told me I was headed straight for hell and strapped me until I could hardly stand. He'd lived through the Destruction himself, and the fear of God was stronger in his heart than it was in mine. That was bitter medicine, Len, but I'm not sure it didn't save me. And if I must, I'll treat you the same way, though I'd rather you didn't make me."

"I won't, Pa," Len said hastily.

"I hope not. Because you see, Len, it's all so useless. Forget for a moment about whether it's sinful or not, and just think about the solid facts. All those things that Gran talks about, the teevees, the cars, the railroads, and the airplanes, depended on the cities." He frowned and made motions with his hands, trying to explain. "Concentration, Len. Organization. Like the works of a clock, every little piece depending on every other little piece to make it go. One man didn't make an automobile, the way a good wainwright makes a wagon. It took thousands of men, all working together, and depending on thousands of other men in other places to make the fuel and the rubber so the automobiles could run when they did build them. It was the cities that made those things possible, Len, and when the cities went they were not possible any more. So we don't have them. We never will have them."

"Not ever, as long as the world?" asked Len, with a wistful sense of loss.

"That's in the hands of the Lord," said Pa. "But we won't live as long as the world. Len, you'd as well hanker after the Pharaohs of Egypt as after the things that were lost in the Destruction."

Len nodded, deep in thought. "I still don't see, though, Pa—why did they have to *kill* the man?"

Pa sighed. "Men do what they believe to be right, or what they think is necessary to protect themselves. A terrible scourge came onto this world. Those of us who survived it have labored and fought and sweat for two generations to recover from it. Now we're prosperous and at peace, and nobody wants that scourge to come back. When we find men who seem to carry the seeds of it, we take steps against them, according to our different ways. And some ways are violent."

He handed Len his jacket. "Here, put it on. And then I want you to go into the fields and look around you, and think about what you see, and I want you to ask God for the greatest gift He has in His power to give, a contented heart. And I want you to think of the dead man as a sign that was given you to remind you of the wages of folly, which are just as bad as the wages of sin."

Len pulled his jacket on. He nodded and smiled at Pa, loving him.

Pa said, "Just one more thing. Esau got you to go to that preaching."

"I didn't say—"

"You don't have to, I know you and I know Esau. Now I'm going to tell you something, and you needn't repeat it. Esau's headstrong, and he makes it a point of pride to be off-ox and ornery about everything just to show he's smart. He was born for trouble as the sparks fly upward, and I don't want you tagging in after him like a pup at his heels. If it happens again, you'll get such a thrashing as you never dreamed of. Understand?"

"Yes, *sir!*"

"Then get."

Len did not make Pa tell him again. He went away across the dooryard. He passed the gate and the cart road and went out over the west field, moving sedately, with his head bowed and the thoughts going round and round in it until it ached.

Yesterday the men had cut corn here, the long sickle-shaped knives going *whick-whick!* against the rustling stalks, and the boys had shocked it. Len liked the harvest. Everybody got together and helped everybody else, and there was a certain excitement to it, a sense of final victory in the battle you had fought since planting time, a feeling of tucking in for the winter that was right and natural as the falling of the leaves and the preparations of the squirrels. Len scuffed along slowly between the stubble rows and the tall shocks, and he got to smelling the sun on the dry corn, and hearing the crows cawing somewhere in the edge of the woods, and then the colors of the trees began to get to him. Suddenly he realized that the whole countryside was ablaze and burning with beauty, and he walked on toward the woods, with his head up to see the crests of red and gold against the sky. There was a clump of sumacs at the edge of the field, so triumphantly scarlet that they made him blink. He stopped beside them and looked back.

From here he could see almost the whole farm, the neat pattern of the fields, the snake fences in good repair, the buildings tight and well-roofed with split shakes, weathered to a silver gray that glistened in the sun. Sheep grazed in the upper pasture, and in the lower one were the cows, the harness mare, and the great thick-muscled draft team, all sleek and fat. The barn and the granary were full. The root cellar was full. The spring house was full, and in the home cellar there were crocks and jars, and flitches of bacon, and hams new from the smokehouse, and they had taken every bit of it from the earth with their own hands. A sense of warmth began to spread all through Len, and with it came a passionate, wordless love for this place that he was looking at, the fields and the house, the barn, the rough woods, the sky. He understood what Pa meant. It was good, and God was good. He understood what Pa meant about a contented heart. He prayed. When he was finished praying he turned and went in between the trees.

He had been this way so often that there had come to be a narrow path beaten through the brush. Len's step was light now, and his head was high. His broad-brimmed hat caught in the low branches, and he took it off. Pretty soon he took off his jacket, too. The path joined a deer trail. Several times he bent to look at fresh signs, and when he crossed a clearing with long grass in it he could see the round crushed places where the deer had bedded.

In a few minutes he came into a long glade. The brush thinned, shaded out by the mighty maples that grew here. Len sat down and rolled up his jacket, and then he lay down on his back with the jacket under his head and looked up at the trees. The branches made a twisty pattern of black, holding a cloud of golden leaves, and above them the sky was so blue and deep and still that you felt you could drown in it. From time to time a little shower of leaves shook down, drifting slow and bright on the quiet air. Len meditated, but his thoughts had no shape to them any more. For the first time since the preaching, they were merely happy. After a while, with a feeling of absolute peacefulness, he dozed off. And then all at once he started bolt upright, his heart thumping and the sweat springing out on his skin.

There was a sound in the woods.

It was not a right sound. It was not made by any animal or bird or wind or tree branch. It was a crackling and hissing and squealing all mixed together, and out of the middle of it came a sudden roar. It was not loud, it sounded small and distant, and yet at the same time it seemed to come from not too far away. Suddenly it was gone, as though cut off sharp with a knife.

Len stood still and listened.

It came again, but very faintly now, very stealthily, blending with the rustle of the breeze in the high branches. Len sat down and took off his shoes. Then he padded barefoot over the moss and grass to the end of the glade, and then as quietly as he could along the bed of a little stream until the brush thinned out again in a grove of butternuts. He passed through these, ducked into a clump of thorn apples, and went on his hands and knees until he could look out the other side. The sound had not grown any louder, but it was closer. Much closer.

Beyond the thorn apples was a bank of grass, where the violets grew thick in the springtime. It was a wedge-shaped bank, made where the run that gave the village its name slid into the slow brown Pymatuning. It had a big tree leaning over at its tip, with half its roots exposed by the cutting out of the earth in time of flood. It was as private a place as you could find on a Sabbath afternoon in October, in the very heart and center of the woods and at the farthest point away from the farms on either side of the river.

Esau was there. He was sitting hunched over a fallen log, and the noise came from something he held between his hands.

FOUR

L en came out of the thorn apples. Esau leaped up in a guilty panic. He tried to run away, and hide the object behind his back, and ward off an expected blow, all at the same time, and when he saw that it was only Len he fell back down on the log as though his knees had given under him.

"What did you want to do that for?" he said between his teeth. "I thought it was Dad."

His hands were shaking. They were still trying to cover up and conceal what they held. Len stopped where he was, startled at Esau's fright.

"What you got there?" he asked.

"Nothing. Just an old box."

It was a poor lie. Len ignored it. He went closer to Esau and looked. The thing was box-shaped. It was small, only a few inches across, and flat. It was made of wood, but there was a different look about it from any wooden object Len had ever seen before. He could not tell quite what the difference was, but it was there. It had curious openings in it, and several knobs sticking out from it, and in one place was a spool of thread fitted into a recess, only this thread was metal. It hummed and whispered softly to itself.

Awed and more than a little scared, Len asked, "What is it?"

"You know the thing Gran talks about sometimes? Where the voices come out of the air?"

"Teevee? But that was big, and it had pictures."

"No," said Esau. "I mean the other thing that just had voices."

Len drew in a long unsteady breath and let it go again in a quivering "Oh-h!" He reached out a finger and touched the humming box, very lightly, just to be sure it was really there. He said,

"A radio?"

Esau rested it on his knees and held it firm with one hand. The other shot out and caught Len by the front of his shirt. His face had such a fierceness in it that Len did not try to break away or fight back. Anyway, he was afraid to struggle, lest the radio get broken.

"If you tell anybody," said Esau, "I'll kill you. I swear I'll kill you."

He looked as though he meant it, and Len did not blame him. He said, "I won't, Esau. Honest, swear-on-the-Book." His eyes were drawn back to the wonderful, terrifying, magical thing in Esau's lap. "Where'd you get it? Does it work? Can you really hear voices from it?" He hunkered down until his chin was almost resting on Esau's thigh.

Esau's hand withdrew from Len's shirt and went back to stroke the smooth wooden surface of the box. At this close range Len could see that it had worn places on it around the knobs, made by the rubbing of fingers, and that one corner was chipped. These intimate things made it suddenly real. Someone had owned it and used it for a long time.

"I stole it," Esau said. "It belonged to Soames, the trader."

The familiar nerve tightened and twanged in Len's middle. He drew back a little and looked up at Esau and then all around, as though he expected stones to come flying at them out of the thorn-apple clump.

"How did you get it?" he asked, unconsciously dropping his voice.

"You remember when Mr. Hostetter put us in the wagon, he went to get something?"

"Yes, he got a box out of Soames' wagon—oh!"

"It was in the box. There was some other, stuff, too, books I think, and little things, but it was dark and I didn't dare make any noise. I could feel that this was something different, like the old things Gran talks about. I hid it in my shirt."

Len shook his head, more in amazement than reproach. "And all the time we thought you were fainted. What made you do it, Esau? I mean, how did you know there was anything in the box?"

"Well, Soames was from Bartorstown, wasn't he?"

"That's what they said at the preaching. But—" Len broke off short as a corollary truth dawned on him, shining with a great light. He looked at the radio. "He was from Bartorstown. And there is a Bartorstown. It's real."

"When I saw Hostetter coming back with that box, I just had to look inside it. Coins or anything like that I wouldn't touch, but this—" Esau caressed the radio, turning it gently in his hands. "Look at those knobs, and the way this part here is done. You couldn't do that by hand in any village smithy, Len. It must have been machined. The way it's all put together, and inside—" He squinted in through the grilled openings, trying to catch the light so it would reflect on what was beyond them. "Inside there's the strangest things." He put it down again. "I didn't know what it was at first. I only felt what it was like. I had to have it."

Len got up slowly. He walked over to the edge of the bank and looked down at the clear brown water, low and slack and half covered over with red and gold leaves. Esau said nervously, "What's the matter? If you think you're going to tell, I'll say you stole it with me. I'll say—"

"I ain't going to tell," said Len angrily. "You've had the thing all this time and never told me, and I can keep a secret as good as you."

Esau said, "I was afraid to. You're young, Lennie, and used to minding your pa." He added with some truth, "Anyway, we've hardly seen each other since the preaching."

"It don't matter," Len said. It did matter, of course, and he felt hurt and indignant that Esau had not trusted him, but he was not going to let Esau know that. "I was just thinking."

"What?"

"Well, Mr. Hostetter knew Soames. He went to the preaching to try and help him, and then he took the box out of Soames' wagon. Maybe—"

"Yes," said Esau. "I thought of that. Maybe Mr. Hostetter is from Bartorstown, too, and not from Pennsylvania at all."

Great vistas of terrifying and wonderful possibility were opened up in Len's mind. He stood there on the bank of the Pymatuning, while the gold and scarlet leaves came down and the crows laughed their harsh derisive laughter, and the horizons widened and shone around him until he was dizzy with them. Then he remembered why he was here, or rather why it was that Pa had sent him into the fields and woods to meditate, and how he had made peace with God and the world just such a little time before, and how good it had felt. And now it was all gone again.

He turned around. "Can you hear voices with it?"

"I haven't yet," said Esau. "But I'm going to keep on till I do."

They tried that afternoon, cautiously turning one knob and then another. Esau had turned one too far, or Len would never have heard it. They had not the remotest idea how a radio worked or what the knobs and openings and the spool of thin wire were for. They could only experiment, and all they got was the now-familiar crackle and hiss and squeal. But even that was a thing of wonder. It was a sound never heard before, full of mystery and a sense of great unseen spaces, and it was made by a machine. They did not leave it until the sun was so low that they were afraid to stay any longer. Then Esau hid the radio carefully in a hollow tree, wrapping it first in a bit of canvas and making sure that the main knob was turned clear around till it clicked and there was no more sound, lest the hum and crackle should attract the attention of some chance hunter or fisherman.

That hollow tree became the pivot of Len's days, and it was the most exciting and wildly frustrating thing imaginable. Now that he had a reason for going, it seemed almost impossible to find time and excuses for going to the woods. The weather turned cold and nasty, with rain and sleet and then snow. The stock had to be put in the barn, and after that there was not much time to do anything but feed, water, and clean up after a great houseful of animals. There was milking, and the henhouse to see to, and then there was helping Ma with the churning and carrying stovewood, and such, around the house.

After morning chores, when it was still hardly light, he tramped the mile and a half to the village over roads that were one day deep in mud and frozen hard as iron the next, with yesterday's ruts immortalized in ice. On the west side of the village square, beyond the smithy but not so far as the cobblers' shop, was the house of Mr. Nordholt, the schoolmaster, and there, with the other young of Piper's Run, Len struggled with his sums and his letters, his reading and his Bible history until noon, when he was turned loose to walk home again. After that there were other things. Len often felt that he had more to do than Pa and brother James put together.

Brother James was nineteen and arranging to marry the oldest daughter of Mr. Spofford, the miller. He was a lot like Pa, square and strong and quiet, proud of his fine new beard in spite of the fact that it was nearly pink. When the weather was right, Len went with him and Pa to the wood lot, or around to mend fence or clear hedgerows, and sometimes they would go hunting, both for meat and for skins, because nothing was ever wasted or thrown away. There were deer, and coon, and possum, and woodchuck at the right time of the year, and squirrel, and rumors of bear in the wilder parts of the Pennsylvania hills that might be expected to drift west into Ohio, and sometimes if the winter was very bad they would hear rumors of wolves up north beyond the lakes. There were foxes to keep out of the henroost, and rats to keep out of the corn, and rabbits out of the young orchard. And every evening there was milking again, and the windup chores, and then dinner and bed. It did not leave much time for the radio.

And yet waking or sleeping it was never out of his mind. Two things were linked with it, a memory and a dream. The memory was the death of Soames. Time had transfigured him until he was taller and more noble and splendid than any ginger-haired trader had ever been, and the firelight on him had merged into the glory of martyrdom. The dream was of Bartorstown. It was pieced together out of Gran's stories, and bits of sermons, and descriptions of heaven. It had big white buildings that went high up in the air, and it was full of colors and sounds, and people strangely dressed, and it blazed with light, and in it there was every kind of thing that Gran had told about, machines and luxuries and pleasures.

The most agonizing part of the little radio was that both he and Esau knew that it was a link with Bartorstown and if they only understood how to use it they could actually hear people talking from it and about it. They might even learn where it was and how a person might get there if he decided to go. But it was as hard for Esau to come to the woods as it was for Len, and in their few stolen moments they got nothing from the radio but meaningless noises.

The temptation to ask Gran questions about radios was almost more than Len could hold in. But he did not dare, and anyway he was sure she wouldn't know any more about it than he did.

"We need a book," said Esau. "That's what we need. A book that tells all about these things."

"Yes," said Len. "Sure. But where are you going to get one?"

Esau didn't answer.

The great cold waves rolled down from the north and northwest, one after the other. Snows fell and then melted in a warmer blow from the south, and then the slush they left behind them froze again as the temperature plunged down. Sometimes it rained, very cold and dreary, and the bare wood dripped. The manure pile behind the barn grew into a brown and strawy alp. And Len thought.

Whether it was the stimulus of the radio, or simply that he was growing up, or both, he saw everything about him in a new way, as though he had managed to get a little distance off so that his sight wasn't blurred by being too close. He did not do this all the time, of course. He was too busy and too tired. But now and then he would see Gran sitting by the fire, knitting with her old, old unsteady hands, and he would think how long she had been alive and all she had seen, and he would feel sorry for her because she was old and Baby Esther, a minute copy of Ma in her tiny cap and apron and full skirts, was young and just beginning.

He would see Ma, always working at something, washing, sewing, spinning, weaving, quilting, making sure the table was loaded with food for hungry men, a thick, solid woman, very kind and quiet. He would see the house he lived in, the familiar whitewashed rooms of which he knew every crack and knothole in the wooden walls. It was an old house. Gran said it had been built only a year or two after the church. The floors ran up and down every which way and the walls leaned, but it was still sound as a mountain, put together out of great timbers by the first Colter who had come here, many generations before the Destruction. Yet it was not too different from the new houses that were built now. The ones that had been built in Gran's childhood or just before were the ones that really looked queer, little flat-roofed things that had mostly to be re-sided with wood, and their great gaping windows boarded in. He would stretch up and try to touch the ceiling, figuring that by next year he could do it. And a great wave of love would come over him, and he would think, I'll never leave here, never! And his conscience would hurt him with a physical pain because he knew he was doing wrong to fool with the forbidden radio and the forbidden dream of Bartorstown.

For the first time he really saw Brother James and envied him. His face was as smooth and placid as Ma's, without a glimmer of curiosity in it. He would not care if there were twenty Bartorstowns just across the Pymatuning. All he wanted was to marry Ruth Spofford and stay right where he was. Len felt dimly that Brother James was one of the happy ones who had never had to pray for a contented heart.

Pa was different. Pa had had to fight. The fighting had left lines in his face, but they were good lines, strong ones. And his contentment was different from Brother James'. It hadn't just happened. Pa had had to sweat for it, like getting a good crop from a poor field. You could feel it when you were around him, if you thought about it, and it was a fine thing, a thing you would like to get hold of for yourself.

But could you? Could you give up all the mystery and wonder of the world? Could you never see it, and never want to see it? Could you stop the waiting, hoping eagerness to hear a voice from nowhere, out of a little square box?

In January, just after the turn of the year, there was an ice storm on a Sabbath evening. On Monday morning Len walked to school just as the sun came up, and every tree and twig and stiff dead weed glittered with a cold glory. He lagged on the way, looking at the familiar woods turned strange and shining like a forest of glass—a sight rarer and lovelier than the clinging snows that made them all a still, hushed white—and he was late when he crossed the village square, past the chunky granite monument that said it was in memory of the veterans of all wars, erected by the citizens of Piper's Run. It had had a bronze eagle on it once, but there was nothing left of that now but a lump of corroded metal in the shape of two claws. It too was all sheathed in ice, and the ground underfoot was slippery. Ashes had been thrown on the steps of Mr. Nordholt's house. Len clambered up onto the porch and went inside.

The room was still chilly in spite of a roaring fire in the grate. It had a tremendously high ceiling and very tall double doors and very long windows, so that more cold leaked in than a fire could handily take care of. The walls were of whitewashed plaster, with a lot of ornamental woodwork polished down to the original dark grain of the native black walnut. The students sat on rough benches, without backs, but with long trestle tables in front of them. They were graded in size, from the littlest ones in front to the biggest in the back, girls on one side, boys on the other. There were twenty-three in all. Each one had a small slab of smooth slate, a squeaky pencil, and a rag, and they were taught everything but their sums from the Bible.

This morning they were all sitting very still with their hands in their laps, each one trying to blend into the room like a rabbit into a hedgerow so as not to be noticed. Mr. Nordholt was standing facing them. He was a tall, thin man, with a white beard and an expression of gentle sternness that frightened only the very young. But this morning he was angry. He was angry clear through with a towering and indignant wrath, and his eyes shot such a glare at Len that he quailed before it. Mr. Nordholt was not alone. Mr. Glasser was there, and Mr. Harkness, and Mr. Clute, and Mr. Fenway. They were the law and council of Piper's Run, and they sat stiffly in a row looking thunder and lightning at the students.

"If," said Mr. Nordholt, "you will be good enough to take your seat, *Mister* Colter—"

Len slid into his place on the back bench without stopping to take off his thick outer jacket or the scarf around his neck. He sat there trying to look small and innocent, wondering what on earth the trouble was and thinking guiltily of the radio.

Mr. Nordholt said, "For three days over the New Year I was in Andover, visiting my sister. I did not lock my door when I went away, because it has never been necessary in Piper's Run to lock our doors against thieves."

Mr. Nordholt's voice was choked with some very strong emotion, and Len knew that something bad had happened. He went rapidly over his own actions on those three days but found nothing that could be brought up against him.

"Someone," said Mr. Nordholt, "entered this house during my absence and stole from it three books."

Len stiffened in his seat. He remembered Esau saying, "We need a book—"

"Those books," said Mr. Nordholt, "are the property of the township of Piper's Run. They are pre-Destruction books, and therefore irreplaceable. And they are not for idle or indiscriminate use. I want them back."

He stood aside, and Mr. Harkness rose. Mr. Harkness was short and thick, and bandy-legged from walking all his life after a plow, and his voice had a rusty creak in it. He always prayed the longest prayers in meeting. Now he looked along the rows of benches with two little steely eyes that were usually as friendly as a beagle's.

"Now then," said Mr. Harkness, "I'm going to ask each one of you in turn, did you take them or do you know who did. And I don't want any lies or any bearing of false witness."

He stumped over to the left-hand corner and began, walking down the benches and back again. Len listened to the monotonous *No Mr. Harkness* coming closer and closer, and he sweated profusely and tried to loosen his tongue. After all, he did not know that it was Esau. Thou shalt not bear false witness, Mr. Harkness just said so, and to look guilty when you're not is a sort of false-witnessing. Besides, if they get to looking around too close they might find out about the—

Harkness' eye and finger were pointed straight at him.

"No," said Len, "Mr. Harkness."

It seemed to him that all the guilt and fear in the world were loud and quivering in those three words, but Mr. Harkness passed on. When he came to the end of the last row he said,

"Very well. Perhaps you're all telling the truth, perhaps not. We'll find out. Now I'll say this. If you see a book that you know does not belong to the person who has it, you are to come to me, or to Mr. Nordholt or to Mr. Glasser or Mr. Clute or Mr. Fenway. You are to ask your parents to do the same. Do you understand that?"

Yes, Mr. Harkness.

"Let us pray. Oh God, Who knowest all things, forgive the erring child, or man, as it may be, who has broken Thy commandment against theft. Turn his soul toward righteousness, that he may return that which is not his, and make him patient of chastisement—"

Len took a chance on his way home and made a circle down through the woods, running most of the way to make up for the extra distance. The sun had melted some of the icy armor on the trees, but it was still bright enough to hurt the eyes, and the footing was treacherous. He was blown and weary by the time he got to the hollow tree.

There were three books in it, wrapped up in canvas beside the radio, dry and safe. The covers and the paper inside fascinated him with faded colors for the eye and unfamiliar textures for the touch. They had an indefinable something in common with the radio.

One was a dark green book called *Elementary Physics*. One was thin and brownish, with a long title: *Radioactivity and Nucleonics: An Introduction*. The third was fat and gray, and its name was *History of the United States*. The words of the first two meant nothing to Len, except that he recognized the *Radio* part. He turned the pages, hastily, with shaking fingers, trying to take it all in at one glance and seeing nothing but a blur of print and pictures and curious line drawings. Here and there on the pages someone had marked and written in the margins, "Monday, test," or "To here," or "Write paper on La. Purchase."

Len felt a hunger and a craving he had not known before, because nothing had ever aroused them. They were up in his head, and they were so strong they made it ache. He wanted to read. He wanted to take the books and wrap himself around them and absorb them to the last word and picture. He knew perfectly well what his duty was. He did not do it. He folded the canvas around the books again and replaced them carefully in the hollow tree. Then he ran back on the circuitous route home, and his mind was spinning all the way with stratagems to deceive Pa and make guilty trips to the woods appear innocent. His conscience made a single peep, no louder than a day-old chick, and then was still.

FIVE

Esau was almost in tears. He flung down the book he was holding and said furiously, "I don't know what the words mean, so what good does it do me? I just took a big risk for nothing!"

He had been over and over the book on physics and the one on radioactivity, and Len had been over and over them with him. The one on radioactivity they had laid aside because it didn't seem to have anything to do with radios, and anyway they could not make head or tail of what it was about. But the book on physics—another puzzling misuse of a word that had almost caused Esau to pass it by in his search through Mr. Nordholt's library—did have a part in it about radio. They had scowled and mumbled over it until the queer-shaped and unpronounceable words were stamped on their brains and they could have drawn diagrams of waves and circuits, triodes and oscillators in their sleep, without in the least understanding what they were.

Len picked the book up from between his feet, where it had landed, and brushed the dirt from its cover. Then he looked inside it and shook his head. He said sadly,

"It doesn't tell you how to make voices come out."

"No. It doesn't tell what the knobs and the spool are for, either." Esau turned the radio gloomily between his hands. One of the knobs they knew made it noisy or quiet—alive or dead, Len thought of it unconsciously. But the others remained a mystery. By making the noise very soft and holding the radio against their ears they had learned that the sound came out of one of the openings. What the other two were for was also a mystery. No one of the three looked like its mates, so it was logical to guess that they were for three different purposes. Len was pretty sure that one of them was to let heat out, like the ventilators in the hayloft, because you could feel it get warm if you held your hand over it for a while. But that still left one, and the enigmatic spool of metal thread. He reached out and took the radio from Esau, just liking the feel of it between his hands, a kind of humming quiver it had like a blade of swamp grass in the wind.

"Mr. Hostetter must know how it works," he said.

They were sure in their hearts that Mr. Hostetter, like Mr. Soames, was from Bartorstown.

Esau nodded. "But we don't dare ask him."

"No."

Len turned the radio over and over, fingering the knobs, the spool, the openings. A chill wind rattled the bare branches overhead. There was ice in the Pymatuning, and the fallen log he sat on was bitter underneath him.

"I just wonder," he said slowly.

"Wonder what?"

"Well, if they talk back and forth with these radios, they wouldn't do it much in the daytime, would they? I mean, people might hear them. If it was me, I'd wait until night, when everybody would be asleep."

"Well, it ain't you," said Esau crossly. But he thought about it, and gradually he got excited. "I'll bet that's right. I'll bet that's just exactly right! We only fooled with it in the daytime, and naturally they wouldn't talk then. Can you see Mr. Hostetter doing it up in the town square, with everybody swarming around and a dozen kids hanging on every wheel?"

He got up and began to pace up and down, blowing on his cold fingers. "We'll have to make plans, Len. We'll have to get away at night."

"Yes," said Len eagerly, and then was sorry he had spoken. That was not going to be so easy.

"Coon hunt," said Esau.

"No. My brother'd want to go. Maybe Pa, too."

Possum hunt was the same thing, and jacklighting deer was no better.

"Well, keep thinking," Esau began to put the books and the radio away. "I got to get back."

"Me, too." Len looked regretfully at the fat gray history, wishing he could take it with them. Esau had picked it up on impulse because it had pictures of machines in it. It was hard going and full of strange names and a lot he did not understand, but it tormented him all the time he was reading it, wondering what was coming on the next page. "Maybe it'd be best just to watch a chance and slip away alone, whichever one of us can, and not try to come together."

"No, sir! I stole it, and I stole the books, and nobody's going to hear a voice without me there!"

He looked so savage that Len said all right.

Esau made sure everything was safe and stepped back. He looked at the hollow tree, scowling. "Not much use to come back here any more till then. And we'll be sugarin' off 'fore long, and there's lambing, and then—"

With a mature depth of bitterness that startled Len, Esau said, "Always something, always some reason why you can't know or learn or do! I'm sick of it. And I'm damned if I'm going to spend my whole life that way, shoveling dung and pulling cow tits!"

Len walked home alone, pondering deeply on those words. He could feel something growing in him, and he knew it was growing in Esau, too. It frightened him. He didn't want it to grow. But he knew that if it stopped growing he would be partly dead, not physically, but like cows or sheep, who eat the grass but do not care what makes it grow.

That was the end of January. In February there was a warm spell, and all over the countryside men and boys went with taps and spiles and buckets to the maple trees. The smoke from the sugarbush blew out on the wind, the first banner of oncoming spring. The last deep snow came and melted off again. There was a period of alternating freeze and thaw that made Pa worry about the winter wheat heaving out of the ground. The wind blew chill from the northwest, and it seemed as though it would never get warm again. The first lamb came bleating into the world. And as Esau had said, there was no spare time for anything.

The willows turned yellow, and then a pale, feathery green. There were some warm days that made you feel all lazy and slithering like a winter snake thawing in the sun. New calves bawled and staggered after their mothers, with more yet to come. The cows were nervous and troublesome, and Len began to get an idea. It was so simple he wondered why he had not thought of it before. After evening chores, when Brother James had closed the barn, Len sneaked back and opened the lower door. An hour later they were all out in the cold dark rounding up cows, and when they got them back inside and counted, two were missing. Pa muttered angrily about the stupid obstinacy of beasts that preferred to run away and calve under a bush, where if anything went wrong there was no help. He gave Len a lantern and told him to run the half mile down the road to Uncle David's house and ask him and Esau to help. It was as easy as that.

Len covered the half mile at a fast lope, his mind busy foreseeing possibilities and preparing for them with a deceitful ease that rather horrified him. He had been given much to laziness, but never to lying, and it was awful how fast he was learning. He tried to excuse himself by thinking that he hadn't told anybody a direct falsehood. But it didn't do any good. He was like one of those white sepulchers they told about in the Bible, fair without and full of wickedness within. And off to his right as he ran the woods showed in the starlight, very black and strange.

Uncle David's kitchen was warm. It smelled of cabbage and steam and drying boots, and it was so clean that Len hesitated to step into it even after he had scraped his feet outside. There was a scrap of rag rug just inside the door and he stood on that, getting his message out between gasping for breath and trying to catch Esau's eye without looking too transparently guilty. Uncle David grumbled and muttered, but he began to pull on his boots, and Aunt Mariah got his jacket and a lantern. Len took a deep gulp of air.

"I think I saw something white moving down in the west field," he said. "Come on, Esau, let's look!"

And Esau came, with his hat on crooked and one arm still out of his jacket. They ran away together before Uncle David could think to stop them, stumbling and leaping over rough pasture where every hollow was full from recent rain, and then into the west field, angling all the time toward the woods. Len muffled the lantern under his coat so that Uncle David could not see from the road when they actually entered the woods, and he kept it hidden for some time afterward, knowing the way pretty well even in the dark, once he found his trail.

"We can say later that the lantern went out," he told Esau.

"Sure," said Esau, in a strange, tight voice. "Let's hurry."

They hurried. Esau grabbed the lantern and ran recklessly on ahead. When they got to the place where the waters met he set the light down and got out the radio with hands that could hardly hold it for shaking. Len sat down on the log, his mouth wide open, his arms pressed to his aching sides. Piper's Run was roaring like a real river, bankfull. It made a riffle and a swirl where it swept into the Pymatuning. The water rushed by foaming, very high now, almost level with the land where they were, dim and disturbed in the starlight, and the night was filled with the sound of it.

Esau dropped the radio.

Len jumped forward with a cry. Esau made a grab, fast and frantic. He caught the radio by the protruding spool. The spool came loose and the radio continued to fall, but slower now, swinging on the end of the wire that unreeled from Esau's hand. It fell with a soft thump into the last year's grass. Esau stood staring at it, and at the spool, and the wire between.

"It's broken," he said. "It's broken."

Len went down on his knees. "No it isn't. Look here." He moved the radio close to the lantern and pointed. "See those two little springs? The spool is meant to come out, and the wire unwinds—"

Enormously excited, he turned the knob. This was something they had not known or tried before. He waited until the humming began. It sounded stronger than it had. He motioned Esau to move back, and he did, reeling out the wire, and the noise got stronger and stronger, and suddenly without warning a man's voice was saying, very scratchy and far away, "—back out to civilization myself next fall, I hope. Anyway, the stuff's on the river ready to load as soon as the—"

The voice faded with a roar and a swoop. Like one half stunned, Esau reeled the wire out to the very end. And a faint, faint voice said, "Sherman wants to know if you've heard from Byers. He hasn't con—"

And that was all. The roaring and whistling and humming went on, so loud that they were afraid it might be heard all the way to where the others were out hunting cows. Once or twice they thought they could hear voices again behind it, but they could not make any more words come clear. Len turned the knob and Esau rolled the wire on the spool and clipped it back in place. They put the radio in the hollow tree, and picked up the lantern, and went away through the woods. They did not speak. They did not even look at each other. And in the dim light of the lantern their eyes were wide and brightly shining.

SIX

The cloud of dust showed first, far down the road. Then the top of the canvas tilt glinted white where the sun fell on it, shining strongly through the green trees. The tilt got higher and rounder, and the wagon began to show underneath it, and the team in front lengthened out from a confused dark blob of motion to six great bay horses stepping along as proud as emperors, their harness gleaming and the trace chains all ajingle.

High up on the wagon seat, handling the long reins lightly, was Mr. Hostetter, his beard rippling in the wind and his hat and shoulders and the trouser legs over his shins all powdered brown from the road.

Len said, "I'm scared."

"What have you got to be scared about?" said Esau. "You ain't going."

"And maybe you're not, either," muttered Len, looking up at the log bridge as the wagon rocked and rattled over it. "I don't think it's that easy."

It was June, in full bright leaf. Len and Esau stood beside Piper's Run just at the edge of the village, where the mill wheel hung slack in the water and kingfishers dropped like bolts of blue flame. The town square was less than a hundred yards away, and the whole township was in it, everybody who was not too young, too old, or too sick to be moved. There were friends and relatives up from Vernon and down from Williamsfield, and from Andover and Farmdale and Burghill and the lonely farmsteads across the Pennsylvania line that were nearer to Piper's Run than to any village of their own. It was the strawberry festival, the first big social event of the summer, where people who had perhaps not seen each other since the first snow could get together and talk and pleasantly stuff themselves, sitting in the dappled sunshine under the elms.

A crowd of boys had run out along the road to meet the wagon. They were running beside it now, shouting up to Mr. Hostetter. The girls, and the boys still too little to run, stood along the edges of the square and waved and called out, the girls in their bonnets and their long skirts blowing in the warm wind, the tiny boys exactly like their fathers in homespun and broad brown hats. Then everybody began to move, flowing across the square toward the wagon, which went slower and slower and finally stopped, the six great horses tossing their heads and snorting as though they had done a mighty thing to get that wagon there and were proud of it. Mr. Hostetter waved and smiled and a boy climbed up and put a dish of strawberries in his hand.

Len and Esau stayed where they were, looking at Mr. Hostetter from a distance. Len felt a curious thrill go through him, partly of sheer guiltiness because of the stolen radio and partly of intimacy, almost of comradeship, because he knew a secret about Mr. Hostetter and was in a sense set apart himself. Somehow, though, he did not want to meet Mr. Hostetter's eyes.

"How are you going to do it?" he asked Esau.

"I'll find a way."

He was staring at the wagon with a fanatic intensity. Ever since that night when they had heard voices Esau had turned somehow strange and wild, not outside but inside, so that sometimes Len hardly knew him any more. *I'm going there*, he had said, meaning Bartorstown, and he had been like one possessed, waiting for Mr. Hostetter.

Esau reached out and took Len by the arm, his grip painfully tight. "Won't you come with me?"

Len hung his head. He stood for a moment, quite still, and then he said, "No, I can't." He moved away from Esau. "Not now."

"Maybe next year. I'll tell him about you."

"Maybe."

Esau started to say something more, but he could not seem to find any words for it. Len moved farther away. He started up the bank, slowly at first and then faster and faster until he was running, with the tears hot in his eyes and his own mind shouting at him, Coward, coward, he's going to Bartorstown and you don't dare!

He did not look back again.

Mr. Hostetter stayed three days in Piper's Run. They were the longest, hardest days Len had ever lived through. Temptation kept telling him, You can still go. And then Conscience would point out Ma and Pa and home and duty and the wickedness of running away without a word. Esau had not given Uncle David and Aunt Mariah a second thought, but Len could not feel that way about Pa and Ma. He knew how Ma would cry, and how Pa would take the blame on himself that he hadn't trained Len right somehow, and that was the biggest part of his cowardice. He didn't want to be responsible for making them unhappy.

There was a third voice in him, too. It lived way back of the others and it had no name. It was a voice he had never heard before, and it only said *No—danger!* whenever he thought of going with Esau to Mr. Hostetter. It spoke so loud and so firm without ever being asked that Len could not ignore it, and in fact when he tried to it became a physical restraint on him just like the reins on a horse, pulling him this way and that past a word or an action that might have been irretrievable. It was Len's first active encounter with his own subconscious. He never forgot it.

He moped and sulked and brooded around the farm, burdened with his secret, hobbling his chores and making excuses not to go into town when the family did, until Ma worried and dosed him heavily with physics and sassafras tea. And all the time his ears were stretched and quivering, waiting to hear hoofbeats on the road, waiting to hear Uncle David rush in saying that Esau was gone.

On the evening of the third day he heard the hoofbeats, coming fast. He was just helping Ma clear off the supper dishes, and the light was still in the sky, reddening toward the west. His nerves jerked taut with a painful snap. The dishes became slippery and enormous in his hands. The horse turned in to the dooryard with the cart rattling behind him, and after that a second horse and cart, and after that a third. Pa went to the door, and Len followed him, with a sickness settling in all his bones. One horse and cart for Uncle David he had expected. But three—

Uncle David was there, all right. He sat in his own cart, and Esau was beside him, sitting still and as white as a sheet, and Mr. Harkness was on the other side of him. Mr. Hostetter was in the second cart with Mr. Nordholt, the schoolmaster, and Mr. Clute was driving. Mr. Fenway and Mr. Glasser were in the third.

Uncle David got down. He motioned to Pa, who had gone out toward the carts. Mr. Hostetter joined them, and Mr. Nordholt, and Mr. Glasser. Esau sat where he was. His head was bent forward and he did not lift it. Mr. Harkness stared at Len, who had stayed in the doorway. His look was outraged, accusing, and sad. Len met it for a fractional second and then dropped his own eyes. He felt very sick now and quite cold. He wanted to run away, but he knew it would not be any use.

The men moved all together to Uncle David's cart, and Uncle David said something to Esau. Esau continued to stare at his hands. He did not speak or nod, and Mr. Nordholt said, "He didn't mean to tell, it just slipped out of him. But he did say it."

Pa turned and looked at Len and said, "Come here."

Len walked out, quite slowly. He would not lift his head to look at Pa, not because of the anger in Pa's face, but because of the sorrow that was there.

"Len."

"Yes, sir."

"Is it true that you have a radio?"

"I—yes, sir."

"Is it true that you tried to use it to get in touch with Bartorstown?"

"Yes, sir."

"Did you read certain books that were stolen? Did you know where they were, and didn't tell Mr. Nordholt? Did you know what Esau was planning to do, and didn't tell me or Uncle David?"

Len sighed. With a gesture curiously like that of an old and tired man, he raised his head and threw his shoulders back. "Yes," he said. "I did all those things."

Pa's face, in the deepening dusk, had become like something cut from a gray rock.

"Very well," he said. "Very well."

"You can ride with us," said Mr. Glasser. "Save harnessing up, just for that little distance."

"All right," said Pa. And he gave Len a cold and blazing glance that meant Come with me.

Len followed him. He passed close to Mr. Hostetter, who was standing with his head half turned away, and under his hat brim Len thought he saw an expression of pity and regret. But they passed without speaking, and Esau never stirred. Pa climbed up into the cart with Mr. Fenway, and Mr. Glasser climbed in after him.

"Up behind," said Pa.

Len climbed slowly onto the shelf, and every movement was an effort. He clung there, and the carts jolted off in line, out of the dooryard and across the road and out around the margin of the west field, toward the woods.

They stopped about where the sumacs grew. They all got out and the men spoke together. And then Pa turned and said, "Len." He pointed at the woods. "Show us."

Len did not move.

Esau spoke for the first time. "You might as well," he said, in a voice heavy with hate. "They'll get it anyway if they have to burn the whole woods."

Uncle David cuffed him backhanded across the mouth and called him something angry and Biblical.

Pa said again, "Len."

Len yielded. He led the way into the woods. And the path looked just the same, and so did the trees, and the tiny stream, and the familiar clumps of thorn apple. But something was changed. Something was gone. They were only trees now, and thorn apples, and the rocky bed of a trickle of water. They no longer belonged to him. They were withdrawn and unwelcoming, and their outlines were harsh, and the big boots of the men crushed down the ferns.

They came out on the point at the meeting of the waters. Len stopped beside the hollow tree.

"Here," he said. His voice sounded unfamiliar in his ears. The bright glow of the west fell clearly here along the open stream, painting the leaves and grass a lurid green, tinting the brown Pymatuning with copper. Crows flapped homeward overhead, dropping their jeering laughter as they went. It seemed to Len that the laughter was meant for him.

Uncle David gave Esau a rough, hard shove. "Get it out."

Esau stood for a minute beside the tree. Len watched him, and the look that was on him in the sunset light. The crows went away, and it was very still.

Esau reached into the hollow of the tree. He brought out the books, wrapped in canvas, and handed them to Mr. Nordholt.

"They're not hurt," he said.

Mr. Nordholt unwrapped them, moving out from under the tree so he could see better. "No," he said. "No, they're not hurt." He wrapped them again and held them against his chest.

Esau lifted out the radio.

He stood holding it, and the tears came up into his eyes and glittered there but did not fall. A hesitancy had come over the men. Mr. Hostetter said, as though he had said it before but was afraid it might not have been understood, "Soames had asked me if anything happened to take his personal belongings and give them to his wife. He had shown me the chest they were in. The people at the preaching were about to loot his wagon. I did not stop to see what was in the chest."

Uncle David stepped forward. He knocked the radio from Esau's hands, driving his fist downward like a hammer. It lay on the turf, and he stamped on it, over and over with his heavy boot. Then he picked up what was left of it and flung it out into the Pymatuning.

Esau said, "I hate you." He looked at them all. "You can't stop me. Someday I'll go to Bartorstown."

Uncle David hit him again, and spun him around, and started to march him back through the woods. Over his shoulder he said, "I'll see to him."

The rest followed in a straggling line, after Mr. Harkness poked his hand around in the hollow of the tree to make sure nothing more was in there. And Mr. Hostetter said,

"I wish my wagon to be searched."

Mr. Harkness said, "We've known you a long time, Ed. I don't think that'll be necessary."

"No, I demand it," said Hostetter, speaking so that everyone could hear. "This boy has made an accusation that I can't let pass. I want my wagon searched from top to bottom, so that there can be no doubt as to whether I possess anything I should not have. Suspicion once started is hard to kill, and news travels. I wouldn't want *other* people to think of me what they thought of Soames."

A shiver ran through Len. He realized suddenly that Hostetter was making an explanation and an apology.

He also understood that Esau had made a fatal mistake.

It seemed a long way back across the west field. This time the carts did not enter the farmyard. They stopped in the road and Len and Pa got down, and the others shifted around so that Esau and Uncle David were alone in their own cart. Then Mr. Harkness said, "We will want to see the boys tomorrow." His voice was ominously quiet. He drove away toward the village, with the second cart behind him. Uncle David started the other way, toward home.

Esau leaned out of the cart and shouted hysterically at Len. "Don't give up. They can't make you stop thinking. No matter what they do to you they can't—"

Uncle David turned the cart sharp around and brought it into the farmyard.

"We'll see about that," he said. "Elijah, I'm going to use your barn."

Pa frowned, but he did not say anything. Uncle David went across to the barn, shoving Esau roughly in front of him. Ma came running out of the house. Uncle David called out, "You bring Len. I want him here." Pa frowned again and then said, "All right." He put out his hands to Ma and drew her aside and said a few words to her, very low, shaking his head. Ma looked at Len. "Oh no," she said. "Oh, Lennie, how could you?" Then she went back to the house with her apron up over her face, and Len knew that she was crying. Pa pointed to the barn. His lips were set tight together. Len thought that Pa did not like what Uncle David was going to do, but that he did not feel he could question it.

Len did not like it either. He would rather have had this just between himself and Pa. But that was like Uncle David. He always figured if you were a kid you had no more rights or feelings than any other possession around the farm. Len shrank from going into the barn.

Pa pointed again, and he went.

It was dark now, but there was a lantern burning inside. Uncle David had taken the harness leather down off the wall. Esau was facing him, in the wide space between the rows of empty stanchions.

"Get down on your knees," said Uncle David.

"No."

"Get down!" And the harness strap cracked.

Esau made a noise between a whimper and a curse. He went down on his knees.

"Thou shalt not steal," said Uncle David. "You've made me the father of a thief. Thou shalt not bear false witness. You've made me the father of a liar." His arm was rising and falling in cadence with his words, so that every pause was punctuated by a sharp *whuk!* of flat leather against Esau's shoulders. "You know what it says in the Book, Esau. He who loveth his child chasteneth him, but he who hateth his son withholdeth the rod. I'm not going to withhold it."

Esau was not able to keep silent any longer. Len turned his back.

After a while Uncle David stopped, breathing hard. "You defied me a bit ago. You said I couldn't make you change your mind. Do you still feel that way?"

Crouched on the floor, Esau screamed at his father. "Yes!"

"You still think you'll go to Bartorstown?"

"Yes!"

"Well," said Uncle David. "We'll see."

Len tried not to listen. It seemed to go on and on. Once Pa stepped forward and said, "David—" But Uncle David only said, "Tend to your own whelp, Elijah. I always told you you were too soft with him." He turned again to Esau. "Have you changed your mind yet?"

Esau's answer was unintelligible but abject in surrender.

"You," said Uncle David suddenly to Len, and jerked him around. "Look at that, and see what boasting and insolence come to in the end."

Esau was groveling on the barn floor, in the dust and straw. Uncle David stirred him with his foot.

"Do you still think you'll go to Bartorstown?"

Esau muttered and moaned, hiding his face in his arms. Len tried to pull away but Uncle David held him, with a hot heavy hand. He smelled of sweat and anger. "There's your hero," he said to Len. "Remember him when your turn comes."

"Let me go," Len whispered. Uncle David laughed. He pushed Len away and handed Pa the harness strap. Then he reached down and got Esau by the neckband of his shirt and pulled him up onto his feet.

"Say it, Esau. Say it out."

Esau sobbed like a little child. "I repent," he said. "I repent."

"Bartorstown," said Uncle David, in the same tone in which Nahum must have pronounced the bloody city. "Get out. Get home and meditate on your sins. Good night, Elijah, and remember—your boy is as guilty as mine."

They went out into the darkness. A minute later Len heard the cart drive off.

Pa sighed. His face looked tired and sad, and deeply angry in a way that was much more frightening than Uncle David's raging. He said slowly, "I trusted you, Len. You betrayed me."

"I didn't mean to."

"But you did."

"Yes."

"Why, Len? You knew those things were wrong. Why did you do them?"

Len cried, "Because I couldn't help it. I want to learn, I want to *know!*"

Pa took off his hat and rolled up his sleeve. "I could preach a long sermon on that text," he said. "But I've already done that, and it was breath wasted. You remember what I told you, Len."

"Yes, Pa." And he set his jaw and curled his two hands up tight.

"I'm sorry," said Pa. "I didn't ever want to have to do this. But I'm going to purge you of your pride, Len, just as Esau was purged."

Inside himself Len said fiercely, No, you won't, you won't make me get down and crawl. I'm not going to give them up, Bartorstown and books and knowing and all the things there are in the world outside of Piper's Run!

But he did. In the dust and straw of the barn he gave them up, and his pride with them. And that was the end of his childhood.

SEVEN

He had slept for a while, a black heavy sleep, and then he had waked again to stare at the darkness, and feel, and think. His body hurt, not with the mere familiar smart of a licking but in a serious way that he would not forget in a hurry. It did not hurt anything like as much as the intangible parts of him, and he lay and wrestled with the agony in the little lopsided room under the eaves that was still stifling from the day's sun. It was almost dawn before anything stood clear from the blind fury of grief and rage and resentment and utter shame that shook around in him like big winds in a small place. Then, perhaps because he was too exhausted to be violent any more, he began to see a thing or two, and understand.

He knew that when he had groveled in Esau's tracks in the dust and forsworn himself, he had lied. He was not going to give up Bartorstown. He could not give it up without giving up the most important part of himself. He did not know quite what that most important part was, but he knew it was there, and he knew that nobody, not even Pa, had the right to lay hands on it. Good or bad, righteous or sinful, it lay beyond whim or attitude or passing play. It was himself, Len Colter, the individual, unique. He could not forswear it and live.

When he understood that, he slept again, quietly, and woke with a salt taste of tears in his mouth to see the window clear and bright and the sun just coming up. The air was full of sound, the screaming of jays and the harsh call of a pheasant in the hedgerow, the piping and chirping of innumerable birds. Len looked out, past the lightning-blasted stub of a giant maple with one indomitable spray of green still sprouting from its side, over the henhouse roof and the home field with the winter wheat ripening on it, to the rough hill slope and the upper wood rising to a crest on which were three dark pines. And a dull sadness came over him, because he was looking at it for the last time. He did not arrive at that decision by any conscious line of reasoning. He only knew it, immediately he waked.

He rose and went stiffly about his chores, white and remote, speaking only when he was spoken to, avoiding people's eyes. With rough kindness, Brother James told him, out of Pa's earshot, to buck up. "It's for your own good, Lennie, and someday you'll look back and be thankful you were caught in time. After all, it's not the end of the world."

Oh yes it is, thought Len. And that's all people know.

After the midday meal he was sent upstairs to wash himself and put on the suit that ordinarily he wore only on the Sabbath. And pretty soon Ma came up with a clean shirt still warm from the iron and made a pretense of looking sternly behind his ears and under his back hair. All the while the tears stole out of her eyes, and suddenly she caught him to her and said rapidly in a whisper, "How could you have done it, Lennie, how could you have been so wicked, to offend the good God and disobey your father?"

Len felt himself beginning to crumble. In a minute or two he would be crying in Ma's arms and all his resolve gone for the time being. So he pushed away from her and said, "Please, Ma, that hurts."

"Your poor back," she murmured. "I forgot." She took his hands. "Lennie, be humble, be patient, and this will all pass away. God will forgive you, you're so young. Too young to realize—"

Pa hollered up the stairs, and that ended it. Ten minutes later the cart was rattling out of the yard, with Len sitting very stiffly beside his father, and neither of them speaking. And Len was thinking about God, and Satan, and the town elders and the preaching man, and Soames and Hostetter and Bartorstown, and it was all confused, but he knew one thing. God was not going to forgive him. He had chosen the way of the transgressor, and he was beyond all hope damned. But he would have all of Bartorstown to keep him company.

Uncle David's cart caught up with them and they went into town together, with Esau huddled in the corner and looking small and fallen-in, as though the bones had all been taken out of him. When they came to the house of Mr. Harkness, Pa and Uncle David got out and stood talking together, leaving Len and Esau to hitch the horses. Esau did not look at Len. He avoided even turning toward him. Len did not look at him, either. But they were side by side at the hitching rack, and Len said fiercely under his breath, "I'll wait for you on the point till moonrise. Then I'm going on."

He could feel Esau start and stiffen. Before he could open his mouth Len said, "Shut up." Then he turned and walked away, to stand respectfully behind his father.

There was a very long, very unhappy session in the parlor of Mr. Harkness' house. Mr. Fenway, Mr. Glasser, and Mr. Clute were there too, and Mr. Nordholt. When they were through, Len felt as though he had been skinned and drawn, like a rabbit with its inmost parts exposed. It made him angry. It made him hate all these slow-spoken bearded men who tore and picked and peeled at him.

Twice he felt that Esau was on the point of betraying him, and he was all ready to make his cousin out a liar. But Esau held his tongue, and after a while Len thought he saw a little stiffening come back into Esau's backbone.

The examination was finished at last. The men conferred. At last Mr. Harkness said to Pa and Uncle David, "I'm sorry that such a disgrace should be brought upon you, for you're both good men and old friends.

But perhaps it will serve as a reminder to everybody that youth is not to be trusted, and that constant watchfulness is the price of a Christian soul."

He swung about very grimly on the boys. "A public birching for both of you, on Saturday morning. And after that, if you should be found guilty a second time, you know what the punishment will be."

He waited. Esau looked at his boots. Len stared steadily past Mr. Harkness' shoulder.

"Well," said Mr. Harkness sharply. "Do you know?"

"Yes," said Len. "You'll make us go away and never come back." He looked Mr. Harkness in the eye and added, "There won't be a second time."

"I sincerely hope not," said Mr. Harkness. "And I recommend that both of you read your Bibles, and meditate, and pray, that God may give you wisdom as well as forgiveness."

There was some more talk among the elders, and then the Colters went out and got into their carts and started home again. They passed Mr. Hostetter's wagon in the town square, but Mr. Hostetter was not in sight.

Pa was silent most of the way, except that all at once he said, "I hold myself to blame in this as much as you, Len."

Len said, "I did it. It wasn't any fault of yours, Pa. It couldn't be."

"Somewhere I failed. I didn't teach you right, didn't make you understand. Somewhere you got away from me." Pa shook his head. "I guess David was right. I spared the rod too much."

"Esau was in it more than me," said Len. "He stole the radio in the first place, and all Uncle David's lickings didn't stop him. It wasn't any way your fault, Pa. It was all mine." He felt bad. Somehow he knew this was the real guilt, and it couldn't be helped.

"James was never like this," said Pa to himself, wondering. "Never a moment's worry. How can the same seed produce two such different fruits?"

They did not speak again. When they got home Ma and Gran and Brother James were waiting. Len was sent to his room, and as he climbed the narrow stairs he could hear Pa telling briefly what had happened, and Ma letting out a little whimpering sob. And suddenly he heard Gran's voice lifted high and shrill in mighty anger.

"You're a fool and a coward, Elijah. That's what you all are, fools and cowards, and the boy is worth the lot of you! Go ahead and break his spirit if you can, but I hope you never do it. I hope you never teach him to be afraid of knowing the truth."

Len smiled and a little quiver went through him, because he knew that was meant for his ears as much as Pa's. All right, Gran, he thought. I'll remember.

That night, when the house was stone-dead quiet, he tied his boots around his neck and crept out the window to the summer-kitchen roof, and from there to the limb of a pear tree, and from there to the ground. He stole out of the farmyard and across the road, and there he put his boots on. Then he walked on, skirting the west field where this season's young oats were growing. The woods loomed very dark ahead. He did not once look back.

It was black and still and lonely in among the trees. Len thought, It's going to be like this a lot from now on, you might as well get used to it. When he reached the point he sat down on the same log where he had sat so often before, and listened to the night music of the frogs and the quiet slipping of the Pymatuning between its banks. The world felt huge, and there was a coldness at his back as though some protective covering had been sheared away. He wondered if Esau would come.

It began to get light down in the southeast, a smudgy grayness brightening slowly to silver. Len waited. He won't come, he thought, he's scared, and I'll have to do this alone. He got up, listening, watching the first thin edge of the moon come up. And a voice inside him said, You can still run home and climb in the window again, and nobody will ever know. He hung on hard to the limb of a tree to keep himself from doing it.

There was a rustle and a thrashing in the dark woods, and Esau came.

They peered at each other for a moment, like owls, and then they caught each other's hands and laughed.

"Public birching," Esau said, panting. "Public birching, hell. The hell with them."

"We'll walk downstream," Len said, "until we find a boat."

"But after that, what?"

"We keep on going. Rivers run into other rivers. I saw the map in the history book. If you keep going long enough you come to the Ohio, and that's the biggest river there is hereabouts."

Esau said stubbornly, "But why the Ohio? It's way south, and everybody knows Bartorstown is west,"

"But where west? West is an awful big place. Listen, don't you remember the voice we heard? The stuff is on the river ready to load as soon as the something. They were Bartorstown men talking, about stuff that was going to Bartorstown. And the Ohio runs west. It's the main highway. After that, there's other rivers. And boats must go there. And that's where we're going."

Esau thought about it a minute. Then he said, "Well, all right. It's a place to start from, anyway. Besides, who knows? I still think we were right about Hostetter, even if he did lie about it. Maybe he'll tell the others, maybe they'll talk about us over their radios, how we ran away to find them. Maybe they'll help us, even, when they find a safe time. Who knows?"

"Yes," said Len. "Who knows?"

They walked off along the bank of the Pymatuning, going south. The moon climbed up to give them light. The water rippled and the frogs sang, and in Len Colter's mind the name of Bartorstown rang with the sound of a great bell.

BOOK TWO

EIGHT

The narrow brown waters of the Pymatuning fatten the Shenango. The Shenango flows down to meet the Mahoning, and the two of them together make the Beaver. The Beaver fattens the Ohio, and the Ohio runs grandly westward to help make mighty the Father of Waters.

Time flows, too. Little units grow into big ones, minutes into months and months into years. Boys become men, and the milestones of a long search multiply and are left behind. But the legend remains a legend, and the dream a dream, glimmering, fading, ever somewhere farther on toward the sunset.

There was a town called Refuge, and a yellow-haired girl, and they were real.

Refuge was not at all like Piper's Run. It was bigger, so much bigger that its boundaries were already straining against the lawful limits, but size was not the chief difference. It was a matter of feeling. Len and Esau had noticed that same feeling in a number of places as they worked their way along the river valleys, particularly where, as in Refuge, highway and waterway conjoined. Piper's Run lived and breathed with the slow calm rhythm of the seasons, and the thoughts of the folk who lived there were calm too. Refuge bustled. The people moved faster, and thought faster, and talked louder, and the streets were noisier at night, with a passing of drays and wagons and the voices of stevedores along the wharves.

Refuge stood on the north bank of the Ohio. It had come by its name, Len understood, because people from a city farther along the river had taken refuge there during the Destruction. It was the terminus now for two main trading routes stretching as far as the Great Lakes, and the wagons rolled day and night while the roads were passable, bringing down baled furs and iron and woolen cloth, flour and cheeses. From east and west along the river came other traffic, bearing other things, copper and hides and tallow and salt beef from the plains, coal and scrap metal from Pennsylvania, salt fish from the Atlantic, kegs of nails, fine guns, paper. The river traffic moved

67

around the clock, too, from spring to early winter, flatboats and launches and tugs towing long strings of loaded barges, going with a fine brave smoke and clatter from their steam engines. These were the first engines Len and Esau had ever seen, and at first they were frightened out of their wits by the noise, but they soon got used to them. They had, one winter, worked in a little foundry near the mouth of the Beaver, making boilers and feeling as though they were already helping to mechanize the world. The New Mennonites frowned on the use of any artificial power, but the riverboat men belonged to different sects and had different problems. They had to get cargoes upriver against the current, and if they could harness steam in a simple and easily handmade engine to help them, they were going to do it, cutting the ethic to fit the need.

On the Kentucky side of the river, just opposite, there was a place called Shadwell. Shadwell was much smaller than Refuge and much newer, but it was swelling out so fast that even Len and Esau could see the difference in the year or so they had been there. The people of Refuge did not care much for Shadwell, which had only happened because traders had begun to come up out of the South with sugar and blackstrap and cotton and tobacco, drawn by the commerce of the Refuge markets. A couple of temporary sheds had gone up, and a ferry dock, and a cabin or two, and before anybody realized it there was a village, with wharves and warehouses of its own, and a name, and a growing population. And Refuge, already as large as a town was permitted by law to be, sat sourly by and watched the overplus of trade it could not handle flow into Shadwell.

There were few Amish or Mennonites in Refuge. The people mostly belonged to the Church of Holy Thankfulness, and were called Kellerites after the James P. Keller who founded the sect. Len and Esau had found that there were few Mennonites anywhere in the settlements that lived by commerce rather than by agriculture. And since they were excommunicated themselves, with no wish to be traced back to Piper's Run, they had long ago discarded the distinctive dress of their childhood faith for the nondescript homespuns of the river towns. They wore their hair short and their chins naked, because it was the custom among the Kellerites for a man to remain clean-shaven until he married, when he was expected to grow the beard that distinguished him more plainly than any removable ring. They went every Sunday to the Church of Holy Thankfulness, and joined in the regular daily devotions of the family they boarded with, and sometimes they forgot that they had ever been anything but Kellerites.

Sometimes, Len thought, they even forgot why they were here and what they were looking for. And he would make himself remember the night when he had waited for Esau on the point above the Pymatuning, and everything that had gone before to bring him there, and it was easy enough to remember the physical things, the chill air and the smell of leaves, the beating, and the way Pa's face had looked as he lifted the strap and brought it whistling down. But the other part of it, the way he had felt inside, was harder to call to mind. Sometimes he could do it only with a real effort. Other times he could not do it at all. And at still other times—and these were the worst—the way he had felt about leaving home and finding Bartorstown seemed to him childish and absurd. He would see home and family so clearly that it was a physical pain in him, and he would think, I threw them all away for a name, a voice in the air, and here I am, a wanderer, and where is Bartorstown? He had found out that time can be a traitor and that thoughts are like mountaintops, a different shape on every side, changing as you move away.

Time had played him another trick, too. It had made him grow up and given him a lot of brand-new things to worry about.

Including the yellow-haired girl.

It was an evening in mid-June, hot and sultry, with the sunset swallowed up in the blackness of an oncoming storm. The two candles on the table burned straight up, with no quiver of air from the open windows to trouble them. Len sat with his hands folded and his head bent, looking down into the remains of a milk pudding. Esau sat on his right, in the same attitude. The yellow-haired girl sat across from them. Her name was Amity Taylor. Her father was saying grace after meat, sitting at the head of the table, and at the foot, her mother listened reverently.

"—didst stretch out the garment of Thy mercy to shelter us in the day of Destruction—"

Amity glanced up from under the shadows of her brows in the candlelight, looking first at Len and then at Esau.

"—our thanks for the limitless abundance of Thy blessing—"

Len felt the girl's eyes on him. His skin was thin and sensitive to that touch, so that without even looking up he knew what she was doing. His heart began to thump. He felt hot. Esau's hands were in his line of vision, folded between Esau's knees. He saw them move and tighten, and he knew that Amity had looked at Esau too, and he got even hotter, thinking about the garden and the shadowy place under the rose arbor.

Wouldn't Judge Taylor ever shut up?

The Amen came at last, muffled in the louder voice of thunder. Hurry, thought Len. Hurry with the dishes or there won't be any walking in the garden. Not for anybody. He jumped up, scraping his chair back over the bare floor. Esau jumped up too, and he and Len went to picking up plates off the table so fast they jostled each other. On the other side of the candlelight, Amity slowly stacked the cups, and smiled.

Mrs. Taylor went out, carrying two serving dishes into the kitchen. At the hall door, the judge seemed on the point of going to his study, as he always did immediately after the final grace. Esau turned suddenly and gave Len a covert glare of anger, and whispered, "Stay out of this."

Amity walked toward the kitchen door, balancing the stack of cups in her two hands. Her yellow hair hung down her back in a thick braid. She wore a dress of gray cotton, high in the neck and long in the skirt, but it did not look on her at all the way a similar dress did on her mother. She had a wonderful way of walking. It made Len's heart come up in his throat every time he saw it. He glared back at Esau and started after her with his own load of plates, making long strides to get ahead. And Judge Taylor said quietly from the hall door, "Len—come into the study when you've put those down. They can get along without you for one washing."

Len stopped. He gave Taylor a startled and apprehensive look, and said, "Yes, sir." Taylor nodded and left the room. Len glanced briefly at Esau, who was openly upset.

"What does he want?" asked Esau.

"How should I know?"

"Listen. Listen, have you been up to anything?"

Amity went slowly through the swinging door, with her skirt moving gracefully around her ankles. Len flushed.

"No more'n you have, Esau," he said angrily. He went after Amity and put his pile of dishes down on the sink board. Amity began to roll her sleeves up. She said to her mother, "Len can't help tonight. Daddy wants him."

Reba Taylor turned from the stove, where a pot of wash water simmered over the coals. She had a mild, pleasant, rather vacuous face, and Len had marked her long ago as one of the incurious ones. Life had passed over her so easily.

"Dear, dear," she said. "Surely you haven't done anything wrong, Len?"

"I hope not, ma'am."

"I'll bet you," said Amity, "that it's about Mike Dulinsky and his warehouse."

"Mr. Dulinsky," said Reba Taylor sharply, "and get about your dishes, young lady. They're your concern. Run along, Len. Very likely the judge only wants to give you some advice, and you could do worse than listen to it."

"Yes, ma'am," said Len, and went out, across the dining room and into the hall and along that to the study, wondering all the way whether he had been seen kissing Amity in the garden, or whether it was about the Dulinsky business, or what. He had often gone to the judge's study, and he had often talked with him, about books and the past and the future and sometimes even the present, but he had never been called in before.

The study door was open. Taylor said, "Come in, Len." He was sitting behind his big desk in the angle of the windows. They faced the west, and the sky beyond them was a dull black as though it had been wiped all over with soot. The trees looked sickly and colorless, and the river lay at one side like a strip of lead. Taylor had been sitting there looking out, with an unlighted candle and an unopened book beside him. He was rather a small man, with smooth cheeks and a high forehead. His hair and beard were always neatly trimmed, his linen was fresh every day, and his dark plain suit was cut from the finest cloth that came into the Refuge market. Len liked him. He had books and read them and encouraged other people to read them, and he was not afraid of knowledge, though he never made a parade of having any more than he needed in his profession. "Don't call undue attention to yourself," he often told Len, "and you will avoid a great deal of trouble."

Now he told Len to come in and shut the door. "I'm afraid we're going to have a really serious talk, and I wanted you here alone because I want you to be free to think and make your decisions without any—well, any other influences."

"You don't think much of Esau, do you?" asked Len, sitting down where the judge had set a chair for him.

"No," said Taylor, "but that is neither here nor there. Except that I'll say further that I do think a great deal of you. And now we'll leave personalities alone. Len, you work for Mike Dulinsky."

"Yes, sir," said Len, and began to bristle up a bit, defensively. So that was it.

"Are you going to continue working for him?"

Len hesitated only a short second before he said again, "Yes, sir."

Taylor thought, looking out at the black sky and the ugly dusk. A beautiful forked blaze ran down the clouds. Len counted slowly, and when he reached seven there was a roll of thunder. "It's still quite a ways off," he said.

"Yes, but we'll catch it. When they come from that direction, we always do. You've done a lot of reading this last year, Len. Have you learned anything from it?"

Len ran his eye lovingly over the shelves. It was too dark to see titles, but he knew the books by their size and place and he had read an awful lot of them.

"I hope so," he said.

"Then apply what you've learned. It isn't any good to you shut up inside your head in a separate cupboard. Do you remember Socrates?"

"Yes."

"He was a greater and a wiser man than you or I will ever be, but that didn't save him when he ran too hard against the whole body of law and public belief."

Lightning flashed again, and this time the interval was shorter. The wind began to blow, tossing the branches of the trees around and riffling the blank surface of the river. Distant figures labored on the wharves to make fast the moorings of the barges, or to hustle bales and sacks under cover. Landward, between the trees, the whitewashed or weathered-silver houses of Refuge glimmered in the last wan light from overhead.

"Why do you want to hasten the day?" asked Taylor quietly. "You'll never live to see it, and neither will your children, nor your grandchildren. Why, Len?"

"Why what?" asked Len, now blankly confused, and then he gasped as Taylor answered him, "Why do you want to bring back the cities?"

Len was silent, peering into the gloom that had suddenly deepened until Taylor was no more than a shadow four feet away.

"They were dying even before the Destruction," said Taylor. "Megalopolis, drowned in its own sewage, choked with its own waste gases, smothered and crushed by its own population. 'City' sounds like a musical word to your ear, but what do you really know about them?"

They had been over this ground before. "Gran used to say—"

"That she was a little girl then, and little girls would hardly see the dirt, the ugliness, the crowded poverty, the vice. The cities were sucking all the life of the country into themselves and destroying it. Men were no longer individuals, but units in a vast machine, all cut to one pattern, with the same tastes and ideas, the same mass-produced education that did not educate but only pasted a veneer of catchwords over ignorance. Why do you want to bring that back?"

An old argument, but applied in a totally unexpected way. Len stammered, "I haven't been thinking about cities one way or the other. And I don't see what Mr. Dulinsky's new warehouse has to do with them."

"Len, if you're not honest with yourself, life will never be honest with you. A stupid man could say that he didn't see and be honest, but not you. Unless you're still too much of a child to think beyond the immediate fact."

"I'm old enough to get married," said Len hotly, "and that ought to be old enough for anything."

"Quite," said Taylor. "Quite. Here comes the rain, Len. Help me with the windows." They shut them, and Taylor lit the candle. The room was now unbearably close and hot. "What a pity," he said, "that the windows always have to be closed just when the cool wind starts to blow. Yes, you're old enough to get married, and I think Amity has a thought or two in that direction herself. It's a possibility I want you to consider."

Len's heart began to pound, the way it always did when Amity was involved. He felt wildly excited, and at the same time it was as though a trap had been set before his feet. He sat down again, and the rain thrashed on the windows like hail.

Taylor said slowly, "Refuge is a good town just the way it stands. You could have a good life here. I can take you off the docks and make a lawyer out of you, and in time you'd be an important man. You would have leisure for study, and all the wisdom of the world is there in those books. And there's Amity. Those are the things I can give you. What does Dulinsky offer?"

Len shook his head. "I do my work, and he pays me. That's all."

"You know he's breaking the law."

"It's a silly law. One warehouse more or less—"

"One warehouse more, in this case, violates the Thirtieth Amendment, which is the most basic law of this land. It won't be overlooked."

"But it isn't fair. Nobody here in Refuge wants to see Shadwell spring up and take a lot of business away because there aren't enough warehouses and wharves and shelters on this side to take care of all the trade."

"One more warehouse," said Taylor, pointedly repeating Len's words, "and then more wharves to serve it, and more housing for the traders, and pretty soon you'll need another warehouse still, and that is the way in which cities are born. Len, has Dulinsky ever mentioned Bartorstown to you?"

Len's heart, which had been beating so hard for Amity, now stopped in sudden fear. He shivered and said, with perfect truthfulness, "No, sir. Never."

"I just wondered. It seems the kind of a thing a Bartorstown man might do. But then I've known Mike since we were boys together, and I can't remember any possible influence—no, I suppose not. But that may not save him, Len, and it may not save you."

Len said carefully, "I don't think I understand."

"You and Esau are strangers. People will accept you as long as you don't run counter to their ways, but if you do, look out." He leaned his elbows on the desk and looked at Len. "You haven't been altogether truthful about yourself."

"I haven't told any lies."

"That isn't always necessary. Anyway, I can pretty well guess. You're a country boy. I would lay odds that you were New Mennonite. And you ran away from home. Why?"

"I guess," said Len, choosing his words as a man on the edge of a pitfall chooses his steps, "that it was because Pa and me couldn't agree on how much was right for me to know."

"Thus far," said Taylor thoughtfully, "and no farther. That has always been a difficult line to draw. Each sect must decide for itself, and to a certain degree, so must every man. Have you found your limit, Len?"

"Not yet."

"Find it," Taylor said, "before you go too far."

They sat for a moment in silence. The rain poured and a lightning bolt came down so close that it made an audible hissing before it hit. The resultant thunder shook the house like an explosion.

"Do you understand," asked Taylor, "why the Thirtieth Amendment was passed?"

"So there wouldn't be any more cities."

"Yes, but do you comprehend the reasoning behind that interdiction? I was brought up in a certain body of belief, and in public I wouldn't dream of contradicting any part of it, but here in private I can say that I do not believe that God directed the cities to be destroyed because they were sinful. I've read too much history. The enemy bombed the big key cities because they were excellent targets, centers of population, centers of manufacture and distribution, without which the country would be like a man with his head cut off. And it worked out just that way. The enormously complex system of supply broke down, the cities that were not bombed had to be abandoned because they were not only dangerous but useless, and everyone was thrown back on the simple basics of survival, chiefly the search for food.

"The men who framed the new laws were determined that that should not happen again. They had the people dispersed now, and they were going to keep them that way, close to their source of supply and offering no more easy targets to a potential enemy. So they passed the Thirtieth Amendment. It was a wise law. It suited the people. They had just had a fearful object lesson in what kind of deathtraps the cities could be. They didn't want any more of them, and gradually that became an article of faith. The country has been healthy and prosperous under the Thirtieth Amendment, Len. Leave it alone."

"Maybe you're right," said Len, scowling at the candle flame. "But when Mr. Dulinsky says how the country has really started to grow again and shouldn't be stopped by outgrown laws, I think he's right, too."

"Don't let him fool you. He's not worried about the country. He's a man who owns four warehouses and wants to own five and is sore because the law says he can't do it."

The judge stood up.

"You'll have to decide what's right in your own mind. But I want to make one thing clear to you. I have my wife and my daughter and myself to think about. If you go on with Dulinsky you'll have to leave my house. No more walks with Amity. No more books. And I warn you, if I am called upon to judge you, judge you I will."

Len stood up too. "Yes, sir."

Taylor dropped a hand on his shoulder. "Don't be a fool, Len. Think it over."

"I will." He went out, feeling sullen and resentful and at the same time convinced that the judge was talking sense. Amity, marriage, a place in the community, a future, roots, no more Dulinsky, no more doubt. No more Bartorstown. No more dreaming. No more seeking and never finding.

He thought about being married to Amity, and what it would be like. It frightened him so that he sweated like a colt seeing harness for the first time. No more dreaming for fair. He thought of Brother James, who by now must be the father of several small Mennonites, and he wondered whether, on the whole, Refuge was very different from Piper's Run, and if Amity was worth having come all this way for. Amity, or Plato. He had not read Plato in Piper's Run, and he had read him in Refuge, but Plato did not seem like the whole answer, either.

No more Bartorstown. But would he ever find it, anyway? Was he crazy to think of exchanging a girl for a phantom?

The hall was dark, except for the intermittent flashes of lightning. There was one of these as he passed the foot of the stairs, and in its brief glare he saw Esau and Amity in the triangular alcove under the treads. They were pressed close together and Esau was kissing her hard, and Amity was not protesting.

NINE

It was the Sabbath afternoon. They were standing in the shadow of the rose arbor, and Amity was glaring at him.

"You did not see me doing any such thing, and if you tell anybody you did I'll say you're lying!"

"I know what I saw," said Len, "and so do you."

She made her thick braid switch back and forth, in a way she had of tossing her head. "I'm not promised to you."

"Would you like to be, Amity?"

"Maybe. I don't know."

"Then why were you kissing Esau?"

"Well, because," she said very reasonably, "how would I know which one of you I like the best, if I didn't?"

"All right," said Len. "All right, then." He reached out and pulled her to him, and because he was thinking of how Esau had done it he was rather rough about it. For the first time he held her really tight and felt how soft and firm she was and how her body curved amazingly. Her eyes were close to his, so close that they became only a blue color without any shape, and he felt dizzy and shut his own, and found her mouth just by touch alone.

After a while he pushed her away a little and said, "Now which is it?" He was shaking all over, but there was only the faintest flush in Amity's cheeks and the look she gave him was quite cool. She smiled.

"I don't know," she said. "You'll have to try again."

"Is that what you told Esau?"

"What do you care what I told Esau?" Again the yellow braid went swish-swish across the back of her dress. "You mind your own business, Len Colter."

"I could make it my business."

"Who said?"

"Your father said, that's who."

"Oh," said Amity. "He did." Suddenly it was as though a curtain had dropped between them. She drew away, and the line of her mouth got hard.

"Amity," he said. "Listen, Amity, I—"

"You leave me alone. You hear, Len?"

"What's so different now? You were anxious enough a minute ago."

"Anxious! That's all you know. And if you think because you've been sneaking around to my father behind my back—"

"I didn't sneak. Amity, listen." He caught her again and pulled her toward him, and she hissed at him between her teeth. "Let me go, I don't belong to you, I don't belong to anybody! Let me go—"

He held her, struggling. It excited him, and he laughed and bent his head to kiss her again.

"Aw, come on, Amity, I love you—"

She squalled like a cat and clawed his cheek. He let her go, and she was not pretty any more, her face was all twisted and ugly and her eyes were mean. She ran away from him down the path. The air was warm and the smell of roses was heavy around him. For a while he stood looking after her, and then he walked slowly to the house and up to the room he shared with Esau.

Esau was lying on the bed, half asleep. He only grunted and rolled over when Len came in. Len opened the door of the shallow cupboard. He took out a small sack made of tough canvas and began to pack his belongings into it, methodically, ramming each article down into place with unnecessary force. His face was flushed and his brows pulled down into a heavy scowl.

Esau rolled back again. He blinked at Len and said, "What do you think you're doing?"

"Packing."

"Packing!" Esau sat up. "What for?"

"What do people usually do it for? I'm leaving."

Esau's feet hit the floor. "Are you crazy? What do you mean, you're leaving, just like that. Don't I have anything to say about it?"

"Not about me leaving, you don't. You can do what you want to. Look out, I want those boots."

"All right! But you can't—Wait a minute. What's that on your cheek?"

"What?" Len swiped at his cheek with the back of his hand. It came away with a little red smear on it. Amity had dug deep.

Esau began to laugh.

Len straightened up. "What's funny?"

"She finally told you off, did she? Oh, don't give me any story about how the cat scratched you, I know claw marks when I see them. Good. I told you to keep away from her, but you wouldn't listen. I—"

"Do you figure," asked Len quietly, "that she belongs to you?"

Esau smiled. "I could have told you that, too."

Len hit him. It was the first time in his life that he had hit anybody in genuine anger. He watched Esau fall backward onto the bed, his eyes bulging with surprise and a thin red trickle springing out of the corner of his mouth, and it all seemed to happen very slowly, giving him plenty of time to feel guilty and regretful and confused. It was almost as though he had struck his own brother. But he was still angry. He grabbed up his bag and started out the door, and Esau sprang off the bed and caught him by the shoulder of his jacket, spinning him around. "Hit me, will you?" he panted. "Hit me, you dirty—" He called Len a name he had picked up along the river docks and swung his fist, hard.

Len ducked. Esau's knuckles slid along the side of his jaw and on into the solid jamb of the door. Esau howled and danced away, holding his hand under his other arm and cursing. Len started to say something like "I'm sorry," but changed his mind and turned again to go. And Judge Taylor was in the hall.

"Stop that," he said to Esau, and Esau stopped, standing still in the middle of the room. Taylor looked from one to the other and to the bag in Len's hand. "I've just spoken to Amity," he said, and Len could see that underneath his judicial manner Taylor was in a seething rage. "I'm sorry, Len. I seem to have made an error of judgment."

"Yes, sir," said Len. "I was just going."

Taylor nodded. "All the same," he said, "what I told you is true. Remember it." He looked keenly at Esau.

"Let him go," Esau said. "I'm staying right here."

"I think not," said Taylor.

Esau said, "But he—"

"I hit him first," said Len.

"That is neither here nor there," said the judge. "Get your things together, Esau."

"But why? I make enough to pay the rent. I haven't done any—"

"I'm not sure yet exactly what you have done, but much or little, that's an end to it. The room is no longer for rent. And if I catch you around my daughter again I'll have you run out of town. Is that clear?"

Esau glowered at him, but he did not say anything. He started to throw his things into a pile on the bed. Len went out past the judge, along the hall and down the stairs. He went out the back way, and as he passed the kitchen he caught a glimpse through the half-open door of Amity bent over the kitchen table, sobbing like a wildcat, and Mrs. Taylor watching her with an expression of blank dismay, one hand raised as though for a comforting pat on the shoulder but stopped in midair and forgotten.

Len let himself out by the back gate, avoiding the rose arbor.

Sabbath lay quiet and heavy on the town. Len stuck to the alleys, walking steadily along in the dust. He did not have any idea where he was going, but habit and the general configuration of Refuge took him down to the river and onto the docks where Dulinsky's four big warehouses stood in line. He stopped there, uncertain and sullen, only just beginning to realize that things had changed very radically for him in the last few minutes.

The river ran green as bottle glass, and among the trees of its farther bank the roofs of Shadwell glimmered in the hot sun. There was a string of river craft tied up along the dock. The men who belonged to them were either in the town or asleep below deck. Nothing moved but the river, and the clouds, and a half-grown cat playing a game with itself on the foredeck of one of the barges. Off to his right, further down, was the big bare rectangle of the new warehouse site. The foundation stones were already laid. Timbers and planks were set by in neat piles, and there was a sawmill with a heap of pale yellow dust below it. Two men, widely separated, lounged inconspicuously in the shade. Len frowned. They looked to him almost as though they were on guard.

Perhaps they were. It was a stupid world, full of stupid people. Fearful people, thinking that if the least little thing was changed the whole sky would fall on them. Stupid world. He hated it. Amity lived in it, and somewhere in it Bartorstown was hidden so it could never be found, and life was dark and full of frustrations.

He was still brooding when Esau came onto the dock after him.

Esau was carrying his own belongings in a hasty bundle, and his face looked red and ugly. His lip was swollen on one side. He threw the bundle down and stood in front of Len and said, "I've got a couple of things to settle with you."

Len breathed hard through his nose. He was not afraid of Esau, and he felt low and mean enough now that a fight would be a pleasant thing. He was not quite as tall as Esau but his shoulders were wider and thicker. He hunched them up and waited.

"What did you want to go and get us thrown out of there for?" Esau said.

"*I* left. It was you that got thrown out."

"Fine cousin you are. What did you say to old man Taylor to make him do that?"

"Nothing. Didn't have to."

"What do you mean by that?"

"He doesn't like you, that's what I mean. Don't come picking a fight with me unless you mean it, Esau."

"Sore, aren't you? Well go ahead and be sore, and I'll tell you something. And you can tell the judge. Nobody can keep me away from Amity. I'll see her anytime I want to, and do anything I want to with her, because she likes me whether her father does or not."

"Big mouth," said Len. "That's all you got, a great big windy mouth."

"I wouldn't talk," said Esau bitterly. "If it hadn't been for you I'd never left home. I'd be there now, probably with the whole farm by now, and a wife and kids if I wanted them, instead of roaming to hell and gone around the country looking for—"

"Shut up," said Len fiercely.

"All right, but you know what I mean, and not even knowing where I'm going to sleep tonight. Trouble, Len. That's all you ever made for me, and now you made it with my girl."

In utter indignation, Len said, "Esau, you're a yellow-bellied liar." And Esau hit him.

Len had got so mad that he had forgotten to be on guard, and the blow took him by surprise. It knocked his hat off and stung most painfully on his cheekbone. He sucked in a sharp breath and went for Esau. They scuffled and banged each other around on the dock for a minute or two and then suddenly Esau said, "Hold it, hold off, somebody's coming and you know what you get for fighting on the Sabbath."

They drew apart, breathing hard. Len picked up his hat, trying to look as though he had not been doing anything. Out of the corner of his eye he saw Mike Dulinsky and two other men coming onto the dock.

"We'll finish this later," he whispered to Esau.

"Sure."

They stood to one side. Dulinsky recognized them and smiled. He was a big powerful man, run slightly to fat around the middle. He had very bright eyes that seemed to see everything, including a lot that was out of sight, but they were cold eyes that never really warmed up even when they smiled. Len admired Mike Dulinsky. He respected him. But he did not particularly like him. The two men with him were Ames and Whinnery, both warehouse owners.

"Well," said Dulinsky. "Down looking over the project?"

"Not exactly," said Len. "We—uh—could we have permission to sleep in the office tonight? We—aren't rooming at the Taylors' any more."

"Oh?" said Dulinsky, raising his eyebrows. Ames made a sardonic sound that was not quite a snicker.

Len ignored that. "Is it all right, sir?"

"Of course. Make yourselves at home. You have the key with you? Good. Come along, gentlemen."

He went off with Whinnery and Ames. Len got his bag and Esau his bundle and they walked back a way up the dock to the office, a long two-story shed where the paper work of the warehouses was done. Len had the key to it because it was part of his job to open the office every morning. While he was fiddling with the lock, Esau looked back and said, "He's got 'em down there showing 'em the foundations. They don't look too happy."

Len glanced back too. Dulinsky was waving his arms and talking animatedly, but Ames and Whinnery looked worried and shook their heads.

"He'll have to do more than talk to convince them," said Esau.

Len grunted and went inside. In a few minutes, after they had gone up into the loft to stow their belongings, they heard somebody come in. It was Dulinsky, and he was alone. He gave them a direct, hard stare and said, "Are you scared too? Are you going to run out on me?"

He did not give them time to answer, jerking his head toward the outside.

"*They're* scared. They want more warehouses, too. They want Refuge to grow and make them rich, but they don't want to take any of the risk. They want to see what happens to me first. The bastards. I've been trying to convince them that if we all work together—Why did the judge make you leave his house? Was it on account of me?"

"Well," said Len. "Yes."

Esau looked surprised, but he did not say anything.

"I need you," said Dulinsky. "I need all the men I can get. I hope you'll stick with me, but I won't try to hold you. If you're worried, you better go now."

"I don't know about Len," said Esau, grinning, "but I'm going to stay." He was not thinking about warehouses.

Dulinsky looked at Len. Len flushed and looked at the floor. "I don't know," he said. "It isn't that I'm afraid to stay, it's just that maybe I want to leave Refuge and go on down-river."

"I'll get along," said Dulinsky.

"I'm sure you will," said Len, stubbornly, "but I want to think about it."

"Stick with me," said Dulinsky, "and get rich. My great-great-grandfather came here from Poland, and he never got rich because things were already built. But now they're ready to be built again, and I'm going to get in on the ground floor. I know what the judge has been telling you. He's a negativist. He's afraid of believing in anything. I'm not. I believe in the greatness of this country, and I know that these outmoded shackles have got to be broken off if it's ever to grow again. They won't break themselves. Somebody, men like you and me, will have to get in there and do it."

"Yes, sir," said Len. "But I still want to think it over."

Dulinsky studied him keenly, and then he smiled. "You don't push easily, do you? Not a bad trait—All right, go ahead and think."

He left them. Len looked at Esau, but the mood was gone and he did not feel like fighting any more. He said, "I'm going for a walk."

Esau shrugged, making no attempt to join him. Len walked slowly along the dock, thinking of the westbound boats, wondering if any of them were secretly bound for Bartorstown, wondering if it was any use to go blindly from place to place, wondering what to do. He reached the end of the dock and stepped off it, going on past the warehouse site. The two men watched him closely until he turned away.

He was perhaps not consciously thinking of going there, but a few minutes more of wandering about brought him to the edge of the traders' compound, an area of hard-packed earth where the wagons were drawn up between long ranks of stable sheds and auction sheds and permanent shelter houses for the men. Len hung around here a good bit. Partly his work for Dulinsky required him to, but there was more to it than that. There was all the gossip and excitement of the roads, and sometimes there was even news of Piper's Run, and there was the never-ending hope that someday he would hear the word he had been waiting all these years to hear. He never had. He had never even seen a familiar face, Hostetter's face in particular, and that was odd because he knew that Hostetter went South in the winter season and therefore would have to cross the river somewhere. Len had been at all the ferry points, but Hostetter had not appeared. He had often wondered if Hostetter had gone back to Bartorstown, or if something had happened to him and he was dead.

The area was quiet now, for no business was done on the Sabbath, and the men were sitting and talking in the shade, or off somewhere to afternoon prayer meeting. Len knew most of them at least by sight, and they knew him. He joined them, glad of some talk to get his mind off his problems for a while. Some of them were New Mennonites. Len always felt shy around them, and a little unhappy, because they brought back to him many things he would just as soon not think about. He had never let on that he had once been one of them.

They talked awhile. The shadows got longer and a cool breeze came up off the river. There began to be a smell of wood smoke and cooking food, and it occurred to Len that he did not have any place to eat supper. He asked if he could stay.

"Of course, and welcome," said a New Mennonite named Fisher. "Tell you what, Len, if you was to go and get some more wood off the big pile it would help."

Len took the barrow and trundled off across to the edge of the compound where the great wood stack was. He had to pass along beside the stable sheds to do this. He filled the barrow with firewood and turned back again. When he reached a certain point beside the stables, the lines of wagons hid him from the shelter houses and the men, who were now all getting busy around the fires. It was dark inside the stables. A sweet warm smell of horse came out of them, and a sound of munching.

A voice came out of them, too. It said his name.

"Len Colter."

Len stopped. It was a hushed and hurried voice, very sharp, insistent. He looked around, but he could not see anything.

"Don't look for me unless you want to get us both in trouble," said the voice. "Just listen. I have a message for you, from a friend. He says to tell you that you'll never find what you're looking for. He says go home to Piper's Run and make your peace. He says—"

"Hostetter," Len whispered. "Are you Hostetter?"

"—get out of Refuge. There will be a bath of fire, and you'll get burned in it. Get out, Len. Go home. Now walk on, as though nothing had happened."

Len started to walk. But he said, into the dark of the stables, in a whispered cry of wild triumph, "You know there's only one place I want to go! If you want me to leave Refuge, you'll have to take me there."

And the voice answered, on a fading sigh. "Remember the night of the preaching. You may not always be saved."

TEN

Two weeks later, the frame of the new warehouse had taken shape and men were starting to work on the roof. Len worked where he was told to, now on the construction gang and now in the office when the papers got stacked too high. He did this in a state of tense excitement, going through a lot of the motions automatically while his mind was on other things. He was like a man waiting for an explosion to happen.

He had moved his sleeping quarters to a hut in the traders' section, leaving Esau in full possession of Dulinsky's loft. He spent every spare minute there, quite forgetting Amity, forgetting everything but the hope that now, any minute, after all these years, things would break for him the way he wanted them to. He went over and over in his mind every word the voice had said. He heard them in his light uneasy sleep. And he would not have left Refuge and Dulinsky now for any reason under the sun.

He knew there was danger. He was beginning to feel it in the air and see it in the faces of some of the men who dropped by to watch as the timbers of the warehouse went up. There were too many strangers among them. The countryside around Refuge was populous and prosperous farm land, and only partly New Mennonite. On market days there were always farmers in town, and the country preachers and the storekeepers and the traders came and went, and it was obvious that the word was spreading around. Len knew he was taking a chance, and he knew that it was perhaps not fair to Hostetter or whoever it was that had risked giving him that warning. But he was fiercely determined not to go.

He was angry with Hostetter and the men of Bartorstown.

It was perfectly apparent now that they must have known where he and Esau were ever since they left Piper's Run. He could think of half a dozen times when a trader had happened along providentially to help them out of a bad spot, and he was sure now that these were not accidents. He was sure that the reason he had never met Hostetter was not accidental either. Hostetter had avoided them, and probably the men of Bartorstown had avoided using the facilities of whatever town the Colter boys happened to be in. That was why there had never been a clue. Hostetter knew perfectly well why they had run away, and he had spread the warning, and for all these years the men of Bartorstown had been deliberately keeping them from all hope of finding what they were after. And at the same time, the men of Bartorstown could easily, at any moment, have simply picked them up and taken them where they wanted to go. Len felt like a child deceived by its elders. He wanted to get his hands on Hostetter.

He had not said anything about this to Esau. He did not like Esau very well any more, and he was not sure of him. He figured there was plenty of time for talking later on, and in the meantime everybody, including Esau, was safer if he didn't know.

Len hung around the traders, not asking any questions or saying anything, just there with his eyes and his ears wide open. But he did not see anybody he knew, and no secret voice spoke to him again. If it was Hostetter, he was still keeping out of sight.

He would hardly be able to do that in Refuge. Len decided that if it was Hostetter, he was staying across the river in Shadwell. And immediately Len felt a compulsion to go there. Perhaps, away from people who knew him too well, another contact might be made.

He didn't have any excuse to go to Shadwell, but it did not take him long to think one up. One evening as he was helping Dulinsky close the office he said, "I've just been thinking it wouldn't be a bad idea if I was to go over to Shadwell and see what they think about what you're doing. After all, if you're successful, it'll mean the bread out of their mouths."

"I know what they think," said Dulinsky. He slammed a desk drawer shut and looked out the window at the dark framework of the building rising against the blue west. After a minute he said, "I saw Judge Taylor today."

Len waited. He was fidgety and nervous all the time these days. It seemed hours before Dulinsky spoke again.

"He told me if I didn't stop building that he and the town authorities would arrest me and everyone connected with me."

"Do you think they will?"

"I reminded him that I hadn't violated any local law. The Thirtieth Amendment is a Federal law, and he has no jurisdiction over that."

"What did he say?"

Dulinsky shrugged. "Just what I expected. He'll send immediately to the federal court in Maryland, asking for authority or a federal officer."

"Oh well," said Len, "that'll take a while. And public opinion—"

"Yes," said Dulinsky. "Public opinion is the only hope I have. Taylor knows it. The elders know it. Old man Shadwell knows it. This thing isn't going to wait for any federal judge to jog trot all the way from Maryland."

"You'll carry the rally tomorrow night," said Len confidently. "Refuge is pretty sore about Shadwell taking business away from them. The people are behind you, most of them."

Dulinsky grunted. "Maybe it wouldn't be amiss if you did go to Shadwell. This rally is important. I'll stand or fall by the way it goes, and if old man Shadwell is fixing to come over and make me some trouble, I want to know it. I'll give you some business to do, so it won't look too much as though you're spying. Don't ask any questions, just see what you can pick up. Oh, and don't take Esau."

Len hadn't been intending to, but he asked, "Why not?"

"You've got wit enough to stay out of trouble. He hasn't. Do you know where he spends his nights?"

"Why," said Len, surprised, "right here, I suppose."

"Maybe. I hope so. You take the morning ferry, Len, and come back on the afternoon. I want you here for the rally. I need every voice I can get shouting Hooray for Mike."

"All right," said Len. "Good night."

He walked past the new warehouse on his way. It smelled fragrantly of new wood and had a satisfying hugeness. Len felt that it was good to build. For the moment he agreed passionately with Dulinsky.

A voice challenged him from the shadow of a pile of planks, and he said, "Hello, Harry, it's me." He walked on. There were four men on guard now. They carried big billets of wood in their hands, and fires burned all night to light the area. He understood that Mike Dulinsky came down there every so often to look around, as though he was too uneasy to sleep.

Len did not sleep well himself. He sat around talking for a while after supper and then rolled in, but he was thinking about tomorrow, thinking how he would walk through Shadwell to the traders' compound and Hostetter would be there, and he would say something to him, something quiet but significant, and Hostetter would nod and say, "All right, it's no use fighting you any longer, I'll take you where you want to go." He played that scene over and over in his mind, and all the time he knew it was only one of those things you dream up when you're a child and haven't learned yet about reality. Then he got to thinking about Dulinsky asking where Esau spent his nights, and sleep was out of the question. Len wanted to know too.

He thought he did know. And it was amazing, considering that he didn't care at all about Amity, how much the idea upset him.

He rose and went out into the warm night. The compound was dark and silent, except for an occasional thump from the stables where the big horses moved in their stalls. He crossed it and went up through the sleeping streets of the town, deliberately taking the long way round so as not to pass the new warehouse. He didn't want to talk to the guards.

The long way round was long enough to take him past Judge Taylor's house. Nothing was stirring there, and no light showed. He picked out Amity's window, and then he felt ashamed and moved on, down to the docks.

The door of Dulinsky's office was locked, but Esau had a key now, so that didn't mean anything. Len hesitated. The wet smell of the river was strong in the air, a presage of rain, and the sky was clouded. The watch fires burned, farther down the bank. It was quiet, and somehow the office shed had the feel of an empty building. Len unlocked the door and went in.

Esau was not there.

Len stood still for quite a while, in a black fury at first, but calming down gradually into a sort of disgusted contempt for Esau's stupidity. As for Amity, if that was what she wanted she was welcome to it. He wasn't angry. Not much.

Esau's cot had not been touched. Len turned back the quilt, folding it carefully. He set Esau's spare boots straight under the edge of the cot, picked up a soiled shirt and hung it neatly on a peg. Then he lit the lamp beside Esau's bed, turned it low, and left it burning. He went out, locking the office door behind him.

It was very late when he got back to the compound. Even so, he sat for a long time on the doorstep, looking at the night and thinking. Lonely thoughts.

In the morning he stopped by to pick up the letter Dulinsky had for him to take to Shadwell, and Esau was there, looking so gray and old about the face that Len almost felt sorry for him.

"What's the matter with you?" he demanded.

Esau snarled at him.

"You look scared to death," said Len deliberately. "Is somebody making you threats about the warehouse?"

"Mind your own damn business," said Esau, and Len smiled inwardly. Let him sweat. Let him wonder who was here last night, when he was where he had no business to be. Let him wonder who knows, and wait.

He went down and got on board the ferry, a great lumbering flat thing with a shack to shelter the boiler and the wood stack. A light, steady rain had begun to fall, and the far shore was obscured in mist. A southbound trader with a load of woolens and leather was crossing too. Len helped him with his team and then sat with him in the wagon, remembering what magic things these wagons had been to him when he was a boy. The Canfield Fair seemed like something that happened a million years ago. The trader was a thin man with a gingery beard that reminded him of Soames. He shuddered and looked away, down-river, where the slow strong current ran forever to the west. A launch was beating its way up against it. The launch made a mournful hooting at the ferry, and the ferry answered, and then from the east a third voice spoke and a string of barges went down well in front of them, loaded with coal that glistened bright and black in the rain.

Shadwell was little and new and raw, and growing so fast that there were half-built buildings wherever Len looked. The waterfront hummed, and up on a rise behind it the big Shadwell house sat watching with all its glassy eyes.

Len walked up to the warehouse office where he had to go to deliver his letter. A lot of the men who would have been building were not working today on account of the rain. There was a little gang of them bunched up on the porch of the general store. It seemed to Len as though they watched him pretty close, but then that was probably only because he was a stranger off the ferry. He went in and gave the letter to a small elderly man named Gerrit, who read it hurriedly and then eyed Len as though he had crept out of the mud at low water.

"You tell Mike Dulinsky," he said, "that I follow the words of the Good Book that forbid me to have any dealings with unrighteous men. And as for you, I'd advise you to do the same. But you're a young man, and the young are always sinful, so I won't waste my breath. Git."

He flung the letter in a box of wastepaper and turned away. Len shrugged and went out. He headed off across the muddy square toward the traders' compound. One of the men on the porch of the general store came down the steps and ambled across to Gerrit's office. It was raining harder, and little streams of yellow water ran everywhere along the naked ground.

There were a lot of wagons in the compound, but none of them bore Hostetter's name. Most of the men were under cover. He did not see anyone he knew, and no one spoke to him. After a while he turned around and went back.

The square was full of men. They stood in the rain, and the yellow water splashed around their boots, but they did not seem to mind. They were all facing one way, toward Len.

One of them said, "You're from Refuge."

Len nodded.

"You work for Dulinsky."

Len shrugged and started to push by him.

Two other men came up on either side of him and caught his arms. He tried to get free, but they held him tight, one on each side, and when he tried to kick they stomped his ankles.

The first man said, "We got a message for Refuge. You tell them. We ain't going to let them take away what is rightfully ours. If they don't stop Dulinsky, we will. Can you remember that?"

Len glared at him. He was scared. He did not say anything.

"Make him remember it, boys," said the first man.

The two men holding him were joined by two more. They threw Len face down in the mud. He got up, and when he was halfway to his feet they kicked him flat again and grabbed his arms and rolled him. Then somebody else grabbed him and then another and another, roughing him around the square between them, perfectly quiet except for the little grunts of effort, not really hurting him too badly but never giving him a chance to fight back. When they were through they went away and left him, dizzy and gasping for breath, spitting out mud and water. He scrambled to his feet and looked around, but the square was deserted.

He went down to the ferry and got aboard, although it was a long time before it was due to go back again. He was wet to the skin and shivering, although he was not conscious of being cold.

The ferry captain was a native of Refuge. He helped Len clean up and gave him a blanket out of his own locker. Then Len looked up along the streets of Shadwell.

"I'll kill 'em," said Len. "I'll kill 'em."

"Sure," said the ferry captain. "And I'll tell you one thing. They better not come over to Refuge and start trouble, or they'll find out what trouble is."

Toward midafternoon the rain stopped, and by five o'clock, when the ferry docked again at Refuge, the sky was clearing. Len reported to Dulinsky, who looked grave and shook his head.

"I'm sorry, Len," he said. "I should have known better."

"Well," said Len, "they didn't do me any damage, and now you know. They'll likely come over to the rally."

Dulinsky nodded. His eyes began to shine and he rubbed his hands together. "Maybe that's just what we want," he said. "Go change your clothes and get some supper. I'll see you later."

Len started home, but Dulinsky was already ahead of him, posting men to watch along the docks and doubling the warehouse guard.

At the compound Fisher spotted Len and asked him, "What happened to you?"

"I had a little trouble with the Shads," said Len, still too sore to want to talk about it. He went into his cabin and shut the door, and began to strip off his clothes, dried stiff with the yellow mud. And he wondered.

He wondered if Hostetter had abandoned him. And he wondered if Hostetter or anyone else would really be able to do much, when the time came. He remembered the voice saying, You may not always be saved.

When it was dark, he walked over to the town square, and the rally.

ELEVEN

The main square of Refuge was wide and grassy, with trees to make shade there in the summer. The church, austere and gaunt and authoritative, dominated the square from its northern side. On the east and west were lesser buildings, stores, houses, a school, but on the southern side the town hall stood, not as tall as the church but broader, spreading out into wings that housed the courtrooms, the archives, the various offices necessary to the orderly running of a township. The shops and the public buildings were now closed and dark, and Len noticed that some of the shopkeepers had put up their storm shutters.

The square was full. It seemed as though all the men and half the women of Refuge were there, standing around on the wet grass or moving back and forth to talk, and there were others there, farmers in from the country, a handful of New Mennonites. A sort of pulpit stood in the middle of the square. It was a permanent structure, and it was used chiefly by visiting preachers at open-air prayer meetings, but political speakers used it too at the time of a local or national election. Mike Dulinsky was going to use it tonight. Len remembered what Gran had told him about the old days, when a speaker could talk to everybody in the country at once through the teevee boxes, and he wondered with a quivering thrill of excitement if tonight was the start of the long road back to that kind of a world—Mike Dulinsky talking to a handful of people in a village named Refuge on the dark Ohio. He had read enough of Judge Taylor's history books to know that that was the way things happened sometimes. His heart began to beat faster, and he walked nervously back and forth, vaguely determined that Dulinsky should talk, no matter who tried to stop him.

The preacher, Brother Meyerhoff, came out of the side door of the church. Four of the deacons were with him, and a fifth man Len did not recognize until they came into the light of one of the bonfires that burned there. It was Judge Taylor. They passed on and Len lost them in the crowd, but he was sure they were heading for the speaker's stand. He followed them, slowly. He was about halfway across the grassy open when Mike Dulinsky came from the other side and there was a general motion toward the center, and the crowd suddenly clotted up so he couldn't get through it without pushing. There were half a dozen men with Dulinsky, carrying lanterns on long poles. They put these in brackets around the speaker's pulpit, so that it stood up like a bright column in the darkness. Dulinsky climbed up and began to speak.

"Tonight," he said, "we stand at a crossroads."

Somebody pulled at Len's sleeve, and he turned around. It was Esau, nodding to him to come away from the crowd.

"There's boats on the river," Esau said, when they were out of earshot. "Coming this way. You warn him, Len, I got to get back to the docks." He looked furtively around. "Is Amity here?"

"I don't know. The judge is."

"Oh Lord," said Esau. "Listen, I got to go. If you see Amity, tell her I won't be around for a while. She'll understand."

"Will she? Anyway, I thought you were bragging how nobody could—"

"Oh, shut up. You tell Dulinsky they're coming. Watch yourself, Len. Don't get in any more trouble than you can help."

"It looks to me," said Len, "as though you're the one in trouble. If I don't see Amity, I'll give the message to her father."

Esau swore and disappeared into the dark. Len began to edge his way through the crowd. They were standing quiet, listening, very grave and intent. Dulinsky was talking to them with a passionate sincerity. This was his one time, and he was giving everything he had to it.

"—that was eighty years ago. No danger menaces us now. Why should we continue to live in the shadow of a fear for which there is no longer any cause?"

A ripple of sound, half choked, half eager, ran across the crowd. Dulinsky gave it no time to die.

"I'll tell you why!" he shouted. "It's because the New Mennonites climbed into the saddle and have hung onto the government ever since. They don't like growth, they don't like change. Their creed rejects them both, and so does their greed. Yes, I said greed! They're farmers. They don't want to see the trading centers like Refuge get rich and fat. They don't want a competitive market, and above all they don't want people like us pushing them out of their nice seats in Congress where they can make all the laws. So they forbid us to build a new warehouse when we need it. Now do you think that's fair or right or godly? You there, Brother Meyerhoff, do you say the New Mennonites should tell us all how to live, or should our own Church of Holy Thankfulness have something to say about it too?"

Brother Meyerhoff answered, "It hasn't to do with them or with us. It has to do with you, Dulinsky, and you're talking blasphemy!"

A cry of voices, mostly female, seconded him. Len pushed himself to the foot of the stand. Dulinsky was leaning over, looking at Meyerhoff. There were beads of sweat on his forehead.

"Blaspheming, am I?" he demanded. "You tell me where."

"You've been to church. You've read the Book and listened to the sermons. You know how the Almighty cleansed the land of cities, and bade His children that He saved to walk henceforth in the path of righteousness, to love the things of the spirit and not the things of the flesh! In the words of the prophet Nahum—"

"I don't want to build a city," said Dulinsky. "I want to build a warehouse."

There was a nervous tittering, quickly hushed. Meyerhoff's face was crimson above his beard. Len mounted the steps and spoke to Dulinsky, who nodded. Len climbed down again. He wanted to tell Dulinsky to lay off the New Mennonites, but he did not quite dare for fear of giving himself away.

"Who," asked Dulinsky of Meyerhoff, "has been telling you about cities?" He paused, and then he pointed and said, "Is it you, Judge Taylor?"

In the glare of the lanterns, Len saw that Taylor's face was oddly pale and strained. His voice, when he spoke, was quiet but it rang all over the square.

"There is an amendment to the Constitution of the United States that forbids you to do this. No amount of talk will change that, Dulinsky."

"Ah," said Dulinsky, in a satisfied voice as though he had made Judge Taylor fall into some trap, "that's where you're wrong. Talk is exactly what *will* change it. If enough people talk, and talk loud enough and long enough, that amendment will be changed so that a man can build a warehouse if he needs it to shelter flour or hides, or a house if he needs it to shelter his family." He raised his voice in a sudden shout. "You think about that, you people! Your own kids have had to leave Refuge, and more and more of them will have to go, because they can't build any more houses here when they get married. Am I right?"

He got a response on that. Dulinsky grinned. Out on the dark edges of the crowd a man appeared, and then another and another, coming softly from the direction of the river. And Meyerhoff said, in a voice shaking with anger, "Always, in every age, the unbeliever has prepared the way for evil."

"Maybe," said Dulinsky. He was looking out over Meyerhoff's head, to the edges of the crowd. "And I'll admit that I'm an unbeliever." He glanced down at Len, giving him the warning, while the crowd gasped over that. Then he went on, fast and smooth.

"I'm an unbeliever in poverty, in hunger, in misery. I don't know anybody who does believe in those things, except the New Ishmaelites, but I can't recall we ever thought much of them. In fact, we drove 'em out. I'm an unbeliever in taking a healthy growing child and strapping it down with bands so it won't get any taller than somebody thinks it should. I—"

Judge Taylor brushed past Len and mounted the steps. Dulinsky looked surprised and stopped in midsentence. Taylor gave him one burning glance and said, "A man can make anything he wants to out of words." He turned to the crowd. "I'm going to give you a fact, and then we'll see if Dulinsky can talk it away. If you break the township law it won't affect Refuge alone. It will affect all the country around it. Now, the New Mennonites are peaceful folk and their creed forbids them from violence. They will proceed by due process of law, no matter how long it takes. But there are other sects in the countryside, and their beliefs are different. They look on it as their duty to take up the cudgel for the Lord."

He paused, and in the stillness Len could hear the breathing of the people.

"You'd better think twice," said Taylor, "before you provoke them into taking it up against you."

There was a burst of applause from the outer edge of the crowd. Dulinsky asked scornfully, "Who are you afraid of, Judge—the farmers or the Shadwell men?" He leaned out over the rail and beckoned. "Come on up here, you Shads, up where we can see you. You don't have to be afraid, you're brave men. I got a lad here who knows how brave you are. Len, climb up here a minute."

Len did as he was told, avoiding Judge Taylor's eyes. Dulinsky pushed him to the rail.

"Some of you know Len Colter. I sent him to Shadwell this morning on business. Tell us what kind of a welcome you gave him, you Shads, or are you ashamed?"

The crowd began to mutter and turn around.

"What's the matter?" cried a deep, rough voice from the background. "Didn't he like the taste of Shadwell mud?" The Shadwell men all laughed, and then another voice, one that Len remembered only too well, called to him, "Did you give them our message?"

"Yes," said Dulinsky. "Give the people that message, Len. Say it real loud, so they can all hear."

Judge Taylor said suddenly, under his breath, "You'll regret this night." He ran down the steps.

Len glared out into the shadows. "They're going to stop you," he told the people of Refuge. "The Shads won't let you grow. That's why they're here tonight." His voice went up a notch until it cracked. "I don't care who's afraid of them," he said, "I'm not." He jumped over the rail onto the ground and charged into the crowd. All the helpless rage of the morning was back on him a hundredfold, and he did not care what anybody else did, or what happened to him. He butted his way through until a path was suddenly opened for him and the Shadwell men were standing in a bunch in front of him. Dulinsky's voice was shouting something in which the names of Shadwell and Refuge were coupled together with the word fear. The crowd was beginning to move. A woman was screaming. The

Shadwell men were pulling clubs out from under their coats. Len sprang like a panther. A great roar went up from the crowd, and the riot was on.

Len bore his man down and pounded him. Legs churned around them and people fell over them. There was a lot of screaming now, and women were running away out of the square. Clubs, fists, and boots flailed wildly. Somebody hit Len on the back of the head. The world turned upside down for a minute, and when it steadied again he was staggering along in the midst of a little boiling whirlpool of hard-breathing men, hanging onto somebody's coat and punching blindly with his free hand. The whirlpool spun and heaved and threw him up against a shuttered window and passed on. He stayed there, confused and shaking his head, blowing blood out of his nose. The crowd had broken up. The lanterns still burned around the pulpit in the middle of the square, but there was nobody in it now, and nothing left on the grassy space around it but some hats and some gouged-out places in the turf. The fighting had moved off. He could hear it streaming away down the streets and alleys that led to the docks. He grunted and began to run after it. He was glad Pa could not see him now. He felt hot and queer inside, and he liked it. He wanted to fight some more.

By the time he reached the docks the Shadwell men were piling into their boats as fast as they could, shaking their fists and cursing. The Refuge men were all lined up at the water's edge, helping them. Three or four Shads were in the river and being hauled up into the boats. The air rang with hoots and catcalls. Mike Dulinsky was right in the middle of it, his good dark coat torn and his hair on end, and a splatter of blood down his shirt from a cut mouth. "You going to stop us, are you?" he was yelling at the Shadwell men. "You going to tell Refuge what to do?"

The men on either side of Dulinsky caught him suddenly and hoisted him up onto their shoulders and cheered him. The Shadwell men pulled slowly and sullenly out into the dark river. When they were out of sight the crowd turned, still carrying Dulinsky and cheering, to where the fires burned around the framework of the warehouse. They marched round and round, and the guards cheered too. Len watched them, feeling dizzy but triumphant. Then, looking around, he saw a blaze of light in the direction of the traders' compound. He stared at it, frowning, and in the intervals of the noise behind him he could hear the distant voices of men and the whickering of horses. He began to walk toward the compound.

Lanterns and torches burned all around to give light. The men were bringing their teams out of the stables and harnessing them, and going over their gear, and getting the wagons ready to go. Len watched a minute

94

or two, and all the feeling of triumph and excitement left him. He felt tired, and his nose hurt.

He saw Fisher and went up to him, standing by the head of the team while Fisher worked.

"Why is everybody going?" he asked.

Fisher gave him a long, stern look from under the brim of his broad hat.

"The farmers went out of here primed for trouble," he said. "They'll bring it, and we don't aim to wait."

He made sure his reins were clear and climbed up onto the seat. Len stood aside, and Fisher looked down at him, in something the same way Pa had looked so long ago.

"I thought better of you, Len Colter," Fisher said. "But them that picks up a burning brand will get burned by it. The Lord have mercy on you!"

He shook the reins and shouted, and his wagon creaked and moved, and the other wagons rolled, and Len stood looking after them.

TWELVE

Two o'clock of a hot, still day. The men were laying up sheeting boards on the north and east sides of the warehouse, working in the shade. Refuge was quiet, so quiet that the sound of the hammers rang out like bells on a Sabbath morning. Most of the shipping was gone from the docks, and the wharves were empty.

Esau said, "Do you think they'll come?"

"I don't know." Len looked searchingly at the distant roofs of Shadwell across the river, and up and down the wide stretch of water. He didn't know exactly what he was looking for, Hostetter, a friendly face, anything to break the emptiness and the sense of waiting. All morning since before sunup, cartloads of women and children had been leaving the town, and there were some men with them too, and bundles of household goods.

"They won't do anything," said Esau. "They wouldn't dare."

His voice carried no conviction. Len glanced at him and saw that his face was drawn and nervous. They were standing at the door of the office, not doing anything, just feeling the heat and the quietness. Dulinsky had gone up into the town, and Len said, "I wish he'd come back."

"He's got men out on the roads. If there's any news, we'll be the first to know it."

"Yes," said Len. "I reckon."

The hammers rang sharp on the new yellow wood. Along the edges of the warehouse site, well back in the trees, men loitered and watched. There were more of them on the docks, restless, uneasy, gathering in little groups to talk and then breaking up again, moving back and forth. They kept looking sidelong at the office, and at Len and Esau standing in the doorway, and at the men working on the warehouse, but they did not come close or speak to them. Len did not like that. It made him feel alone and conspicuous, and it worried him because he could feel the doubt and uncertainty and apprehension of these men who were up against something new and did not quite know what to do about it. From time to time a jug of corn was pulled out of a hiding place behind a stump or a stack of barrels, passed around, and put away again, but only one or two of them were drunk.

On impulse, Len stepped to the end of the dock and shouted to a group standing under a tree and talking. "What's the news from town?"

One of them shook his head. "Nothing yet." He was one who had shouted the loudest for Dulinsky last night, but today his face showed no enthusiasm. Suddenly he stooped and picked up a stone and threw it at a little gang of boys who were skulking in the background watching hopefully for trouble. "Get out of here!" he yelled at them. "This ain't no game for your amusement. Go on, git!"

They went, but not far. Len returned to the doorway. It was very hot, very still. Esau shuffled, kicking his heel against the doorpost.

"Len."

"What?"

"What'll we do if they do come?"

"How do I know? Fight, I guess. See what happens. How do I know?"

"Well, I know one thing," said Esau defiantly. "I ain't going to get my neck broke for Dulinsky. The hell with that."

"All right, you figure something." There was an anger in Len now, a vague thing as yet, and undirected, but enough to make him irritable and impatient. Perhaps it was because he was afraid, and that made him angry. But he knew the way Esau's thoughts were running, and he didn't want to have to go through every step of it out loud.

"You bet I'll figure something," said Esau. "You bet I will. It's his warehouse, not mine. Let him fight for it. He sure wouldn't risk his skin for anything of mine. I—"

"Shut up," said Len. "Look."

Judge Taylor was coming along the dock. Esau swore nervously and slid back through the door, out of sight. Len waited, conscious that the men were watching, as though what happened might have great significance.

Taylor came up to the door and stopped. "Tell Mike I want to see him," he said.

Len answered, "He isn't here."

The judge looked at him, deciding whether or not he was lying. There was a pinched grayness about the corners of his mouth, and his eyes were curiously hard and bright.

"I've come," he said, "to offer Mike his last chance."

"He's somewhere up in the town," said Len. "Maybe you can find him there."

Taylor shook his head. "It's the Lord's will," he said, and turned and walked away. At the corner of the office he stopped and spoke again. "I warned you, Len. But none are so blind as those who will not see."

"Wait," said Len. He went up to the judge and looked into his eyes, and shivered. "You know something. What is it?"

"The Lord's will," said the judge, "will be made clear to you when it is time."

Len reached out and caught him by the collar of his fine cloth coat and shook him. "Speak for yourself," he said angrily. "The Lord must be sick to death of everybody hiding behind Him. Nothing happens in this town that you don't have a finger in. What is it?"

Some of the fey light went out of Taylor's eyes. He looked down with a kind of shocked surprise at Len's hands laid roughly upon him, and Len let him go.

"I'm sorry," he said. "But I want to know."

"Yes," said Judge Taylor quietly, "you want to know. That was always your trouble. Didn't I tell you to find your limit before it was too late?"

His face softened, became compassionate and full of a genuine sorrow. "It's too bad, Len. I could have loved you like my own son."

"What have you done?" asked Len, moving a step closer, and the judge answered, "There will be no more cities. There is a law, and the law must be obeyed."

"You're scared," said Len, in a slow, astonished voice. "I understand now, you're scared. You think if a city grows up here the bombs will come again, and you'll be under them. Did you tell the farmers you wouldn't try to stop them if—"

"Hush," said the judge, and held up his hand.

Len turned to listen. So did the men under the trees and along the docks. Esau came out from the doorway. And at the warehouse, one by one the hammers stopped.

There was a sound of singing.

It was faint, but that was only because it was still a long way off. It was deep, and sonorous, a masculine sound, martial and somehow terrifying, coming with the solemn inevitability of a storm that does not stop or swerve. Len could not make out any words, but after he had listened for a minute he knew what they were. Mine eyes have seen the glory of the coming of the Lord. "Good-by, Len," said the judge, and was gone, walking with his head up high and his face white and stern in the heat of the July sun.

"We've got to go," whispered Esau. "We've got to get out of here."

He bolted back into the office, and Len could hear his feet clattering up the wooden stairs to the loft. Len hesitated a minute. Then he began to run, up toward the town, toward the distant, oncoming hymn. I have read a fiery gospel writ in burnished rows of steel … Glory! glory! Hallelujah, His truth is marching on. A tight, cold knot of fear cramped up in Len's belly, and the air turned icy against his skin. The men along the docks and under the trees began to move too, straggling up by other ways, uncertainly at first and then faster, until they were running too. People had come out of their houses. Women, old men, children, listening, shouting at each other and at the men passing in the street, asking what it was, what was going to happen. Len came into the square, and a cart rushed past him so close that the foam from the horse's bit spattered him. There was a whole family in it, the man whipping up the horse and yelling, the women screaming, the kids all clinging together and crying. There was a scattering of people in the square, some heading toward the main north road, some running around aimlessly, women asking if anybody had seen their husbands or their boys, asking, always asking, what is it, what's happening? Len dodged through them and ran out on the north road.

Dulinsky was out on the edge of town, where the wide road ran between fields of wheat almost ripe for the cutting. There were perhaps two hundred men with him, armed with clubs and iron bars, with rifles and duck guns, with picks and frows. They looked grim and anxious. Dulinsky's face, burned brick red by the sun, was only ruddy on the surface. Underneath it was white. He kept wiping his hands on his trousers, one after the other, shifting his grip on the heavy club he held. Len came up beside him. Dulinsky glanced at him but did not speak. His attention was northward, where a solid yellow-brown wall of dust advanced, spreading across the road and into the wheat on either side. The sound of the hymn came out of it, and a rhythmic thud and trample of feet, and across its leading edge there was a pricking here and there of brilliance, as though some bright thing of metal caught the sun.

"It's our town," said Len. "They've got no right in it. We can beat 'em."

Dulinsky wiped his face oil his shirt sleeve. He grunted. It might have been a question or a laugh. Len looked around at the Refuge men.

"They'll fight," he said.

"Will they?" said Dulinsky.

"They were all for you last night."

"That was last night. This is now."

The wall of dust rolled up, and it was full of men. It stopped, and the dust blew away or settled, but the men remained, standing in a great heavy solid blot across the road and in the trampled wheat. The spots of brilliance became scythe blades, and corn knives, and here and there a gun barrel. "Some of them must have walked all night," said Dulinsky. "Look at 'em. Every goddamned dung-head farmer in three counties." He wiped his face again and spoke to the men behind him. "Stand steady, boys. They're not going to do anything." He stepped forward, his expression lofty and impassive, his eyes darting hard little glances this way and that.

A man with white hair and a stern leathery face came forward to meet him. He carried a shotgun in the crook of his arm, and his walk was a farmer's walk, heavy and rolling. But he stretched up his head and yelled out at the Refuge men waiting in the road, and there was something about his harsh strident voice that made Len remember the preaching man.

"Stand aside!" he shouted. "We don't want killing, but we can if we have to, so stand aside, in the name of the Lord!"

"Wait a minute," said Dulinsky. "Just a minute, now. This is our town. May I ask what business you think you have in it?"

The man looked at him and said, "We will have no cities in our midst."

"Cities," said Dulinsky. "Cities!" He laughed. "Now look here, sir. You're Noah Burdette, aren't you? I know you well by sight and reputation. You have quite a name as a preacher in the section around Twin Lakes."

He stepped a little closer, speaking in an easier tone, as a man talks when he knows he is going to turn the argument his way.

"You're a sincere and honest man, Mr. Burdette, and I realize that you're acting on what you believe to be truthful information. So I know you're going to be thankful to learn that your information is wrong, and there's no need for any violence at all. I—"

"Violence," said Burdette, "I don't seek. But I don't run from it, neither, when it's in good cause." He looked Dulinsky up and down, slowly, deliberately, with a face as hard as flint. "I know you, too, by sight and reputation, and you can save your wind. Are you going to stand aside?"

"Listen," said Dulinsky, with a note of desperation coming into his voice. "You've been told that I'm trying to build a city here, and that's crazy. I'm only trying to build a warehouse, and I've got as good a right to it as you've got to a new barn. You can't come here and order me around any more than I could go to your farm and do it!"

"I'm here," said Burdette.

Dulinsky glanced back over his shoulder. Len moved toward him, as though to say, I'm with you. And then Judge Taylor came up through the loose ranks of the Refuge men, saying, "Disperse, go to your homes, and stay there. No harm will come to you. Lay down your weapons and go home."

They hesitated, looking at one another, looking at Dulinsky and the solid mass of the farmers. And Dulinsky said to the judge in weary scorn, "You sheepfaced coward. You were in on this."

"You've done enough harm, Mike," said the judge, very white and standing very stiff and straight. "No need to make everybody in Refuge suffer for it. Stand aside."

Dulinsky glared at him and then at Burdette. "What are you going to do?"

"Cleanse the evil," said Burdette slowly, "as the Book instructs us to, by burning it with fire."

"In plain English," said Dulinsky, "you're going to burn my warehouses, and anything else that happens to take your fancy. The hell you are." He turned around and shouted to the Refuge men. "Listen, you fools, do you think they're going to stop at my warehouses? They'll have the whole town flaming around your ears. Don't you see this is the time, the act that's going to decide how you live for decades yet to come? Are you going to be free men or a gang of belly-crawling slaves?"

His voice rose up to a howl. "Come on and fight, God damn you, fight!"

He spun around and rushed at Burdette, raising his club high in the air.

Without haste and without pity, Burdette swung the shotgun over and fired.

It made a very loud noise. Dulinsky stopped as though he had struck against a solid wall. He stood for a second or two, and then the club dropped out of his hands and he lowered his arms and folded them over his belly. His knees bent and he sank down onto them in the dust.

Len ran forward.

Dulinsky looked up at him with an expression of stunned surprise. His mouth opened. He seemed to be trying to say something, but only blood came out between his lips. Then suddenly his face became blank and remote, like a window when somebody blows out the candle. He fell forward and was still.

"Mike," said Judge Taylor. "Mike?" He looked at Burdette, his eyes widening. "What have you done?"

"Murderer," said Len, and the word encompassed both Burdette and the judge. His voice broke, rising to a harsh scream. "Goddamned yellow-bellied murderer!" He put up his fists and ran toward Burdette, but the line of farmers had begun to move, as though the death of Dulinsky was a signal they had waited for, and Len was caught up in it as in the forefront of a wave. Burdette was gone, and facing him instead was a burly young farmer with a long neck and sloping shoulders and the kind of a mouth that had cried out the accusation against Soames. He carried a length of peeled wood like those used for fence posts, and he brought it down on Len's head, laughing with a sort of cackling haste, his eyes gleaming with immense excitement. Len fell down. Boots clumped and kicked and stumbled over him and he curled up instinctively with his arms over his head and neck. It had become very dark and the Refuge men were far off behind a wavering veil, but he could see them going, melting away until the road was empty in front of the farmers and there was nothing between them and the town any more. They went on into Refuge in the hot afternoon, raising up the dust again as they moved, and when that settled there was only Len, and Dulinsky's body lying three or four feet away from him, and Judge Taylor standing still in the middle of the road, just standing and looking at Dulinsky.

THIRTEEN

Len got slowly to his feet. His head hurt and he felt sick, but his compulsion to get away from there was so great that he forced himself to walk in spite of it. He went carefully around Dulinsky, avoiding the dark stains that were in the dust there, and he passed Judge Taylor. They did not speak, nor look at each other. Len went on toward Refuge until just a little bit before the square, where there was an apple orchard beside the road. He turned off among the trees, and when he felt that he was out of sight he sat down in the long grass and put his head between his knees and vomited. An icy coldness came over him, and a shaking. He waited until they passed, and then he got up again and went on, circling west through the trees.

There was a confused noise in the distance, toward the river. A puff of smoke rose in the clear air, and then another, and suddenly there was a dull booming roar and the whole river front seemed to burst into flame and the smoke poured up black and greasy and very thick, lighted on its underside by the kind of flames that come from stored-up barrels of pitch and lamp oil. The streets of the town were choked with carts and horses and people running. Here and there somebody was helping carry a hurt man. Len avoided them, sticking to the back alleys and the peripheral fields. The smoke came blacker and heavier, rolling over the sky and blotting the sun to an ugly copper color. There were sparks in it now, and bits of flaming stuff tossed up. When he came to a high place, Len could see men on some of the roofs of the houses, and on the church and the town hall, making up bucket lines to wet the buildings down. He could see the waterfront, too. The new warehouse was burning, and the four others that had belonged to Dulinsky, but things had not stopped there. There was a scurrying, a tossing of weapons and a swaying back and forth of little knots of men, and all along the line of docks and warehouses new fires were springing up.

Across the river Shadwell watched but did not stir.

The stables of the traders' compound were blazing when Len came by them. Sparks had fallen in the straw and the hay piles, and other sparks were smoldering on the roofs of the shelters. Len ran into the one he had been occupying and grabbed up his canvas bag and his blanket. When he came out the door he heard men coming and he fled hastily in among the trees at one side. The green leaves were already crisping, and the boughs were shaken by a strange unhealthy wind. A gang of farmers came up from the river. They paused at the edge of the compound, panting, staring about with bright hard eyes. The auction sheds were untouched. One of them, a huge red-bearded man with inflamed cheeks and a roaring voice, pointed to the sheds and bellowed something about money-changers. They made a hungry breathless sound like a pack of dogs after a coon and ran to the long line of sheds, smashing everything they could smash and piling it together and setting fire to it with a torch that one of them was carrying. Then they passed on, kicking over and trampling and breaking down anything in their path. Len thought of Judge Taylor, standing alone in the middle of the road, looking at Dulinsky's body. He would have a lot of things to look at when this day was over.

He went on cautiously between the trees, edging down to the river through a weird sulphurous twilight. The air was choked with the smells of burning, of pitch and wood and oil and hides. Ash fell like a gray and scorching snow. He could hear the fire bell ringing desperately up in the town, but he could not see much that way because of the smoke and the trees. He came out on the riverbank well below the site of the new warehouse and began to work his way back, looking for Esau.

The whole riverbank as far as he could see ahead of him was a solid mass of flame. The heat had driven everybody away and some of them had come downstream past the wreck of the new warehouse, men with their eyes white and staring in blackened faces, men with burned hands and torn clothing and a look of desperation. Three or four were bent over one who lay on the ground moaning and twisting, and there were others sitting down here and there, as though they had come that far and then quit. Most of them were just standing and watching. One man still carried a bucket half full of water.

Len did not see Esau, and he began to be afraid. He went up to several of the men and asked, but they only shook their heads or did not seem to hear him at all. Finally one of them, a clerk named Watts, who had come to the office frequently on business, said bitterly, "Don't worry about him. He's safe if anybody is."

"What do you mean?"

"I mean nobody's seen him since the trouble began. He took off, him and the girl both."

"Girl?" asked Len, startled out of his resentment at Watts' tone.

"Judge Taylor's girl, who else? And where were you, hiding in a hole somewhere? And where's Dulinsky? I thought that son of a bitch was such a mighty fighter, to hear him tell it."

"I was up on the north road," said Len. "And Dulinsky's dead. So I guess he fought harder than you did."

A man standing nearby had turned around at the sound of Dulinsky's name. Under the grime and the soot, the singed hair and the clothing burned partly off him, it was a minute before Len recognized Ames, the warehouse owner who had come down with Dulinsky and the other man that morning to look at the new warehouse and shake his head at Dulinsky's plea for unity.

"Dead," said Ames. "Dead, is he?"

"They shot him. A farmer named Burdette."

"Dead," said Ames. "I'm sorry. He should have lived. He should have lived long enough for a hanging." He lifted his hands and shook them at the blaze and smoke. "Look what he's done to us!"

"He wasn't alone," said Watts. "The Colter boys were in with him, from the beginning."

"If you'd stuck by him this wouldn't have happened," Len said. "He asked you, Mr. Ames. You and Whinnery and the others. He asked the whole town. And what happened? You all danced around and cheered last night—yes, you too, Watts, I saw you!—and then you all ran like rabbits at the first smell of trouble. There wasn't a man of 'em up in the north road that lifted a hand. They left it up to Mike to get killed."

Len's voice had got loud and harsh without his realizing it. The men within earshot had closed in to listen.

"It seems to me," said Ames, "that for a stranger, you take an almighty interest in what we do. Why? What makes you think it's up to you to try and change things? I worked all my life to build up what I had, and then you come, and Dulinsky—"

He stopped. Tears were running out of his eyes and his mouth trembled like a child's.

"Yeah," said Watts. "Why? Where did you come from? Who sent you to call us cowards because we don't want to break the law?"

Len looked around. There were men on all sides of him now. Their faces were grotesque masks of burns with fury. The smoke rolled in a sooty cloud and the flames roared softly with a purring sound as they ate the wealth of Refuge. Up in the town the fire bell had stopped ringing.

Somebody spoke the name of Bartorstown, and Len began to laugh.

Watts reached out and cuffed him. "Funny, is it? All right, where did you come from?"

"Piper's Run, born and raised."

"Why'd you leave it? Why'd you come here to make trouble?"

"He's lying," said another man. "Sure he comes from Bartorstown. They want the cities back."

"It doesn't matter," said Ames, in a low, still voice. "He was in on it. He helped." He turned around, his hands moving as though they groped for something. "There ought to be one piece of rope left unburned in Refuge."

Instantly an eagerness came over the men. "Rope," said somebody. "Yeah. We'll find some." And somebody else said, "Look for the other bastard. We'll hang them both." Some of them ran off down the riverbank, and others began to beat the bushes looking for Esau. Watts and two others tackled Len and bore him down, savaging him with their fists and knees. Ames stood by and watched, looking alternately from Len to the fire.

The men came back. They had not found Esau, but they had found a rope, the mooring line of a skiff tied to the bank farther down. Watts and the others hauled Len to his feet. One of the men tied a clumsy slipknot in the rope and made a noose and put it over Len's head. The rope was damp. It was old and soft and frayed, and it smelled of fish. Len kicked out violently and tore his arms free. They caught him again and hustled him toward the trees, a close-bunched confusion of men lurching along in short erratic bursts of motion with Len struggling in the center, kicking, clawing, banging them with his knees and elbows. And even so, he sensed dimly that it was not men he was fighting at all, but the whole vast soggy smothering continent from sea to sea and from north to south, millions of houses and people and fields and villages all sleeping comfortably and not wanting to be disturbed. The rope was cold and scratchy around his neck, and he was afraid, and he knew he couldn't fight off the idea, the belief and way of life of which these men were only a tiny, tiny part.

He was very dizzy, from the pounding and the blow on the head he had already had up on the north road, so that he was not sure what happened except that suddenly there seemed to be more men, more bodies around him, more upheaval. He was thrown sharply aside. The hands seemed to have let go of him. He hit a tree trunk and slid down it to the ground. There was a face above him. It had blue eyes and a sandy beard with two wide streaks of gray in it, one at each corner of the mouth. He said to the face, "If there weren't so many of you I could kill you all." And it answered him, "You don't want to kill me, Len. Come on, boy, get up."

Tears came suddenly into Len's eyes. "Mr. Hostetter," he said. "Mr. Hostetter." He put up his hands and caught hold of him, and it seemed like a long time ago, in another hour of darkness and fear. Hostetter gave him a strong pull up to his feet and jerked the rope from around his neck.

"Run," he said. "Run like the devil."

Len ran. There were several other men with Hostetter, and they must have charged in hard with the poles and boat hooks they had, because the Refuge men were pretty well scattered. But they were not going to give Len up without a fight, and the intrusion of Hostetter and his party had convinced them that they were right about Bartorstown. They were determined now to get Hostetter too, shouting and cursing, gathering together again and searching for anything they could use as weapons, stones, fallen branches, clods. Len staggered and stumbled as he went, and Hostetter put a hand under his arm and rushed him along.

"Boat waiting," he said. "Farther down."

Things began to fly through the air around them. A stone bounced off

Hostetter's back and he hunched his head down until his broad-brimmed hat seemed to sit flat on his shoulders. They ran in among a grove of trees and out on the other side, and Len stopped suddenly.

"Esau," he said. "Can't go without Esau."

"He's already aboard," said Hostetter. "Come on!"

They ran again, across a pasture sloping down to the water's edge, and the cows went bucketing away with their tails in the air. At the lower end of the pasture was another clump of trees, growing right on the bank, and in their partial concealment a big steam barge was tied up, with a couple of men standing on the deck holding axes, ready to chop the lines free. Smoke began to puff up suddenly from the single low stack, as though a banked fire had been stirred swiftly to life. Len saw Esau hanging over the rail, and there was someone beside him, someone with yellow hair and a long skirt.

There was a board laid from the bank to the rail. They scrambled up over it onto the deck and Hostetter shouted at the men with the axes. Stones were flying again, and Esau caught Amity and hurried her around to the other side of the deckhouse. The axes flashed. There was more shouting, and the Refuge men, with Watts in the lead, rushed right down to the bank and Watts and two others ran out onto the plank. Len did not see Ames among them. The lines parted and went snaking into the water. Hostetter and Len and some others grabbed up long poles and pushed off hard. The plank fell into the water with Watts and the other men that were on it. There was a roar and a clatter from below, the deck shook and sparks burst up through the stack. The barge began to move out into the current. Watts stood waist-deep in the muddy water by the bank and shook his fists at them.

"We know you now!" he shouted, his voice coming thin across the widening gap. "You won't get away!"

The men on the bank behind him shouted too. Their voices grew fainter but the note of hatred remained in them, and the ugliness in the gestures of their hands. Len looked back at Refuge. They were well out in the river now and he could see past the waterfront. Smoke obscured much of the town, but he could see enough. What Burdette's farmers had left untouched the spreading fire was taking for its own.

Len sat down on the deck with his back against the house. He put his arms across his knees and laid his head on them and felt an overwhelming desire to cry like a little boy, but he was too tired even to do that. He just sat and tried to make his mind as blank as the rest of him felt. But he could not do it, and over and over he saw Dulinsky stop and fall down slowly into the hot dust of the north road, and he smelled the smell of a great burning, and Burdette's harsh voice sounded in his ears, saying, "We will have no cities in our midst."

After a while he became aware that somebody was standing over him. He looked up, and it was Hostetter, holding his hat in his hand and wiping his forehead wearily on his coat sleeve.

"Well, boy," he said, "you've got your wish. You're on your way to Bartorstown."

FOURTEEN

It was night, warm and tranquil. There was a moon, lighting the surface of the river and turning the two banks into masses of black shadow. The barge slipped along, chuffing gently as it added a bit to the thrust of the current. There was a lot of cargo on the deck, tied down securely and covered with canvas against the rain. Len had found a place in it. He had slept for a while, and he was sitting now with his back against a bale, watching the river go by.

Hostetter came by, walking slowly along the narrow space left clear on the foredeck, trailing of tobacco smoke from an old pipe. He saw Len sitting up, and stopped. "Feel better?"

"I feel sick," Len said, so viciously that Hostetter knew what he meant. He nodded.

"You know now how I felt the night they killed Bill Soames."

"Murderers," said Len. "Cowards. Bastards." He cursed them until the words choked in his throat. "You should have seen them standing there across the road. And then Burdette shot him. He shot him just the way you'd shoot some vermin you found in the corn."

"Yes," said Hostetter slowly, "we'd have had you out of there sooner if you hadn't gone up after Dulinsky. Poor devil. But I'm not surprised."

"Couldn't you have helped him?"

"Us? You mean Bartorstown?"

"He wanted the same things you want. Growth, progress, intelligence, a future. Couldn't you have helped?"

There was an edge to Len's voice, but Hostetter only took the pipe out of his mouth and asked quietly, "How?"

Len thought about that. After a while he said, "I suppose you couldn't."

"Not without an army. We don't have an army, and if we did have we wouldn't use it. It takes an almighty force to make people change their whole way of thinking and living. We had a force like that just yesterday as time goes for a nation, and we don't want any more of them."

"That's what the judge was afraid of. Change. And he just stood there and watched Dulinsky die." Len shook his head. "He died for nothing. That's what he died for, *nothing*."

"No," said Hostetter, "I wouldn't say that. But it takes more than one Dulinsky. It takes a lot of them, one after the other, in different places—"

"And more Burdettes, and more burnings."

"Yes. And someday one will come along at the right time, and the change will be made."

"That's a lot to look forward to."

"That's the way it is. And then all the Dulinskys will become martyrs to a great ideal. In the meantime, you're disturbers of the peace. And damn it, Len, you know in a way they're right. They're comfortable and happy. Who are you—or any of us—to tell them it's all got to be torn up and changed?"

Len turned and looked at Hostetter in the moonlight. "Is that why you just stand by and watch?"

Hostetter said, with just the faintest note of impatience in his voice, "I don't think you understand about us yet. We're not supermen. We've got all we can do just to stay alive, without trying to remake a country that doesn't want to be remade."

"But how can you say they're right? Ignorant butchers like Burdette, hypocrites like the judge—"

"Honest men, Len, both of them. Yes, they are. Both of them got up this morning all fired up with nobility and good purpose and went and did the right as they saw it. There's never been an act done since the beginning, from a kid stealing candy to a dictator committing genocide, that the person doing it didn't think he was fully justified. That's a mental trick called rationalizing, and it's done the human race more harm than anything else you can name."

"Burdette, maybe," said Len. "He's another one like the man at the preaching that night. But not the judge. He knew better."

"Not at the time. That's the hell of it. The doubts always come later, and they're usually too late. Take yourself, Len. When you ran away from home, did you have any doubts about it? Did you say to yourself, I am now going to do an evil thing and make my parents very unhappy?"

Len looked down at the gleaming water for a long time without answering. Finally he said, in an oddly quiet voice, "How are they? Are they all right?"

"The last I heard they were fine. I didn't go up this spring myself."

"And Gran?"

"She died, a year ago last December."

"Yes," said Len. "She was terrible old." It was strange how sad he felt about Gran, as though a part of his life had gone. Suddenly, with painful clarity, he saw her again sitting on the stoop in the sunlight, looking at the flaming October trees and talking about the red dress she had had so long ago, when the world was a different place.

He said, "Pa couldn't ever quite make her shut up."

Hostetter nodded. "My own grandmother was much the same way."

Silence again. Len sat and watched the river, and the past lay heavy on him, and he did not want to go to Bartorstown. He wanted to go home.

"Your brother's doing fine," said Hostetter. "Has two boys of his own now."

"That's good."

"Piper's Run hasn't changed much."

"No," said Len. "I reckon not." And then he added, "Oh, shut up!"

Hostetter smiled.

"That's the advantage I have over you. I'm going home. It's been a long time."

"Then you didn't come from Pennsylvania at all."

"My people did, originally. I was born in Bartorstown."

An old anger rose and pricked at Len. "Listen," he said, "you knew why we ran away. You must have known all along where we were and what we were doing."

"I felt sort of responsible," Hostetter admitted. "I kept tabs."

"All right," said Len, "why did you make us wait so long? You knew where we wanted to go."

Hostetter said, "Do you remember Soames?"

"I'll never forget him."

"He trusted a boy."

"But," said Len, "I wouldn't—" Then he remembered how Esau had put Hostetter in a bad place. "I guess I see what you mean."

"We've got one unbreakable law in Bartorstown. That law is Hands Off, and because of it we've been able to keep going all these years when the very name of Bartorstown is enough to hang you. Soames broke it. I'm breaking it now, but I got permission. And believe me, that was the feat of the century. For one solid week I talked myself hoarse to Sherman—"

"Sherman," said Len, straightening up. "Yes, Sherman. Sherman wants to know if you've heard from Byers—"

"What the hell are you talking about?" asked Hostetter, staring.

"Over the radio," said Len, and the old excitement came back on him like a stroke of summer lightning. "The voices talking that night I let the cows out of the barn and we went after them down to the creek, and Esau dropped the radio. The spool thing reeled out, and the voices came— Sherman wants to know. And something about the river. That's why we went down to the Ohio."

"Oh yes," said Hostetter. "The radio. That was the start of the whole thing, wasn't it? I owed Esau something for stealing it. I owed him for the blood I sweated when I found it was gone." Hostetter shivered. "Christ. When I think how close he came to exposing me—I'd never have made it back alive, you know. Your own people would have told me to go and never show my face again, but the word would have spread. I had to throw Esau to the wolves, and I won't say I was sorry. But it was too bad you got dragged into it."

"I never blamed you. I told Esau it wasn't going to be that easy."

"Well, you can thank the farmers, because if it hadn't been for them I'd never have talked Sherman into letting me pick you up. I told him you were sure to get it from one side or the other, and I didn't want your blood on my conscience. He finally gave in, but I'll tell you, Len, the next time somebody gives you a piece of good advice, you take it."

Len rubbed his neck where the rope had scratched it. "Yes, sir. And thanks. I won't forget what you did."

Quite sternly, speaking as Pa had used to speak sometimes, Hostetter said, "Don't. Not for me particularly, or for Sherman, but because of a lot of people and ideas that might just depend on your not forgetting."

Len said slowly, "Are you afraid you can't trust me?"

"It isn't exactly a question of trust."

"What is it, then?"

"You're going to Bartorstown."

Len frowned, trying to understand what he was getting at. "But that's where I want to go. That's why—all this happened."

Hostetter pushed the flat-brimmed hat back from his forehead so that his face showed clear in the moonlight. His eyes rested shrewdly and steadily on Len.

"You're going to Bartorstown," he repeated. "You have a place all dreamed up inside your head, and you call it by that name, but that isn't where you're going. You're going to the real Bartorstown, and it's probably not going to be very much like the place in your head at all. You may not like it. You may come to have pretty strong feelings about it. And that's why I say, don't forget you owe us something."

"Listen," said Len. "Can you learn in Bartorstown? Can you read books and talk about things, and use machines, and really *think*?"

Hostetter nodded.

"Then I'll like it there." Len looked out at the dark still country slipping by in the night, the sleeping, murderous, hateful country. "I never want to see any of this again. Ever."

"For my sake," said Hostetter, "I hope you'll fit in. I'm going to have trouble enough as it is, explaining the girl to Sherman. She wasn't included. But I couldn't see what else to do."

"I was wondering about her," Len said.

"Well, she'd come down there to Esau, to try and help him get away. She said she couldn't go back to her parents. She said she was going to stay with Esau. And it seemed like she pretty well had to."

"Why?" asked Len.

"Don't you know?"

"No."

"Best reason in the world," said Hostetter. "She's got his child."

Len sat staring with his mouth open. Hostetter got up. And a man came out of the deckhouse and said to him, "Sam's talking to Collins on the radio. Maybe you'd better come down, Ed."

"Trouble?"

"Well, it seems like our friend we dumped in the water back there meant what he said. Collins says two towboats went by together just after moonrise. They didn't have any tow, and they were chock full of men. One was from Refuge, the other from Shadwell."

Hostetter scowled, knocking the ashes out of his pipe and crushing them carefully under his boots. He said to Len, "We asked Collins to keep watch, just in case. He's got a shanty-boat and acts as a mobile post. Well, come on. This is all part of being a Bartorstown man. You might as well get used to it."

FIFTEEN

L en followed Hostetter and the other man, whose name was Kovacs, into the deckhouse. This was about two thirds the length of the boat, and it was built more as a roof over the cargo hold than it was to provide any elegance for the crew. There were some narrow bunks built in around the walls, and Amity was lying in one of them, her hair all tumbled around her head and her face pale and swollen with tears. Esau was siting on the edge of the bunk, holding her hand. He looked as though he had been sitting there a long time, and he had an expression Len could not remember seeing on him before, haggard and careworn and concerned.

Len looked at Amity. She spoke to him, not meeting his eyes, and he said hello, and it was like speaking to a stranger. He thought, with an already fading pang, of the yellow-haired girl he had kissed in the rose arbor and wondered where she had gone so swiftly. This was a woman here, somebody else's woman, already marked by the cares and troubles of living, and he did not know her.

"Did you see my father, Len?" she asked. "Is he all right?"

"He was, the last I saw of him," Len told her. "The farmers weren't after him. They never touched him."

Esau got up. "You get some sleep now. That's what you need." He patted her hand and then pulled down a thin blanket that had been nailed overhead by way of a curtain. She whimpered a little, protestingly, and told Esau not to go too far away. "Don't worry about that," said Esau, with just the faintest trace of despair. "There isn't any place to go." He glanced quickly at Len, and then at Hostetter, and Len said, "Congratulations, Esau."

A slow red flush crept up over Esau's cheekbones. He straightened his shoulders and said almost defiantly, "I think it's great. And you know how it was, Len. I mean, why we couldn't get married before, on account of the judge."

"Sure," said Len. "I know."

"And I'll tell you one thing," said Esau. "I'll be a better father to it than my dad ever was to me."

"I don't know," said Len. "My father was the best in the world, and I didn't turn out so good either."

He followed Hostetter and Kovacs down a steep hatch ladder into the cargo hold.

The barge did not draw much water, but she was sixty feet long and eighteen wide, and every foot of space in her was crammed with chests and bales and sacks. She smelled strongly of wood and river water, flour and cloth, old tallow and pitch, and a lot of things Len could not identify. From beyond the after bulkhead, sounding muffled and thunderous, came the thumping rhythm of the engine. Just under the hatch a sort of well had been left so that a man could come down the ladder and see that nothing had broached or shifted, and the ladder looked like a solid piece of construction butting onto a solid deck. But a square section of the planking had been swung aside and there was a little pit there, and in the pit was a thing that Len recognized as a radio, although it was larger than the one he and Esau had had, and different in other ways. A man was sitting beside it, talking, with a single lantern hung overhead to give him light.

"Here they are now," he said. "Wait a minute." He turned and spoke to Hostetter. "Collins reckons the best thing would be to contact Rosen at the falls. The river's fairly low now, and he figures with a little help we could slip them there."

"Worth trying," said Hostetter. "What do you think, Joe?"

Kovacs said he thought Collins was right. "We sure don't want any fights, and they're bound to catch up to us, running light."

Esau had come down the ladder, too. He was standing by Len, listening.

"Watts?" he asked.

"I guess so. He must have gone scurrying around clear over to Shadwell to get men."

"They're crazy mad," said Kovacs. "They can't very well get back at the farmers, so they'll take it out on us. Besides, we're fair game whenever you find us." He was a big burly young man, very brown from the sun. He looked as though it would take a great deal to frighten him, and he did not seem frightened now, but Len was impressed by his great determination not to be caught by the boats from Refuge.

Hostetter nodded to the man at the radio. "All right, Sam. Let's talk to Rosen."

Sam said good-by to Collins and began to fiddle with the knobs. "God," said Esau, almost sobbing, "do you remember how we worked with that thing and couldn't raise a whisper, and I stole those books—" He shook his head.

"If you hadn't happened to listen in at night," said Hostetter, "you never would have heard anything." He was crouched down beside the pit now, hanging over Sam's shoulder.

"That was Len's idea," said Esau. "He figured you'd run too much risk of being seen or overheard in the daytime."

"Like now," said Kovacs. "We've got the aerial up—pretty obvious, if you had light enough to see it."

"Shut up," said Sam, bending over the radio. "How do you expect me to—Hey, will you guys give me a clear channel for a minute? This is an emergency." A jumble of voices coming in tinny confusion from the speaker clarified into a single voice which said, "This is Petto at Indian Ferry. Do you want me to relay?"

"No," said Sam. "I want Rosen. He's within range. Lay low, will you? We've got bandits on our tail."

"Oh," said the voice of Petto. "Sing out if you want help."

"Thanks." Sam fiddled with the knobs some more and continued to call for Rosen. Len stood by the ladder and watched and listened, and it seemed in retrospect that he had spent nearly all of his life in Piper's Run down by the Pymatuning trying to make voices come out of an obstinate little box. Now, in a daze of wonder and weariness, he heard, and saw, and could not realize yet that he was actually a part of it.

"This is so much bigger than the one we had," said Esau, moving forward. His eyes shone, the way they had before, so that his handsome, willful face looked like a boy's face again, and the subtle weakness of the mouth was lost in eagerness. "How does it work? What's an aerial? How—"

Kovacs began to explain rather vaguely about batteries and transistors. His mind was not on it. Len's gaze was drawn to Hostetter's face, half shaded by the brim of his hat—the familiar brown Amish hat, the familiar square cut of the hair and the shape of the beard—and he thought of Pa, and he thought of Brother James and his two boys, and of Gran who would not regret the old world any more, and of Baby Esther who must be grown tall by now, and he turned his head away so that he could not see Hostetter but only the impersonal dark beyond the lantern's circle, full of dim and meaningless cargo shapes. The engine thumped, slow and steady, with a short sighing like the breathing of someone asleep. He could hear the paddle blades strike the water, and now he could hear other sounds too, the woody creaking of the barge itself and the sloughing and bubbling of the river sliding underneath the hull. One of those moments of disorientation came to him, a wild interval of wondering what he was doing in this place, ending in a realization that a lot had happened in the last twenty-four hours and he was tired out.

Sam was talking to Rosen.

"We're going to crack on some speed now. It should be right after daybreak, if we don't run onto a sand bar."

"Well, watch it," said the scratchy voice of Rosen from the speaker. "The channel's tricky now."

"Is anything getting down the rapids?"

"Nothing but driftwood. It's all locking through, and I've got them piled up at both ends of the canal. I don't want to tamper with the gates unless I'm forced to it. I've spent years building myself up here, but the slightest breath of suspicion—"

"Yeah," said Sam. "It would look a little coincidental, I guess. Of course, we could just ram through—"

"Not with my barge," said Kovacs. "We've got a long way to go in her yet, and I like her bottom in one piece. There must be another way."

"Let me think," said Rosen.

There was a long pause while he thought. The men waited around the radio, breathing heavily.

Rather timidly, a voice spoke, saying, "This is Petto again, at Indian Ferry."

"Okay. What?"

"Well, I was just thinking. The river's low now, and the channel's narrow. It ought to be easy to block."

"Do you have anything in mind?" asked Hostetter.

"There's a dredge working right off the end of the point," said Petto. "The men come in at night to the village, so we don't have to worry about anyone drowning. Now, if you could pass here while it's still dark, and I could be out by the dredge ready to turn her loose, the river makes a bend right here and the current would swing her on broadside, and I'll bet nothing but a canoe would get by her till she was towed off again."

"Petto," said Sam, "I love you. Did you hear that, Rosen?"

"I heard. Sounds like a solution."

"It does," said Kovacs, "but when we get there, lock us through fast, just in case."

"I'll be watching," said Rosen. "So long."

"All right," said Sam. "Petto?" They began to talk, arranging signals and timing, discussing the condition of the channel between their present position and Indian Ferry. Kovacs turned and looked at Len and Esau. "Come on," he said. "I've got a job for you. Know anything about steam engines?"

"A little," said Len.

"Well, all you have to know about this one is to keep the fire up. We're in a hurry."

"Sure," said Len, glad of something to do. He was tired, but he could stand to be more tired if it would stop his mind from whirling around over old memories and unhappy thoughts, and the picture of Dulinsky's dying face, which was already becoming confused with the face of Soames. He scrambled up the ladder after Kovacs. In the deckhouse, Amity had apparently fallen asleep, for she made no move when they passed, Esau going on his tiptoes and looking nervously at the blanket curtaining her bunk. For a minute the night air touched them, clean and cool, and then they went down again into the pit where the boiler was. Here there was a smell of hot iron and coal dust, and a very sweaty-looking man with a broad shovel moving between the bin and the fire door. Kovacs said, "Here's some help, Charlie. We're going to move."

Charlie nodded. "Extra shovels over there." He kicked open the door and began to pile in the coal. Len took his shirt off. Esau started to, but stopped with it half unbuttoned and said, looking at the boiler, "I thought it would be different."

"What?" said Kovacs.

"Well, the engine. I mean, coming from Bartorstown, you could have any kind of an engine you want, and I thought—"

Kovacs shook his head. "Wood and coal are all the fuel there is. We have to use 'em. Besides, you stop a lot of places along the river, and a lot of people come aboard, and the first thing they want to see is your engine. They'd know in a minute if it was different. And suppose you have a breakdown? What would you do then, send all the way back to Bartorstown for parts?"

"Yeah," said Esau. "I suppose so." He was obviously disappointed. Kovacs went away. Esau finished taking his shirt off, got a shovel, and fell in beside Len at the coalbin. They fed the fire while Charlie worked the draft and watched the safety valve. The thump of the piston came faster and faster, churning the paddle wheel, and the barge picked up speed, going away with the current. Finally Charlie motioned them to hold it for a while, and they stopped, leaning on their shovels and wiping the sweat off their faces. And Esau said, "I don't think Bartorstown is going to turn out much like we thought it would."

"Nothing," said Len, "ever seems to."

It seemed like an awfully long time before another man came with word that the race was over and told Len and Esau they could quit. They stumbled up on deck, and Len felt the barge jerk and quiver as the paddles were reversed. It was not the first time that night, and Len thought that Kovacs must either have, or be himself, the devil and all of a pilot.

He leaned against the deckhouse, shivering in the cool air. It was that slack, dark time when the moon has left the sky and the sun hasn't come yet. The bank was a low black smudge with an edge of mist along it. Ahead it seemed to curve in like a solid wall, as though the river ended there, and in a minute the barge would run head on into it. Len yawned and listened to the frogs. The barge swung, and there was a bend in the river. In the hollow of the bend there was a village, the square shapes of the houses sensed rather than seen. Close by the end of the point a couple of red lights burned, hung apparently in midair.

Up on the foredeck, a lantern was shown and then covered three times in quick succession. From very low down on the water came an answering series of blinks. Because he knew it was there, Len was able to make out a dim canoe with a man in it, and then all at once the huge spectral shape of the dredger seemed to spring at him out of the gloom. It slid by, a skeletal thing like a partly dismantled house set on a flat platform, very massive and weighted with the heavy iron scoop. Then it was behind them, and Len watched the red lights. For a long time they did not seem to move, and then they seemed to shift a little, and then a little more, and then with a ponderous and mighty slowness they swung in a long arc toward the opposite shore and stopped, and the noise came down the river a moment later.

Esau said, "They'll be lucky if they have her out of there by this time tomorrow."

Len nodded. He could feel the tension lifting, or perhaps it was only because for the first time in weeks he felt safe himself. The Refuge men could not follow now, and whatever word they might send ahead would be too late to stop them.

"I'm going to turn in," he said, and went into the deckhouse. Amity still slept behind her curtain. Len picked a bunk as far away from hers as he could get, and fell almost instantly asleep. The last thought he had was of Esau being a father, and it didn't seem right at all, somehow. Then the face of Watts intruded, and a horrible smell of damp rope. Len choked and whimpered, and then the darkness flowed over him, still and deep.

SIXTEEN

They went through the canal next morning, one of a long line of craft, towboats, steam barges, flatboats, going down with the current all the way to the gulf, traders' floating stores that were like the shoregoing wagons, going to lonely little towns where the river was the only road. It was a slow process, even though Kovacs said that Rosen was locking them through faster than usual, and there was a lot of time just to sit and watch. The sun had come up in a welter of mist. That was gone now, but the quality of the heat had changed from the dry burning clarity of the day before. The air was thick and heavy, and the slightest movement brought a wash of sweat over the skin. Kovacs sniffed and said it smelled of storm.

"About midafternoon," said Hostetter, squinting at the sky.

"Yup," said Kovacs. "Better start figuring a place to tie up."

He went away, busy nursing his barge. Hostetter was sitting on the deck in what shade he could find under the edge of the house, and Len sat beside him. Amity had gone back to her bunk, and Esau was with her. From time to time Len could hear the murmur of their voices through the small slit windows, but not any of the words they said.

Hostetter glanced enviously after Kovacs and then looked at his own big hands with the thick pads of callus on them from the long handling of reins. "I miss 'em," he said.

"What?" said Len, who had been thinking his own thoughts.

"My horses. The wagon. Seems funny, after all these years, just to sit. I wonder if I'm going to like it."

"I thought you were happy, going home."

"I am. And high time, too, while most of my old friends are still around. But this business of leading two lives has its drawbacks. I've been away from Bartorstown for close onto thirty years and only been back once in all that time. Places like Piper's Run seem more like home to me now. When I told them last fall I was quitting the road, they asked me to settle there—and you know something? I could have done it."

He brooded, watching the men at work on the lock without really seeing them.

"I suppose it'll all come back to me," he said. "After all, the place you were born and grew up in—But it'll seem funny to shave again. And I've worn these clothes so long—"

Water sucked and purled out of the lock and the barge sank slowly until you had to look up to see the top of the bank. The sun beat down, and no breeze stirred in that sunken pocket. Len half shut his eyes and drew his feet in under him because they were in the sun and burning.

"What are you?" he asked.

Hostetter turned his head and looked at him. "A trader."

"I mean really. What are you in Bartorstown?"

"A trader."

Len frowned. "I guess I don't understand. I thought all the Bartorstown men were something—scientists, or machine makers—something."

"I'm a trader," repeated Hostetter. "Kovacs, he's a river-boat man. Rosen is a good administrator and keeps the canal in repair and running smoothly because it's vital to us. Petto, back there at Indian Ferry—I used to know Petto's father, and he was a pretty good man in electronics, but the boy is a trader like me, except that he stays more in one place. There are only so many potential scientists and technicians in Bartorstown, like any community. And they need the rest of us to keep them going."

"You mean," said Len slowly, revising some deep-rooted ideas, "that all these years you've really been—"

"Trading," said Hostetter. "Yes. There are over four hundred people in Bartorstown, not counting us outside. They all have to eat and wear clothes. Then there's other things too, iron and alloys and chemicals and drugs, and so on. It all has to be brought in from outside."

"I see," said Len. There was a long pause. Then he said sadly, "Four hundred people. That isn't even half as many as there were in Refuge."

"It's about ninety per cent more than there were ever supposed to be. Originally there were thirty-five or forty men, all specialists, working on this hush-hush project for the government. Then when the reaction came after the war and things began to get nasty, they brought in a lot of other men and their families, scientists, teachers, people who weren't very popular on the outside any more. We've been lucky. There were a lot of other secret installations in the country, but Bartorstown is the only one that wasn't discovered or betrayed, or didn't have to be abandoned."

Len's hands tightened on his knees, and his eyes were bright. "What were they doing there—the forty men, the specialists?"

A kind of a peculiar look came into Hostetter's face. But he only said, "They were trying to find an answer to something, I can't tell you what it was, Len. All I can tell you is, they didn't find it."

"Are they still trying?" asked Len. "Or can't you tell me that, either?"

"You wait till you get there. Then you can ask all the questions you want to, from the men who are authorized to answer them. I'm not."

"When I get there," Len murmured. "It sure sounds strange. When I get to Bartorstown—I've said it a million times in my mind, but now it's real. When I get to Bartorstown."

"Be careful how you throw that name around."

"Don't worry. But—what's it like there?"

"Physically," said Hostetter, "it's a hole. Piper's Run, Refuge, Louisville over there, they've all got it beat a mile."

Len looked at the pleasant village strung out along the canal, and at the wide green plain beyond it, dotted with farmsteads and grazing cattle, and he said, remembering a dream, "No lights? No towers?"

"Lights? Well, yes and no. Towers—I'm afraid not."

"Oh," said Len, and was silent. The barge glided on. Pitch bubbled gently in the deck seams and it was an effort to breathe. After a while Hostetter took off his broad hat and wiped his forehead and said, "Oh no, it's too hot. This can't last."

Len glanced up at the sky. It was cloudless and intensely blue, but he said, "It's going to break. We'll get a good one." He turned his attention back to the village. "That used to be a city, didn't it?"

"A big one."

"I remember now, it was named after the king of France. Mr. Hostetter—"

"Hm?"

"Whatever happened to those countries—I mean, like France?"

"They're just about like us—the ones on the winning side. Lord knows what happened to the ones that lost. The whole world has jogged back to pretty much what it was when Louisville was this size before, and this canal was first dug. With a difference, though. Then they were anxious to grow and change."

"Will it always stay like this?"

"Nothing," said Hostetter, "ever stays always like anything."

"But not in my time," Len murmured, echoing Judge Taylor's words, "nor in my children's." And in his mind was the far, sad sound of the falling down of high buildings built on clouds.

"In the meantime," said Hostetter, "it's a good world. Enjoy it."

"Good," said Len bitterly. "When it's full of men like Burdette, and Watts, and the people who killed Soames?"

"Len, the world has always been full of men like that, and it always will be. Don't ask the impossible." He looked at Len's face, and then he smiled. "I shouldn't ask the impossible either."

"What do you mean?"

"It's a matter of age," said Hostetter. "Don't worry. Time will take care of it."

They passed through the lower locks and out onto the river again below the great falls. By midafternoon the whole northern sky had turned a purplish black, and a silence had fallen over the land. "Line squalls," said Kovacs, and sent Len and Esau down to stoke again. The barge went boiling downstream, her paddles lashing up the spray. It got stiller yet, and hotter, until it seemed the world would have to burst with it, and then the first crackings and rumblings of that bursting made themselves heard over the scrape of the shovels and the clang of the fire door. Finally Sam put his head down the ladder and shouted to Charlie to let off and bank up. Drenched and reeling, Len and Esau emerged into a portentous twilight, with the sky drawn down over the country like a black cowl. They were tied up now in midstream in the lee of an island, and the north bank rose up in a protecting bluff.

"Here she comes," said Hostetter.

They ducked for the shelter of the house. The wind hit first, laying the trees over and turning up the lighter sides of their leaves. Then the rain came, riding the wind in a white smother that blotted everything from sight, and it was mixed with leaves and twigs and flying branches. After that was the lightning, and the thunder, and the cracking of trees, and then after a long time only the rain was left, pouring down straight and heavy as though it was tipped out of a bucket. They went out on deck and made sure everything was fast, shivering in the new chill, and then took turns sleeping. The rain slacked and almost stopped, and then came on again with a new storm, and during his watch Len could see lightning flaring all along the horizon as the squalls danced on the forward edge of the cool air mass moving down from the north. About midnight, through diminished rain and distant thunder, Len heard a new sound, and knew that it was the river rising.

They started on again in a clear bright dawn, with a fine breeze blowing and a sky like scoured porcelain dotted with white clouds, and only the torn branches of the trees and the river water roiled with mud and debris were left to show the wildness of the night. Half a mile below where Kovacs had tied up they passed a towboat and a string of barges, tossed up all along the south bank, and below that again a mile or two was a trader's boat sunk in the shallows where she had run onto a snag.

That was the beginning of a long journey, and a long strange period for Len that had the quality of a dream. They followed the Ohio to its mouth and turned north into the Mississippi. They were breasting the current now, beating a slow and careful way up a channel that switched constantly back and forth between the banks, so that the barge seemed always to be about to run onto the land beside some whitewashed marker. They used up the coal, and took on wood at a station on the Illinois side, and beat on again to the mouth of the Missouri, and after that for days they wallowed their way up the chutes of the Big Muddy. Mostly it was hot. There were storms, and rain, and around the middle of August there came a few nights cold enough to hint of fall. Sometimes the wind blew so hard against them they had to tie up and wait, and watch the down-river traffic go past them flying. Sometimes after a rain the water would rise and run so fast that they could make no headway, and then it would fall just as quickly and show them too late how the treacherous channel had shifted, and they would have to work the barge painfully and with much labor and swearing off the sand bar where she had stuck fast. The muddy water fouled the boiler, and they had to stop and clean it, and other times they had to stop for more wood. And Esau grumbled, "This is a hell of a way for Bartorstown men to travel."

"Esau," said Hostetter, "I'll tell you. If we had planes we'd be glad to fly them. But we don't have planes, and this is better than walking—as you will find out."

"Do we have much farther to go?" asked Len.

Hostetter made a pushing movement with his head against the west. "Clear to the Rockies."

"How much longer?"

"Another month. Maybe more if we run into trouble. Maybe less if we don't."

"And you won't tell us what it's like?" asked Esau. "What it's really like, the way it looks, how it is to live there."

But Hostetter only said curtly, "You'll find out when you get there."

He refused to talk to them about Bartorstown. He made that one statement about Piper's Run being a pleasanter place, and then he would not say any more. Neither would the other men. No matter how the question was phrased, how subtly the conversation was twisted around to trap them, they would not talk about Bartorstown. And Len realized that it was because they were afraid to.

"You're afraid we might give it away," he said to Hostetter. And then, not in any spirit of reproach but merely as a statement of fact, "I guess you don't trust us yet."

"It isn't a question of trust. It's just that no Bartorstown man ever talks about it, and you ought to know better than to ask."

"I'm sorry," said Len, "It's just that we've thought about it so long. I guess we've got a lot to learn."

"Quite a lot," said Hostetter thoughtfully. "It won't be easy, either. So many things will jar against every belief you've grown up with, and I don't care how you scoff at it, some of it sticks to you."

"That won't bother me," said Esau.

"No," said Hostetter, "I doubt if it will. But Len's different."

"How different?" demanded Len, bristling a bit.

"Esau plays it all by ear," said Hostetter. "You worry." Later, when Esau was gone, he put his hand on Len's shoulder and smiled, giving him a close, deep look at the same time, and Len smiled back and said, "There's times when you make me think an awful lot of Pa."

"I don't mind," said Hostetter. "I don't mind at all."

SEVENTEEN

The character of the country changed. The green rolling forest land flattened out and thinned away, and the sky became an enormous thing, stretched incredibly across a gray-green plain that seemed to go on and on over the rim of the world, drawing a man's gaze into its emptiness until his eyes ached with it, and until he searched hungrily for a tree or even a high bush to break the blank horizon. There were prosperous villages along the river, and Hostetter said it was good farming country in spite of how it looked, but Len hated the flat monotony of it, after the lush valleys he was used to. At night, though, there was a grandeur to it, a feeling of windy vastness all ablaze with more stars than Len had ever seen before.

"It takes a while to get used to it," Hostetter said. "But it has its own beauty. Most places do, if you don't shut your eyes and your mind against it. That's why I'm sorry I made that crack about Bartorstown."

"You meant it, though," said Len. "You know what I think? I think you're sorry you're going back."

"Change is always a sorry thing," said Hostetter. "You get used to doing things in a certain way, and it's always a wrench to break it up."

A thought came to Len which had curiously enough never come to him before. He asked, "Do you have a family in Bartorstown?"

Hostetter shook his head. "I've always had too much of a roving foot. Never wanted any ties to it."

They both, unconsciously, looked forward along the deck to where Esau sat with Amity.

"And they're so easy to get," said Hostetter.

There was something possessive in Amity's posture, in the way her head was bent toward Esau and the way her hand rested on his. She was getting plump, and her mouth was petulant, and she was taking her approaching, if still distant, motherhood very seriously. Len shivered, remembering the rose arbor.

"Yes," said Hostetter, chuckling. "I agree. But you've got to admit they sort of deserve each other."

"I just can't figure Esau as a father, somehow."

"You might be surprised," said Hostetter. "And besides, she'll keep him in line. Don't be too toplofty, boy. Your time will come."

"Not if I know it first," said Len.

Hostetter chuckled again.

The barge thrashed its way on toward the mouth of the Platte. Len worked and ate and slept, and between times he thought. Something had been taken away from him, and after a while he realized what it was and why its going made him unhappy. It was the picture of Bartorstown he had carried with him, the vision he had followed all the long way from home. That was gone now, and in its place was only a little collection of facts and a blank waiting to be filled in. Bartorstown—a pre-war, top-secret military installation for some kind of research, named for Henry Waltham Bartor, the Secretary of Defense who had it built—was undergoing a painful translation from dream to reality. The reality was yet to come, and in the meantime there was nothing, and Len felt vaguely as though somebody had died. Which, of course, Gran had, and the two things were so closely connected in his mind that he couldn't think about Bartorstown without thinking about Gran too, and remembering the defiant things she had said that made Pa so mad. He wondered if she knew he was going there. He hoped so. He thought she would be pleased.

They tied up one night by a low bank in the middle of nowhere, with nothing in sight but the prairie grass and the endless sky, and no sound but the wind that never got tired of blowing, and the ceaseless running of the river. In the morning they started to unload the barge, and around noon Len paused a moment to catch his breath and wipe the sweat out of his eyes. And he saw a pillar of dust moving far off on the prairie, coming toward the river.

Hostetter nodded. "It's our men, bringing the wagons. We'll angle up from here to the valley of the Platte, and pick up the rest of our party at a point on the South Fork."

"And then?" asked Len, with a stir of the old excitement making his heart beat faster.

"Then we're on the last stretch."

A few hours later the wagons came in, eight of them, great lumbering things made for the hauling of freight and drawn by mules. The men who drove them were brown and leathery, with the tops of their foreheads all white when they took their hats off, and a network of pale lines around their eyes where the sun hadn't got to the bottom of the squinted-up wrinkles. They greeted Kovacs and the bargemen as old friends, and shook Hostetter's hand warmly as a sort of welcome home. Then one of them, an old fellow with a piercing glance and a pair of shoulders that looked as though they could carry a wagon alone if the mules gave out, peered closely at Len and Esau and said to Hostetter, "So these are your boys."

"Well," said Hostetter, coloring slightly.

The old man walked around them slowly, his head on one side. "My son was in the Ohio country couple-three years ago. He said all you heard about was Hostetter's boys. Where were they, what were they doing, let him know when they moved on."

"It wasn't that bad," said Hostetter. His face was now brick red. "Anyway, a couple of kids—And I'd known them since they were born."

The old man finished his circuit and stood in front of Len and Esau. He put out a hand like a slab of oak and shook with them gravely in turn. "Hostetter's boys," he said, "I'm glad you got here before my old friend Ed had a total breakdown."

He went away laughing. Hostetter snorted and began to throw boxes and barrels around. Len grinned, and Kovacs burst out laughing.

"He isn't just joking, either," said Kovacs, jerking his head toward the old man. "Ed kept every radio in that part of the country hot."

"Well, damn it," grumbled Hostetter, "a couple of kids. What would you have done?"

They camped that night beside the river, and next day they loaded the wagons, taking great care with the stowage of each piece in the beds, and leaving a place in one where Amity could ride and sleep. Kovacs was going on into the Upper Missouri, and shortly after noon they got up steam on the barge and chuffed away. The mules were rounded up by two or three of the men, riding small wiry horses of a type Len had not seen before. He helped them to harness up and then took his seat in one of the wagons. The long whips cracked and the drivers shouted. The mules leaned their necks into the collars and the wagons rolled slowly over the prairie grass, with a heavy creaking and complaint of axles. At nightfall, across the flat land, Len could still see the barge on the river. In the morning it was still there, but farther off, and sometime during the day he lost it. And the prairie became immensely large and lonely.

The Platte runs wide and shallow between hills of sand. The sun beats down and the wind blows, and the land goes on forever. Len remembered the Ohio with an infinite longing. But after a while, when he got used to it, he became aware of a whole new world here, a way of living that didn't seem half bad, once you shucked off a habit of thought that called for green woods and green grass, rain and plowing. The dusty cottonwoods that grew by the water became as beautiful as oaks, and the ranch houses that clung close to the river were more welcome than the villages of his own country because they were so much more infrequent. They were rough and sun-bitten, but they were comfortable enough, and Len liked the people, the brown hardy women and the men who seemed to have lost some of themselves when they came apart from their horses. Beyond the sand hills was the prairie, and on the prairie were the great wild herds of cattle and the roving horse bands that made the living of these hunters and traders. Hostetter said that the wild herds were the descendants of the pre-war range stock, turned loose in the great upheaval that followed the abandonment of the cities and the consequent breakdown of the system of supply and demand.

"Their range runs clear down to the Mexican border," he said, "and there isn't a fence on it now. The dry-farmers all quit long ago. For generations there hasn't been a single plow to scratch up the plains, and the grass is coming back even in the worst of the man-made deserts, like the good Lord meant it to be." He took a deep breath, looking all around the horizon. "There's something about it, isn't there, Len? I mean, in some ways the East is closed in, with hills and woods and the other side of a river valley."

"You ain't going to get me to say I don't like the East," said Len. "But I'm getting to like this too. It's just so big and empty I keep feeling like I'm going to fall in."

It was dry, too. The wind beat and picked at him, sucking the moisture out of him like a great leech. He drank and drank, and there was always sand in the bottom of the cup, and he was always thirsty. The mules rolled the miles back under the wagon wheels, but so gradually and through such a sameness of country that Len got a feeling they hadn't moved. Through deep ravines in the sand hills the wild cattle came down to drink, and at night the coyotes yapped and howled and then fell into respectful silence before the deeper and more blood-chilling voice of some wayfaring wolf. Sometimes they would go for days without seeing a ranch house or any sign of human life, and then they would pass a camp where the hunters had made a great kill and were busy jerking or salting down the beef and rough-curing the hides. And time passed. And like the time on the river, it was timeless.

They reached the rendezvous on the South Fork, in a meadow faded and sun-scorched, but still greener than the glaring sandy desolation that spread around it as far as the eye could reach, broken only by the shallow rushing of the river. When they went on again there were thirty-one wagons in the party, and some seventy men. Some of them had come directly across the Great Plains, others had come from the north and west, and they were loaded with everything from wool and iron pigs to gunpowder. Hostetter said that other freight trains like this came up from Arkansas and the wide country to the south and west, and that others still followed the old trail through the South Pass from the country west of the mountains. All the supplies had to be fetched before winter, because the Plains were a cruel place when the northers blew and the single pass into Bartorstown was blocked with snow.

From time to time, at particular points, they would find groups of men encamped and waiting for them, and they would stop to trade, and at one place, where another stream trickled into the South Fork and there was a village of four houses, they picked up two more wagons loaded with hides and dried beef. And Len asked, when he was sure he was alone with Hostetter, "Don't these people ever get suspicious? I mean, about where we're going."

Hostetter shook his head.

"But I should think they'd guess."

"They don't have to. They know."

"They *know* we're going to Bartorstown?" said Len incredulously.

"Yes," said Hostetter, "but they don't know they know it. You'll see what I mean when you get there."

Len did not ask any more, but he thought about it, and it didn't seem to make any kind of sense.

The wagons lumbered on through the heat and the glare. And on a late afternoon when the Rockies hung blue and misty like a curtain across the west, there came a sudden shout from up ahead. It was flung back all along the line, from driver to driver, and the wagons jolted to a stop. Hostetter reached back for a gun, and Len asked, "What is it?"

Hostetter said, "I suppose you've heard of the New Ishmaelites."

"Yes."

"Well, now you're going to see them."

Len followed Hostetter's gesture, squinting against the reddening light. And on top of a low and barren bluff he saw a gathering of people, perhaps half a hundred of them, looking down.

EIGHTEEN

He jumped to the ground with Hostetter. The driver stayed put, so he could move the wagon into a defensive line if the order came. Esau joined them, and some other men, and the old chap with the bright eyes and the mighty shoulders, whose name was Wepplo. Most of them had guns.

"What do we do?" asked Len, and the old man answered, "Wait."

They waited. Two men and a woman came slowly down from the bluff, and the leader of the train went just as slowly out to meet them, with half a dozen armed men behind to cover him. And Len stared.

The people gathered on the bluff were like an awkward frieze of scarecrows put together out of old bones and strips of blackened leather. There was something horrible about seeing that there were children among them, peering with a normal childlike wonder and excitement at the strange men and the wagons. They wore goatskins, very much like old Bible pictures of John the Baptist, or else long wrappings of dirty white cloth like winding sheets. Their hair hung long and matted down their backs, and the men had beards to their waists. They were gaunt, and even the children had a wild and starveling look. Their eyes were sunken, and perhaps it was only a trick of the lowering sun, but it seemed to Len that they burned and smoldered with an actual glow, like the eyes he had seen once on a dog that had the mad sickness.

"Will they fight us?" he asked.

"Can't tell yet," said Wepplo. "Sometimes yes, other times no. Depends."

"What do you mean," demanded Esau, "it depends?"

"On whether they've been 'struck' or not. Mostly they just wander and pray and do a lot of real holy starving. But then all of a sudden one of 'em'll start screaming and frothing and fall down kicking, and that's a sign they've been struck by the Lord's special favor. So the rest of 'em whoop and screech and beat themselves with thorny branches or maybe whips—whips, you see, is the only personal article their religion allows them to own—and when they're worked up enough they all pile down and butcher some rancher that's affronted the Lord by pampering his flesh with a sod roof and a full belly. They can do a real nice job of butchering, too."

Len shivered. The faces of the Ishmaelites frightened him. He remembered the faces of the farmers when they marched into Refuge, and how their stony dedication had frightened him then. But they were different. Their fanaticism roused up only when it was prodded. These people lived by it, lived for it, and served it without rhyme, reason, or thought.

He hoped they would not fight.

They did not. The two wild-looking men and the woman—a wiry creature with sharp shin bones showing under her shroud when she walked, and a tangle of black hair blowing over her shoulders—were too far away for any of their talk to be heard, but after a few minutes the leader of the train turned and spoke to the men behind him, and two of them turned and came back to the train. They sought out a particular wagon, and Wepplo grunted.

"Not this time. They only want some powder."

"Gunpowder?" asked Len incredulously.

"Their religion don't seem to call for them starving quite to death, and every gang of them—this is only one band, you understand—does own a couple of guns. I hear they never shoot a young cow, though, but only the old bulls, which are tough enough to mortify anybody's flesh."

"But powder," said Len. "Don't they use it on the ranchers, too?"

The old man shook his head. "They're knife-and-claw killers, when they kill. I guess they can get closer to their work that way. Besides, they only get enough powder to barely keep them going." He nodded toward the two men, who were going back again carrying a small keg. A thin sound, half wailing and half waspish, penetrated from the second wagon down, and Esau said, "Oh Lord, there's Amity calling me. She's probably scared to death." He turned and went immediately. Len watched the New Ishmaelites.

"Where did they come from?" he asked, trying to remember what he had heard about them. They were one of the very earliest extreme sects, but he didn't know much more than that.

"Some of them were here to begin with," Hostetter said. "Under other names, of course, and not nearly so crazy because the pressure of society sort of held them down, but a fertile seed bred. Others came here of their own accord when the New Ishmaelite movement took shape and really got going. A lot more were driven here out of the East, being natural-born troublemakers that other people wanted to be rid of."

The small keg of powder changed hands. Len said, "What do they trade you for it?"

"Nothing. Buying and selling are no part of holiness and, anyway, they don't have anything. When you come right down to it, I don't know why we do give it to them. I guess," said Wepplo, "probably it's on account of the kids. You know, once in a while you find one of 'em like a coyote pup, lost in the sagebrush. If they're young enough, and brought up right, they turn out just as smart and nice as anyone."

The woman lifted her arms up high, whether for a curse or a blessing Len couldn't tell. The wind tossed the lank hair back from her face, and he saw with a shock that she was young, and might have been handsome if her cheeks were full and her eyes less hunger-bright and staring. Then she and the two men climbed back to the top of the bluff, and in five minutes they were all gone, hidden by the cut-up hills. But that night the Bartorstown men doubled the watch.

Two days later they filled every cask, bottle, and bucket with water and left the river, striking south and west into a waste and very empty land, sun-scorched, wind-scourged, and dry as an old skull. They were climbing now, toward distant bastions of red rock with tumbled masses of peaks rising blue and far away behind them. The mules and the men labored together, toiling slowly, and Len learned to hate the sun. And he looked up at the blank, cruel peaks, and wondered. Then, when the water was almost gone, a red scarp swung away to the west and showed an opening about as wide as two wagons, and Hostetter said, "This is the first gate."

They filed into it. It was smooth like a made road, but it was steep, and everybody was walking now to ease the mules, except Amity. After a little while, without any order that Len could hear, or for any reason that he could see, they stopped.

He asked why.

"Routine," Hostetter said. "We're not exactly overrun with people, as you might guess from the country, but not even a rabbit can get through here without being seen, and it's customary to stop and be looked over. If somebody doesn't, we know right away it's a stranger."

Len craned his neck, but he could not see anything but red rock. Esau was walking with them, and Wepplo. Wepplo laughed and said, "Boy, they're looking at you right now in Bartorstown. Yes, they are. Studying you real close, and if they don't like your looks, all they have to do is push one little button and *boom!*" He made a sweeping gesture with his hand, and Len and Esau both ducked. Wepplo laughed again.

"What do you mean, *boom?*" said Esau angrily, glaring around. "You mean somebody in Bartorstown could kill us here? That's crazy."

"It's true," said Hostetter. "But I wouldn't get excited. They know we're coming."

Len felt the skin between his shoulders turn cold and crawl. "How can they see us?"

"Scanners," said Hostetter, pointing vaguely at the rock. "Hidden in the cracks, where you can't see 'em. A scanner is kind of like an eye, way off from the body. Whoever comes through here, they know it in Bartorstown, and it's still a day's journey away."

"And all they have to do is push something?" said Esau, wetting his lips.

Wepplo swung his hand again, and repeated, *"Boom!"*

"They must have really had something almighty secret here," said Esau, "to go to all that trouble."

Wepplo opened his mouth, and Hostetter said, "Give a hand with the wagon here, will you?" Wepplo shut his mouth again and leaned onto the tail gate of a wagon that seemed already to be rolling smoothly. Len looked sharply at Hostetter, but his head was bent and his whole attention appeared to be on the pushing. Len smiled. He did not say anything.

Beyond the cut was a road. It was a good, wide road, and Hostetter said it had been made a long time ago before the Destruction. He called it a switchback. It zigzagged right up the side of a mountain, and Len could still see the marks on the rock where huge iron teeth had bitten it away. They moved up slowly, the teams grunting and puffing, and the men helping them, and Hostetter pointed to a ragged notch very high up against the sky. He said, "Tomorrow."

Len's heart began to beat fast and the nerves pricked all through his stomach. But he shook his head, and Hostetter asked, "What's the matter?"

"I never thought there'd be a road to it. I mean, just a road."

"How did you think we'd get in and out?"

"I don't know," said Len, "but I thought there'd be at least walls or guards or something. Of course they can stop people in the cut back there—"

"They *could*. They never have."

"You mean people walk right through there? And up this road? And through that pass into Bartorstown?"

"They do," said Hostetter, "and they don't. Didn't you ever hear that the best way to hide something is to leave it right out in the open?"

"I don't understand," said Len. "Not at all."

"You will."

"I guess so." Len's eyes were shining again in that particular way, and he said softly, "Tomorrow," as though it was a beautiful word.

"It's been a long way, hasn't it?" said Hostetter. "You really wanted to come, to stick to it like that." He was silent a minute, looking up at the pass. Then he said, "Give it time, Len. It won't be all that you've dreamed about, but give it time. Don't make any snap decisions."

Len turned and studied him gravely. "You keep sounding all the time like you're trying to warn me about something."

"I'm just trying to tell you to—not be impatient. Give yourself a chance to get adjusted." Suddenly, almost angrily, he said, "This is a hard life, that's what I'm trying to tell you. It's hard for everybody, even in Bartorstown, and it doesn't get any easier, and don't expect a shiny tinsel heaven and then break your heart because it isn't there."

He looked hard at Len, very briefly, and then looked away, breathing hard and doing the mechanical things with his hands that a man does when he's upset and trying not to show it. And Len said slowly, "You hate the place."

He could not believe it. But when Hostetter said sharply, "That's ridiculous, of course I don't," he knew that it was true.

"Why did you come back? You could have stayed in Piper's Run."

"So could you."

"But that's different."

"No, it isn't. You had a reason. So have I." He walked on for a minute with his head bent down. Then he said, "Just don't ever plan on going back."

He went ahead fast, leaving Len behind, and Len did not see him alone again the rest of that day and night. But he felt as shocked as he would have if, in the old days, Pa had suddenly told him that there was no God.

He did not say anything to Esau. But he kept glancing up at the pass, and wondering. Toward late afternoon they were high enough up on the mountain that he could see back the other way, over the ridge of the scarp, to where the desert lay all lonely and burning. A terrible feeling of doubt came over him. The red and yellow rock, the sharp peaks that hung against the sky, the gray desert and the dust and the dryness, the pitiless light that was never softened by a cloud or gentled by rain, the vast ringing silences where nothing lived but the wind, all seemed to mock him with their cheerlessness and lack of hope. He wished he was back—no, not home, because he would have to face Pa there, and not in Refuge, either. Just somewhere where there was life and water and green grass. Somewhere where the ugly rock did not stand up every way you looked, like—

Like what?

Like the truth, when all the dreams are torn away from it?

It wasn't a happy thought. He tried to ignore it, but every time he saw Hostetter it came to him again. Hostetter seemed broody and withdrawn, and after they camped and had supper he disappeared. Len started to look for him and then had sense enough to stop.

They were camped in the mouth of the pass, where there was a wide space on both sides of the road. The wind blew and it was bitterly cold.

Just before dark Len noticed some letters cut in the side of a cliff above the road. They were crumbling and weatherworn, but they were big, and he could make them out. They said FALL CREEK 13 mi.

Hostetter was gone, so Len hunted up Wepplo and asked him what they meant.

"Can't you read, boy? They mean just what they say. Fall Creek, thirteen miles. That's from here to there."

"Thirteen miles," said Len, "from here to Fall Creek. All right. But what's Fall Creek?"

"Town," said Wepplo.

"Where?"

"In Fall Creek Canyon." He pointed. "Thirteen miles."

He was grinning. Len began to hate the old man's sense of humor. "What about Fall Creek?" he asked. "What does it have to do with us?"

"Why," said Wepplo, "it's got damn near everything to do with us. Didn't you know, boy? That's where we're going."

Then he laughed. Len walked away fast. He was mad at Wepplo, mad at Hostetter, mad at Fall Creek. He was mad at the world. He rolled up in his blanket and lay shivering and cursing. He was dog-tired. But it was a long time before he fell asleep, and then he dreamed. He dreamed that he was trying to find Bartorstown. He knew he was almost there, but there was fog and darkness and the road kept shifting its direction. He kept asking an old man how to get there, but the old man had never heard of Bartorstown and would only say over and over that it was thirteen miles to Fall Creek.

They went through the pass the next day. Both Len and Hostetter were now morose and did not talk much. They crossed the saddleback before noon, and after that they went much faster, going down. The mules stepped out smartly as though they knew they were almost home. The men got cheerful and eager. Esau kept running up as often as he could get away from Amity and asking, "Are we almost there?" And Hostetter would nod and say, "Almost."

They came out of the pass with the afternoon sun in their eyes. The road pitched down in another switchback along the side of a cliff, and way at the bottom of the cliff there was a canyon, with the blue shadow of the opposite wall already sliding across it. Hostetter pointed. His voice was neither excited, nor happy, nor sad. It was just a voice, saying, "There it is."

BOOK THREE

NINETEEN

The wagons went down the wide steep road with the brake shoes screeching and the mules braced back on their haunches. Len looked over the edge, into the canyon. He looked a long time without speaking. Esau came and walked beside him, and they both looked. And it was Esau who turned around with his face all white and angry and shouted at Mr. Hostetter, "What do you think this is, a joke? Do you think this is real funny, bringing us all this way—"

"Oh, shut up," said Hostetter. He sounded tired now, all of a sudden, and impatient, and he spoke to Esau the way a man speaks to an annoying child. Esau shut up. Hostetter glanced at Len. Len did not turn or lift his head. He was still staring down into the bottom of the canyon.

There was a town there. Seen from this height and angle it was mostly a collection of roofs, clustered along the sides of a stream bed where some cottonwoods grew. They were ordinary roofs of ordinary little houses such as Len had been used to seeing all his life, and he thought that many of the houses were made of logs, or slab. At the north end of the canyon was a small dam with a patch of blue water behind it. Beside the dam, straggling up a slope, there were a couple of high, queer-looking buildings. Close by them rails ran up and down the slope, leading from a hole in the cliff to a dump of broken rock. There were tiny cars on the rails. At the foot of the slope were several more buildings, low and flat ones this time, with a curving top. They were a rusty color. From the other side of the dam a short road led to another hole in the cliff, but there were no rails or cars or anything connected with this one, and rocks had rolled down across the road.

Len could see people moving around. Smoke came from some of the chimneys. A team of tiny mules brought a string of tiny cars down the rails on the slope, and the carts were dumped. After a minute or two the sound drifted up to him, faint and thin like an echo.

He turned and looked at Hostetter.

"Fall Creek," said Hostetter. "It's a mining town. Silver. Not very high-grade ore, but good enough and a lot of it. We still take it out. There's no secret about Fall Creek, never has been." He swept his hand out in a brief, curt gesture. "We live here."

Len said slowly, "But it isn't Bartorstown."

"No. That's kind of a wrong name, anyway. It isn't really a town at all."

Even more slowly, Len said, "Pa told me there was no such place. He told me it was only a state of mind."

"Your Pa was wrong. There is such a place, and it's real. Real enough to keep hundreds of people working for it all their lives."

"But where?" said Esau furiously. "Where?"

"You've waited this long. You can wait a few hours longer."

They went on, down the steep road. The shadow of the mountain widened and filled the canyon, and began to flow up the eastern wall to meet them. Farther down, on the breast of an old fall, a stand of pines caught the light and turned a harsh green, too bright against the red and ochers of the rock.

Len said, "Fall Creek is just another town."

"You can't get clear out of the world," Hostetter said. "You can't now and you couldn't then. The houses are built of logs and slab because we had to build them out of what there was. Originally Fall Creek had electricity because it was the fashion then. Now it isn't the fashion, so we don't have it. Main thing is to look like everybody else, and then they don't notice you."

"But a real secret place," said Len. "A place nobody knew about." He frowned, trying to puzzle it out. "A place you don't dare let anybody know about now—and yet you just live openly in a town, with a road to it, and strangers come and go."

"When you start barring people out they know you have something to hide. Fall Creek was built first. It was built quite openly. What few people there were in this Godforsaken part of the country got used to it, got used to the trucks and a particular kind of plane going to and from it. It was only a mining town. Bartorstown was built later, behind the cover of Fall Creek, and nobody ever suspected it."

Len thought that over. Then he asked, "Didn't they even guess it when all the new people started coming in?"

"The world was full of refugees, and thousands of them headed for places just like this, as far back in the hills as they could get."

The shadow reached up and they went into it, and it was twilight. Lamps were being lit in the town. They were just lamps, such as were lit in Piper's

Run, or Refuge, or a thousand other towns. The road flattened out. The mules were tired, but they pricked their long ears forward and swung along fast, and the drivers yelled and made their whips crack like rifle shots. There was quite a crowd waiting for them under the cottonwoods, lanterns burning, women calling out to their men on the wagons, children running up and down and shouting. They did not look any different from any other people Len had seen in this part of the country. They wore the same kinds of clothes, and their manners were the same. Hostetter said again, as though he knew what Len was thinking, "You have to live in the world. You can't get away from it."

Len said with a quiet bitterness, "There isn't even as much here as we had in Piper's Run. No farms, no food, nothing but rocks all around. Why do people stay here?"

"They have a reason."

"It must be a mighty damn big one," retorted Len, in a tone that said he did not believe in anything any more.

Hostetter did not answer.

The wagons stopped. The drivers got down and everybody that was riding got out, Esau lifting down a pale and rumpled Amity, who stared about her distrustfully. Boys and young men ran up and took the mules and led them away with the wagons. There were a terrible lot of strange faces, and after a while Len realized that they were nearly all staring at him and Esau. They hung together instinctively, close to Hostetter. Hostetter was craning his head around, yelling for Wepplo, and the old man came up grinning, with his arm around a girl. She was kind of a small girl, with dark hair and snapping dark eyes like Wepplo's, and a face that was perhaps a little too sharp and determined. She wore a shirt with the neck open and the sleeves rolled up, and a skirt that came down just over the tops of a pair of soft high boots. She looked first at Amity, and then at Esau, and then at Len. She looked the longest at Len, and her eyes were not at all shy about meeting his.

"My granddaughter," said Wepplo, as though she was made of pure gold. "Joan. Mrs. Esau Colter, Mr. Esau Colter, Mr. Len Colter."

"Joan," said Hostetter, "will you take Mrs. Colter with you for a while?"

"Sure," said Joan, rather sulkily. Amity hung onto Esau and started a protest, but Hostetter shut her up.

"Nobody's going to bite you. Go along, and Esau will come as soon as he can."

Amity went, reluctantly, leaning on the dark girl's shoulder. She looked as big as a house, and not from the baby, either, which was still a long way off. The dark girl gave Len a sly laughing glance and then disappeared in the crowd. Hostetter nodded to Wepplo and hitched up his pants and said to Len and Esau, "All right, come on."

They followed him, and all along the way people stared at them and talked, not in an unfriendly way, but as though Len and Esau were of tremendous interest to them. Len said, "They don't seem to be very used to strangers."

"Not strangers coming to live with them. Anyway, they've been hearing about you two for a long time. They're curious."

"Hostetter's boys," said Len, and grinned for the first time in two days.

Hostetter grinned too. He led them down a dark lane between scattered houses to where a fairly large frame house with a porch across its front was set on a slope, higher than the others and facing the mine. The clapboards were old and weathered, and the porch had been shored up underneath with logs.

"This was built for the mine superintendent," said Hostetter. "Sherman lives in it now."

"Sherman is the boss?" asked Esau.

"Of a lot of things, yes. There's Gutierrez and Erdmann, too. They have the say about other things."

"But Sherman let us come," said Len.

"He had to talk to the others. They all had to agree to that."

There was lamplight in the house. They went up the steps onto the porch, and the door opened before Hostetter could knock on it. A tall thin gray-haired woman with a pleasant face stood in the doorway, smiling and holding out her arms to Hostetter. He said, "Hello, Mary," and she said, "Ed! Welcome home!" and kissed him on the cheek. "Well," said Hostetter. "It's been a long time." "Eleven, no twelve years," said Mary. "It's good to have you back."

She looked at Len and Esau.

"This is Mary Sherman," said Hostetter, as though he felt he had to explain, "an old friend. She used to play with my sister when we were all young—my sister's dead now. Mary, these are the boys."

He introduced them. Mary Sherman smiled at them, half sadly, as though she had much she could say. But all she did say was, "Yes, they're waiting for you. Come inside."

They stepped into the living room. The floor was bare and clean, the pine boards worn down to the grain. The furniture was old, most of it, and plain, of a kind Len had seen before that was made before the Destruction. There was a big table with a lamp on it, and three men were sitting around it. Two of them were about Hostetter's age, and one was younger, perhaps forty or so. One of the older ones, a big square blocky man with a clean-shaven chin and light eyes, got up and shook hands with Hostetter. Then Hostetter shook hands with the others, and there was some talk. Len looked around uncomfortably and saw that Mary Sherman was already gone.

"Come here," said the big blocky man, and Len realized that he was being spoken to. He stepped into the circle of lamplight, close to the table. Esau came with him. The big man studied them. His eyes were the color of a winter sky just before snow, very keen and penetrating. The younger man sat beside him, leaning forward on the table. He had reddish hair and he wore spectacles and his face looked tired, not as though he needed to rest right now but as though it always looked tired. Behind him, in the shadows between the table and the big iron stove, was the third man, small, swarthy and bitter, with a neat pointed beard as white as linen. Len stared back at them, not knowing whether to be angry or awed or what, and beginning to sweat from sheer nervousness.

The big man said abruptly, "I'm Sherman. This is Mr. Erdmann"— the younger man nodded—"and Mr. Gutierrez." The small bitter man grunted. "I know you're both Colters. But which is which?"

They named themselves. Hostetter had withdrawn into the shadows, and Len heard him filling his pipe.

Sherman said to Esau, "Then you're the one with the—ah—expectant mother."

Esau started to explain, and Sherman stopped him. "I know all about it, and I've already given Hostetter his tongue-lashing for exceeding authority, so we can forget it, except for one thing. I want you to bring her here at exactly ten o'clock tomorrow morning. The minister will be here. Nobody needs to know about it. Is that understood?"

"Yes, sir," said Esau. Sherman was not threatening or unpleasant. He was just used to giving orders, and the answer was automatic.

He looked from Esau to Len, and asked, "Why did you want to come here?"

Len bent his head and did not say anything.

"Go ahead," said Hostetter. "Tell him."

"How can I?" said Len. "All right. We thought it would be a place where people were different, where they could think about things and talk about them without getting into trouble. Where there were machines and—oh, all the things there used to be."

Sherman smiled. It made him no longer a cold-eyed blocky man used to giving orders, but a human being who had lived a long time and learned not to fight it. Like Hostetter. Like Pa. Len recognized him, and suddenly he felt that he was not entirely among strangers.

"You thought," said Sherman, "that we'd have a city, just like the old ones, with everything in it."

"I guess so," said Len, and he was not angry now, only regretful.

"No," said Sherman. "All we have is the first part of what you wanted."

Erdmann said, "And we're looking for the second."

"Oh yes," said Gutierrez. His voice was thin and bitter like the rest of him. "We have a cause. You'll understand about that—you young men have had a cause yourselves. Do you want me to tell them, Harry?"

"Later," Sherman said. He leaned forward and spoke to Len and Esau, and his eyes were hard again, and cold. "You have Hostetter to thank—"

"Not entirely," said Hostetter, breaking in. "You had your reason."

"A man can always find a reason to justify himself," said Sherman cynically. "But all right, I admit I had one. However, most of it was Hostetter. Otherwise you would both be dead now, at the hands of the mob in that town—what's the name—?"

"Refuge," said Len. "Yes, we know that."

"I'm not rubbing it in, merely getting the facts straight. We've done you a favor, and I won't try to impress upon you what a very big favor it is because you won't be able to understand until you've been here awhile. Then I won't have to tell you. In the meantime, I'm going to ask you to repay it by doing as you're told and not asking too many questions."

He paused. Erdmann cleared his throat nervously in the silence, and Gutierrez muttered, "Give them the shaft, Harry. Swift and clean."

Sherman turned around. "Have you been drinking, Julio?"

"No. But I will."

Sherman grunted. "Well, anyway, what he means is this. You're not to leave Fall Creek. Don't do anything that even looks like leaving. We have a great deal at stake here, more than you can possibly imagine as yet, and we can't risk it."

He finished simply with three words. "You'll be shot."

TWENTY

There was another silence. Then Esau said, just a little too loudly, "We worked hard enough to get here, we're not likely to run away."

"People change their minds. It was only fair to tell you."

Esau put his hands on the table and said, "Can I ask just one question?"
"Go ahead."

"Where the hell *is* Bartorstown?"

Sherman leaned back in his chair and looked hard at Esau, frowning. "You know something, Colter? I wouldn't answer that, now or later, if there was any way to keep it from you. You boys have made us quite a problem. When strangers come in here we keep our mouths shut and are careful, and that isn't much of a worry because there are very few strangers and they don't stay long. But you two are going to live here. Sooner or later, inevitably, you're going to find out all about us. And yet you don't really belong here. Your whole life, your training, your background, your conditioning, are totally at odds with everything we believe in."

He glanced at Len, harshly amused. "No use getting red around the ears, young fellow. I know you're sincere. I know you've gone through hell to get here, which is more than a lot of us would do. But—tomorrow is another day. How are you going to feel then, or the day after?"

"I should think you're pretty safe," said Len, "as long as you have plenty of bullets."

"Oh," said Sherman. "That. Yes. Well, I suppose so. Anyway, we decided to take a chance on you, and so we haven't any choice. So you'll be told about Bartorstown. But not tonight." He got up and shoved his hand unexpectedly at Len. "Bear with me."

Len shook hands with him and smiled.

Hostetter said, "I'll see you, Harry." He nodded to Len and Esau, and they went out again, into full dark and air that had a crisp edge of chill on it, and a lot of unfamiliar smells. They walked back through the town. Lamps were going on in every house, people were talking loud and laughing, and going from place to place in little groups. "There's always a celebration," said Hostetter. "Some of the men have been away a long time."

They wound up in a neat, solid log house that belonged to the Wepplos, the old man and his son and daughter-in-law, and the girl Joan. They ate dinner and a lot of people drifted in and out, saying hello to Hostetter and nipping out of a big jug that got to passing around. The girl Joan watched Len all evening, but she didn't say much. Quite late, Gutierrez came in. He was dead drunk, and he stood looking down at Len so solemnly and for such a long time that Len asked him what he wanted.

Gutierrez said, "I just wanted to see a man who wanted to come here when he didn't have to."

He sighed and went away. Pretty soon Hostetter tapped him on the shoulder. "Come on, Lennie," he said, "unless you want to sleep on Wepplo's floor."

He seemed in a jovial frame of mind, as though coming home had not after all been as bad as he thought it would be. Len walked along beside him through the cold night. Fall Creek was quieter now, and the lamps were going out. He told Hostetter about Gutierrez.

Hostetter said, "Poor Julio. He's in a bad frame of mind."

"What's wrong with him?"

"He's been working on this thing for three years. Actually, he's been working on it most of his life, but this particular point of attack, I mean. Three years. And he's just found out it's no good. Clear the slate, try again. Only Julio's beginning to think he isn't going to live long enough."

"Long enough for what?"

But Hostetter only said, 'We'll have to bunk in the bachelor's shack. But that isn't bad. Lots of company."

The bachelor's shack turned out to be a long two-story frame building, part of the original construction of Fall Creek, with some later additions running out from it in clumsy wings. The room Hostetter led him into was at the back of one of these wings, with its own door and some stubby pine trees close by to scent the air and whisper when the breeze blew. They had brought their blanket rolls from Wepplo's. Hostetter pitched his into one of the two bunks and sat down and began to take off his boots.

"How do you like her?" he said.

"Like who?" asked Len, spreading his blankets.

"Joan Wepplo."

"How should I know? I hardly saw her."

Hostetter laughed. "You hardly took your eyes off her all evening."

"I've got better things to think about," said Len angrily, "than some girl."

He rolled into the bunk. Hostetter blew out the candle, and a few minutes later he was snoring. Len lay wide awake, every surface of him exposed and sensitive and quivering, feeling and hearing. The bunk was a new shape. Everything was strange: the smells of earth and dust and pine needles and pine resin and walls and floor and cooking, the dim sounds of movement and of voices in the night, everything. And yet it was not strange, either. It was just another part of the world, another town, and no matter what Bartorstown turned out to be now it would not be anything at all that he had hoped for. He felt awful. He felt so awful, and he was so angry with everything for being as it was that he kicked the wall, and then he felt so childish that he began to laugh. And in the middle of his laughing, the face of Joan Wepplo floated by, watching him with bright speculative eyes.

When he woke up it was morning, and Hostetter had already been out somewhere because he was just coming back.

"Got a clean shirt?"

"I think so."

"Well, get busy and put it on. Esau wants you to stand up with him."

Len muttered something under his breath about it being late in the day for formalities like that, but he washed and shaved and put on the clean shirt, and walked up with Hostetter to Sherman's house. The village seemed quiet, with not many people around. He got the feeling that they were watching him from inside the windows of the houses, but he did not mention it.

The wedding was short and plain. Amity was wearing a dress somebody must have loaned her. She looked smug. Esau did not look any way at all. He was just there. The minister was a young man and quite short, with an annoying habit of bobbing up and down on his toes as though he were trying all the time to stretch himself. Sherman and his wife and Hostetter stood in the background, watching. When it was over Mary Sherman put her arms around Amity, and Len shook hands rather stiffly with Esau, feeling silly. He was ready to go then, but Sherman said, "If you don't mind, I'd like you to stay awhile. All of you."

They were in a small room. He crossed it and opened the door into the living room, and Len saw that there were seven or eight men inside.

"Now there's nothing to worry about," Sherman said, and motioned them through the door. "Those three chairs right there at the table— that's right. Sit down. I want you to talk to some people."

They sat down, close together in a row. Sherman sat next to them, with Hostetter just beyond him, and the other men crowded in until they were all clumped around the table. There were pens and paper on it, and some other things, and in the middle a big wicker basket with the lid down. Sherman named over the men, but Len could not remember them all, except for Erdmann and Gutierrez, whom he already knew. They were nearly all middle-aged, and keen-looking, as though they were used to some authority. They were all very polite to Amity.

Sherman said, "This isn't an inquisition or anything, we're just interested. How did you first hear of Bartorstown, what made you so determined to come here, what happened to you because of it, how did it all start. Can you start us off, Ed? I think you were in on the beginning."

"Well," said Hostetter, "I guess it began the night Esau stole the radio."

Sherman looked at Esau, and Esau looked uncomfortable. "I guess that was wrong to do, but I was only a kid then. And they killed this man because they said he was from Bartorstown—it was an awful night. And I was curious."

"Go on," said Sherman, and they all leaned forward, interested. Esau went on, and pretty soon Len joined in, and they told about the preaching and how Soames was stoned to death, and how the radio got to be a fixation with them. And with Hostetter nudging them along here and there, and Sherman or one of the other men asking a question, they found themselves telling the whole story right up to the time Hostetter and the bargemen had taken them out of the smoke and anger of Refuge. Amity had something to tell about that too, and she made it graphic enough. When they were all through it seemed to Len that they had put up with a terrible lot for all they had found when they got here, but he didn't say so.

Sherman got up and opened another door on the far side of the room. There was a room there with a lot of equipment in it, and a man sitting in the midst of it with a funny-looking thing on his head. He took this off and Sherman asked him, "How did it go?" and he said, "Fine."

Sherman closed the door again and turned around. "I can tell you now that you've been talking to all of Fall Creek, and Bartorstown." He lifted the lid of the wicker basket and showed what was inside. "These are microphones. Every word you said was picked up and broadcast." He let the lid fall and stood looking at them. "I wanted them all to hear your story, in your own words, and this seemed like the best way. I was afraid if I put you up on a platform with four hundred people staring at you you'd freeze up. So I did this."

"Oh my," said Amity, and put her hand over her mouth.

Sherman glanced at the other men. "Quite a story, isn't it?"

"They're young," said Gutierrez. He looked sick enough to die with it, and his voice was weak, but still bitter. "They have faith, and trust."

"Let them keep it," said Erdmann shrilly. "For God's sake, let *somebody* keep it."

Kindly, patiently, Sherman said, "You both need a rest. Will you do us all a great favor? Go and take one."

"Oh no," said Gutierrez, "not for anything. I wouldn't miss this for the world. I want to see their little faces shine when they catch their first glimpse of the fairy city."

Looking at the microphones, Len said, "Is this the reason you said you had for letting us come?"

"Partly," said Sherman. "Our people are human. Most of them have no direct contact with the main work to keep them feeling important and interested. They live a restricted life here. They get discontented. Your story is a powerful reminder of what life is like on the outside, and why we have to keep on with what we're doing. It's also a hopeful one."

"How?"

"It shows that eighty years of the most rigid control hasn't been able to stamp out the art of independent thinking."

"Be honest, Harry," said Gutierrez. "There was a measure of sentiment in our decision."

"Perhaps," said Sherman. "It did seem like a betrayal of everything we like to think we stand for to let you get hung up for believing in us. Everybody in Fall Creek seemed to think so, anyway."

He looked at them thoughtfully. "It may have been a foolish decision. You certainly aren't likely, either one of you, to contribute anything to our work, and you do constitute a problem out of all proportion to your personal importance. You're the first strangers we've taken in for more years than I can remember. We can't let you go again. We don't want to be forced to do what I warned you we would do. So we'll have to take pains, far more than with any of our own, to see that you're thoroughly integrated into the fabric of our living, our thoughts, our particular goal. Unless we're to keep a watch on you forever, we have to turn you into trustworthy citizens of Bartorstown. And that means practically a complete re-education."

He cast a sharp, sardonic glance at Hostetter. "He swore you were worth the trouble. I hope he was right."

He leaned over then and shook Amity by the hand. "Thank you, Mrs. Colter, you've been very helpful. I don't think you'd find this trip interesting, so why don't you come and have some lunch with my wife? She can help you on a lot of things."

He led Amity to the door and handed her over to Mary Sherman, who always seemed to be where she was wanted. Then he came back and nodded to Len and Esau.

"Well," he said, "let's, go."

"To Bartorstown?" asked Len. And Sherman answered, "To Bartorstown."

TWENTY-ONE

The explanation was simple when you knew it. So simple that Len realized it was no wonder he hadn't guessed it. Sherman led the way up the canyon, past the mine slope and on to the other side of the little dam. Gutierrez was with them, and Erdmann, and Hostetter, and two of the other men. The rest had gone about their business somewhere else. The sun was hot down here in the bottom of the valley, and the dust was dry. The air smelled of dust and cottonwoods and pine needles and mules. Len glanced at Esau. His face was kind of pale and set, and his eyes roved restlessly, as though they didn't want to see what was in front of them. Len knew how he felt. This was the end, the solid inescapable truth, the last of the dream. He should have been excited himself. He should have felt something. But he did not. He had already been through all the feelings he had in him, and now he was just a man walking.

They turned up the disused slope that the rocks had rolled on. They walked between the rocks in the hot sun, up to the hole in the face of the cliff. It had a wooden gate across it, weathered but in good repair, and a sign above it saying:

DANGER
MINE TUNNEL UNSAFE
Falling Rock
Keep Out

The gate was locked. Sherman opened it and they went through, and he locked it again behind him.

"Keeps the kids out," he said. "They're the only ones that ever bother."

Inside the tunnel, as far as the harsh reflected sunlight showed, there was a clutter of loose rock on the tunnel floor and a crumbly look about the walls. The shoring timbers were rotted and broken, and some of the roof props were hanging down. It was not a place anybody would be likely to force his way into. Sherman said that every mine had abandoned workings, and nobody thought anything about it. "This one, naturally, is perfectly safe. But the mock-up is convincing."

"Too damn convincing," said Gutierrez, stumbling. "I'll break a leg here yet."

The light shaded off into darkness, and the tunnel bent to the left. Suddenly, without any warning, another light blazed up ahead. It was bluish and very brilliant, not like any Len had seen before, and now for the first time excitement began to stir in him. He heard Esau catch his breath and say, "Electric!" The tunnel here was smooth and unencumbered. They walked along it quickly, and beyond the dazzle of the light Len saw a door.

They stopped in front of it. The light was overhead now. Len tried to look straight into it and it made him blind like the sun. "Isn't that something," Esau whispered. "Just like Gran used to say."

"There are scanners here," said Sherman. "Give them a second or two. There. Go on now."

The door opened. It was thick and made of metal set massively into the living rock. They went through it. It closed quietly behind them, and they were in Bartorstown.

This part of it was only a continuation of the tunnel, but here the rock was dressed very smooth and neat, and lights were set all along it in a trough sunk in the roof. The air had a funny taste to it, flat and metallic. Len could feel it moving over his face, and there was a soft, soft hushing sound that seemed to belong to it. His nerves had tightened now, and he was sweating. He had a brief and awful vision of the outside of the mountain that was now on top of him, and he thought he could feel every pound of it weighing down on him. "Is it all like this?" he asked. "Underground, I mean."

Sherman nodded. "They put a lot of places underground in those days. Under a mountain was about the only safe place you could get."

Esau was peering down the corridor. It seemed to go a long way in. "Is it very big?"

Gutierrez answered this time. "How big is big? If you look at Bartorstown one way it's the biggest thing there is. It's all yesterday and all tomorrow. Look at it another way, it's a hole in the ground, just big enough to bury a man in."

About twenty feet away down the corridor a man stepped out of a doorway to meet them. He was a young fellow, about Esau's age. He spoke with easy respect to Sherman and the others, and then stared frankly at the Colters.

"Hello," he said. "I saw you coming through the lower pass. My name's Jones." He held out his hand.

They shook it and moved closer to the door. The rock-cut chamber beyond was fairly large, and it was crammed with an awful lot of things, boards and wires and knobs and stuff like the inside of a radio. Esau looked around, and then he looked at Jones and said, "Are you the one that pushes the button?"

They were all puzzled for a minute, and then Hostetter laughed. "Wepplo was joshing them about that. No, Jones would have to pass that responsibility on."

"Matter of fact," said Sherman, "we've never pushed that button yet. But we keep it in working order, just in case. Come here."

He motioned them to follow him, and they did, with the cautious tenseness of men or animals who find themselves in a strange place and feel they may want to get out of it in a hurry. They were careful not to touch anything. Jones went ahead of them and began casually doing things with some of the knobs and switches. He did not quite swagger. Sherman pointed to a square glass window, and Len stared into it for a confused second or two before he realized that it could hardly be a window at all, and if it were it couldn't be looking into the narrow rocky cut that was away on the other side of the ridge.

"The scanners pick up the image and transmit it back to this screen," Sherman said, and before he could go on Esau cried out in a child's tone of delighted wonder, "Teevee!"

"Same principle," said Sherman. "Where'd you hear about that?"

"Our grandmother. She told us a lot of things."

"Oh yes. You mentioned her, I think—talking about Bartorstown." Smoothly, but with unmistakable firmness, he drew their attention to the screen again. "There's always somebody on duty here, to watch. Nobody can get through that gateway unseen, in—or out."

"What about nighttime?" asked Len. He supposed Sherman had a right to keep reminding them, but it made him resentful. Sherman gave him a sharp, cool glance.

"Did your grandmother tell you about electric eyes?"

"No."

"They can see in the dark. Show them, Jones."

The young man showed them a board with little glass bulbs on it, in two rows opposite each other. "This is like the lower pass, see? And these little bulbs, they're the electric-eye pairs. When you walk between them you break beam, and these bulbs light up. We know right where you are."

If Esau got the byplay, he didn't show it. He was staring with bright envious eyes at Jones, and suddenly he asked, "Could I learn to do that too?"

"I don't see why not," said Sherman, "if you're willing to study."

Esau breathed heavily and smiled.

They went out and down the corridor again, under the brilliant lights. There were some other doors with numbers on them that Sherman said were storerooms. Then the corridor branched into two. Len was confused now about direction, but they took the right-hand branch. It widened out into a staggering series of rooms, cut smooth out of the rock with heavy columns of it left in regular rows to bear the weight of the low roof. The rooms were separate from each other but interconnecting, like the segments of a wheel, and they seemed to have smaller chambers opening from their outer edges. They were full of things. Len did not try, after the first few minutes, to understand what he saw because he knew it would take him years to do that. He just looked, and felt, and tried to get hold of the full realization that he had entered into a totally different world.

Sherman was talking. Sometimes Gutierrez, too, and sometimes Erdmann, and sometimes one of the other men. Hostetter didn't say much.

Bartorstown had been made, they said, as self-supporting as such a place could be. It could repair itself, and make new parts for itself, and there were still some of the original materials it had been supplied with for that purpose. Sherman pointed out the various rooms, the electronics lab, the electrical maintenance shop, the radio shop, rooms full of strange machines and strange glittering shapes of glass and metal, and endless panels of dials and winking lights. Sometimes a man or several men would be in them, sometimes not. Sometimes there were chemical smells and unfamiliar sounds, and sometimes there was nothing but an empty quiet, with the hush-hush of the moving air making them seem even quieter and lonelier. Sherman talked about air ducts and pumps and blowers. Automatic was a word he used over and over, and it was a wonderful word. Doors opened automatically when you came to them, and lights went on and off. "Automatic," said Hostetter, and snorted. "No wonder the Mennonites got to be such a power in the land. Other folks were so spoiled they could hardly tie their shoelaces any more by hand."

"Ed," said Sherman, "you're a poor advertisement for Bartorstown."

"I don't know," said Hostetter. "Seems I was good enough for some."

Len looked at him. He knew Hostetter's moods pretty well now, and he knew he was worried and ill at ease. A nervous chill crawled down Len's back, and he turned to stare again at the strange things all around him. They were wonderful, and fascinating, and they didn't mean a thing until somebody named a purpose for them. Nobody had.

He said so, and Sherman nodded. "They have a purpose. I wanted you to see all of Bartorstown, and not just a part of it, so you would realize how important the government of this country thought that purpose was, even before the Destruction. So important that they saw to it that Bartorstown would survive no matter what happened. Now I'll show you another part of their planning, the power plant."

Hostetter started to speak, and Sherman said quietly, "We'll do this my way, Ed." He walked them a little way more around the central corridor that Len had come to think of as the hub of a wheel, and with a sidelong glance at Len and Esau he said, "We'll use the stair instead of the elevator."

All the way down the echoing steel stair, Len tried to remember what an elevator might be, but couldn't. Then he stopped with them on a floor, and looked around.

They were in a cavernous place that echoed with a deep and mighty throbbing, overtoned and undertoned with other sounds that were strange to Len's ear but that blended all together into one unmistakable voice, saying a word that he had heard spoken before only by the natural voices of wind and thunder and flood. The word was power. The rock vault had been left rougher here, and all the space was flooded with a flat white glare, and in that glare a line of mighty structures stood, squat, bulbous, Gargantuan, dwarfing the men who worked around them. Len's flesh picked up the throbbing and quivered with it, and his nose twitched to the smell of something that was in the air.

"These are the transformers," Sherman said. "You can see the cables there—they run in sunken conduits to carry power all over Bartorstown. These are the generators, and the turbines—"

They walked in the bright white glare under the flanks of the great machines.

"—the steam plant—"

Here was something they could understand. It was enormously bigger than any they had dreamed of, but it was steam, and steam they knew as an old friend among these foreign giants. They clung to it, making comparisons, and one of the two men whose names Len was not sure of patiently explained the differences in design.

"But there's no firebox," said Esau. "No fire, and no fuel. Where's the heat come from?"

"There," said the man, and pointed. The steam plant joined onto a long, high, massive block of concrete. "That's the heat exchanger."

Esau frowned at the concrete. "I don't see—"

"It's all shielded, of course. It's hot."

"Hot," said Esau. "Well, sure, it would have to be to make the water boil. But I still don't see—" He looked around, into the recesses of the cavern. "I still don't see what you use for fuel."

There was a moment of silence, as silent as it ever was in that place. The thrumming beat on Len's ears, and somehow he knew that he stood on a moment's edge before some unguessable pit of darkness, he knew it from the schooled and watchful faces of the men and the way Esau's question hung loud and echoing in the air and would not die away.

"Why," said Sherman, very gently, very casually, and Hostetter's eyes were sharp and anguished in the light, "we use uranium."

And the moment was gone, and the pit gaped wide and black as perdition, and Len shouted, but the shout was swallowed up and drowned until it was only the ghost of a whisper, saying. "Uranium. But that was—that was—"

Sherman's hand rose up and pointed to where the concrete structure heightened and widened into a great thick wall.

"Yes," he said. "Atomic power. That concrete wall is the outer face of the shield. Behind it is the reactor."

Silence again, except for the throbbing of that great voice that never stopped. The concrete wall loomed up like the wall of hell, and Len's heart slowed and the blood in him turned cold as snow water.

Behind it is the reactor.

Behind it is evil and night and terror and death.

A voice screamed in Len's ears, the voice of the preaching man, standing on the edge of his wagon with the sparks flying past him on the night wind—*They have loosed the sacred fire which only I, the Lord Jehovah, should dare to touch—and God said—Let them be cleansed of their sin—*

Esau's voice spoke in shrill denial. "No. There ain't any more of that left in the world."

Let them be cleansed, said the Lord, and they were cleansed. They were burned with the fires of their own making, yea, and the proud towers vanished in the blazing of the wrath of God, and the places of iniquity were made not—

"You're lying," Esau said. "There ain't any more of that, not since the Destruction."

And they were cleansed. But not wholly—

"They're not lying," Len said. He backed slowly away from that staring wall of concrete. "They saved it, and it's there."

Esau whimpered. Then he turned and ran.

Hostetter caught him. He spun him around and Sherman caught his other arm and they held him, and Hostetter said fiercely, "Stand still, Esau."

"But it'll burn me," Esau cried, staring wild-eyed. "It'll burn me inside, and my blood will turn white and my bones will rot and I'll die."

"Don't be a fool," said Hostetter. "You can see it hasn't hurt any of us."

"He's got a right to be afraid of it, Ed," said Sherman, more gently. "You ought to know their teaching better than I. Give them a chance. Listen, Esau. You're thinking of the bomb. This isn't a bomb. It isn't hurtful.

We've lived with it here for nearly a hundred years. It can't explode, and it can't burn you. The concrete makes it safe. Look,"

He let go of Esau and went up to the shield and put his hands on it.

"See? There's nothing here to fear."

And the devil speaks with the tongues of foolish men and works with the hands of the rash ones. Father, forgive me, I didn't know!

Esau licked his lips. His breath came hard and uneven between them. "You go and do it too," he said to Hostetter, as though Hostetter might be of a different flesh from Sherman, being a part of the world that Esau knew and not solely of Bartorstown.

Hostetter shrugged. He went and put his hands on the shield.

And you, thought Len. This is what you wouldn't tell me, what you wouldn't trust me with.

"Well," said Esau, choking, hesitant, sweating and shaking like a frightened horse but not running now, standing his ground, beginning to think. "Well—"

Len clenched his icy fists and looked at Sherman standing against the shield.

"No wonder you're so afraid," he said, in a voice that did not sound like his own at all. "No wonder you shoot people if they try to leave. If anybody went out and told what you've got here they'd rise up and hunt you out and tear you to pieces, and there wouldn't be a mountain in the world big enough to hide yourselves under."

Sherman nodded. "Yes. That's so."

Len shifted his gaze to Hostetter. "Why couldn't you have told us about this, before we ever came here?"

"Len, Len," said Hostetter, shaking his head. "I didn't want you to come. And I warned you, every way I could."

Sherman was watching, intent to see what he would do. They were all watching, Gutierrez with a weary pity, Erdmann with embarrassed eyes, and Esau in the middle of them like a big scared child. He understood dimly that it had all been planned this way and that they were interested in what words he would say and how he would feel. And in a sudden black revulsion of all the hopes and dreams and childhood longings, the seeking and the faith, he shouted at them, "Wasn't one burning of the world enough? Why did you have to keep this thing alive?"

"Because," said Sherman quietly, "it wasn't ours to destroy. And because destroying it is the child's way, the way of the men who burned Refuge, the way of the Thirtieth Amendment. That's only an evasion. You can't destroy knowledge. You can stamp it under and burn it up and forbid it to be, but somewhere it will survive."

"Yes," said Len bitterly, "as long as there are men foolish enough to keep it going. I wanted the cities back, yes. I wanted the things we used to have, and I thought it was stupid to be afraid of something that was gone years and years ago. But I never knew that it wasn't all gone—"

"So now you think they were right to kill Soames, right to kill your friend Dulinsky and destroy a town?"

"I—" The words stuck in Len's throat, and then he cried out, "That isn't fair. There was no atom power in Refuge."

"All right," said Sherman reasonably. "We'll put it another way. Suppose Bartorstown was destroyed, with every man in it. How could you be sure that somewhere in the world, hidden under some other mountain, there wasn't another Bartorstown? And how could you be sure that some forgotten professor of nuclear physics hadn't hoarded his textbooks—you had one in Piper's Run, you said. Multiply that by all the books there must be left in the world. What chance have you got to destroy them all?"

Esau said, slowly, "Len, he's right."

"Book," said Len, feeling the blind fear, feeling the crouching of the Beast behind the wall. "Book, yes, we had one, but we didn't know what it meant. Nobody knew."

"Somebody, somewhere, would figure it out in time. And remember another thing. The first men who found the secret of atomic power didn't have any books to go by. They didn't even know if it could be done. All they had was their brains. You can't destroy all the brains in the world, either."

"All right," cried Len, driven into a corner and seeing no escape. "What other way is there?"

"The way of reason," said Sherman. "And now I can tell you why Bartorstown was built."

TWENTY-TWO

There were three levels in Bartorstown. They climbed now to the middle one, below the laboratories and above the cavern where the old evil hid behind its concrete wall. Len walked ahead of Hostetter, and the others were all around him, Esau still trembling and wiping his mouth over and over with the back of his hand, the Bartorstown men silent and grave. And Len's mind was a wild dark emptiness like a night sky without stars.

He was looking at a picture. The picture was on a long curving piece of glass taller than a man and lit from inside someway so that the picture was like real, with depth and distance in it, and color, and every tiny thing sharp and clear to see. It was a terrible picture. It was a blasted and fragmented desolation, with one little lost building still standing in it, leaning over as though it was tired and wanted to fall.

"You talk about the bomb and what it did, but you never saw it," said Sherman. "The men who built Bartorstown had, or their fathers had. It was a reality, a thing of their time. They put this picture here to remind them, so that they wouldn't be tempted to forget their job. That was what the first bomb did. That was Hiroshima. Now go on, around the end of the wall."

They did, and Gutierrez was already ahead of them, walking with his head down. "I've already seen them too often," he said. He disappeared, through a door at the end of a wide passageway that had more pictures on either side. Erdmann started after him, hesitated, and then dropped back. He did not look at the pictures either.

Sherman did. He said, "These were some of the people who survived that first bombing, after a fashion."

Esau muttered, "Holy Jesus!" He began to shake more violently, hanging his head down and looking sidelong out of the corners of his eyes so as not to see too much.

Len did not say anything. He gave Sherman a straight and smoldering look, and Sherman said, "They felt very strongly about the bomb in those days. They lived under its shadow. In these victims they could see themselves, their families. They wanted very much that there should not be any more victims, any more Hiroshimas, and they knew that there was only one way to make sure of that."

"They couldn't," said Len, "have just destroyed the bomb?"

It was a stupid thing to say, and he was angry with himself instantly for saying it, because he knew better; he had talked about those times with Judge Taylor and read some of the books about them. So he forestalled Sherman's retort by saying quickly, "I know, the enemy wouldn't destroy his. The thing to have done was never to get that far, never to make a bomb."

Sherman said, "The thing to have done was never to learn how to make a fire, so no one would ever get burned. Besides, it was a little too late for that. They had a fact to deal with, not a philosophical argument."

"Well, then," said Len, "what was the answer?"

"A defense. Not the imperfect defense of radar nets and weapon devices, but something far more basic and all-embracing, a totally new concept. A field-type force that could control the interaction of nuclear particles right on their own level, so that no process either of fission or fusion could take place wherever that protecting force-field was in operation. Complete control, Len. Absolute mastery of the atom. No more bombs."

Quiet, and they watched him again to see how he would take it. He closed his eyes against the pictures so that he could try to think, and the words sounded in his head, loud and flat, momentarily without meaning. Complete control. No more bombs. The thing to have done was never to build them, never build fires, never build cities—

No.

No, say the words again, slowly and carefully. Complete control, no more bombs. The bomb is a fact. Atomic power is a fact. It is a living fact close down under my feet, the dreadful power that made these pictures. You can't deny it, you can't destroy it because it is evil and evil is like a serpent that dieth not but reneweth itself perpetually—

No. No. No. These are the words of the preaching man, of Burdette. Complete control of the atom. No more bombs. No more victims, no more fear. Yes. You build stoves to hold the fire in, and you keep water handy to put it out with. Yes.

But—

"But they didn't find the defense," he said. "Because the world got burned up anyway."

"They tried. They pointed the way. We're still following it. Now go on."

They passed through the door where Gutierrez had gone, into a space hollowed like the other spaces out of the solid rock, smoothed and pillared and reaching away on all sides under a clear flood of light. There was a long wall facing them. It was not really a wall, but a huge panel as big as a wall and set by itself, with a couple of small machines linked to it. It was nearly six feet high, not quite reaching the roof. It had a maze of dials and lights on it. The lights were all dark, and the needles of the dials did not move. Gutierrez was standing in front of it, his face twisted into a deep, sad, pondering scowl.

"This is Clementine," he said, not turning his head as they came in. "A foolish name for something on which may hang the future of the world."

Len dropped his hands, and it was as though in that dropping he cast from him many things too heavy or too painful to be carried. Inside my head there is nothing, let it stay that way. Let the emptiness fill up slowly with new things, and old things in new patterns, and maybe then I'll know—what? I don't know. I don't know anything, and all is darkness and confusion and only the Word—

No, not that Word, another one. Clementine.

He sighed and said aloud, "I don't understand."

Sherman walked over to the big dark panel.

"This is a computer. It's the biggest one ever built, the most complex. Do you see there—"

He pointed off beyond the panel, into the pillared spaces that stretched away there, and Len saw that there were countless rows of arrangements of wires and tubes set all orderly one after the other, interrupted at intervals by big glittering cylinders of glass.

"That's all part of it."

Esau's passion for machines was beginning to stir again under the fog of fright.

"All one machine?"

"All one. In it, in those memory banks, is stored all the knowledge about the nature of the atom that existed before the Destruction, and all the knowledge that our research teams have gained since, all expressed in mathematical equations. We could not work without it. It would take the men half their lifetimes just to work out the mathematical problems that Clementine can do in minutes. She is the reason Bartorstown was built, the purpose of the shops upstairs and the reactor down below. Without her, we wouldn't have much chance of finding the answer within any foreseeable time. With her—there's no telling. Any day, any week, could bring the solution to the problem."

Gutierrez made a sound that might have been the beginning of a laugh. It was quickly silenced. And once more Len shook his head and said, "I don't understand."

And I don't think I want to understand. Not today, not now. Because what you're telling me is not a description of a machine but of something else, and I don't want to know any more about it.

But Esau blurted out, "It does sums and remembers them? That don't sound like any machine, that sounds like—a—a—"

He caught himself up sharp, and Sherman said with no particular interest, "They used to call them electronic brains."

Oh Lord, and is there no end to it? First the hell-fire and now this.

"A misnomer," said Sherman. "It doesn't think, any more than a steam engine. It's just a machine."

And now suddenly he rounded on them, his face stern and cold-eyed and his voice as sharp as a whiplash to bring their attention to him, startled and alert.

"I won't push you," he said. "I won't expect you to understand it all in a minute, and I won't expect you to adjust overnight. I'll give you reasonable time. But I want you to remember this. You kicked and clawed and screamed to be let into Bartorstown, and now you're here, and I don't care what you thought it was going to be like, it's what it is, so make your peace with it. We have a certain job to do here. We didn't particularly ask for it, it just happened that way, but we're stuck with it and we're going to do it, in spite of what your piddling little farm-boy consciences may feel about it."

He stood still, regarding them with those cold hard eyes, and Len thought, He means that just the way Burdette meant it when he said, There shall be no cities in our midst.

"You claim you wanted to come here so you could learn," said Sherman. "All right. We'll give you every chance. But from here on, it's up to you."

"Yes, sir," said Esau hastily. "Yes, *sir.*"

Len thought, There is still nothing in my head, it feels like a wind was blowing through it. But he's looking at me, waiting for me to say something—what? Yes, no—and oh Lord, he's right, they did everything under the sun to keep us out and we would bull our way in, and now we're caught in a pit of our own digging—

But the whole world is caught in a pit. Isn't that what we wanted out of, the pit that killed Dulinsky and nearly killed us? The people are afraid and I hated them for it and now—I don't know what the answer is, oh Lord, I don't know, let me find an answer because Sherman is waiting and I can't run away.

"Someday," he said, wrinkling his brows in a frown of effort, so that he looked once more like the brooding boy who had sat with Gran on that October day, "someday atomic power will come back no matter what anybody does to stop it."

"A thing once known always comes back."

"And the cities will come back too."

"In time, inevitably."

"And it will all happen over again, the cities and the bomb, unless you find that way to stop it."

"Unless men have changed a lot by tomorrow, yes."

"Then," said Len, still frowning, still somber, "then I guess you're trying to do what ought to be done. I guess it might be right."

The word stuck to his tongue, but he got it off, and no bolt of lightning came to strike him dead, and Sherman did not challenge him any further.

Esau had moved toward the panel, magnetized by the lure of the machine. He reached hesitantly out and touched it, and asked, "Could we see it work?"

It was Erdmann who answered. "Later. She's just finished a three-year project, and she's shut down now for a complete overhaul."

"Three years," said Gutierrez. "Yes. I wish you could shut me down too, Frank. Pick my brain to pieces and put it together again, all fresh and bright." He began to raise and lower his fist, striking the panel each time, lightly as a feather falling. "Frank," he said, "she could have made a mistake."

Erdmann looked at him sharply. "You know that isn't possible."

"A vagrant charge," said Gutierrez. "A speck of dust, a relay too worn to function right, and how could you ever know?"

"Julio," said Erdmann. "You know better. If the slightest thing goes wrong with her she stops automatically and asks for attention."

Sherman spoke, and the talking stopped, and everybody began to move out into the passageway again. Gutierrez came close behind Len, and even through the doubt and fear that clouded in so thick around him Len could hear him muttering to himself, "She *could* have made a mistake."

TWENTY-THREE

Hostetter was a lamp in the darkness, a solid rock in the midst of flood. He was the link, the carry-over from Piper's Run to Bartorstown, he was the old friend and the strong arm that had already reached out twice to save him, once at the preaching, once at Refuge. Len clung to him, mentally, with a certain desperation.

"You think it's right?" he asked, knowing the inevitable answer, but wanting the assurance anyhow.

They were walking down the road from Bartorstown in the late afternoon. Sherman and the others had lingered behind, perhaps deliberately, so that Hostetter was alone with Len and Esau. And now Hostetter glanced at Len and said, "Yes, I think it's right."

"But," said Len softly, "to work with it, to keep it going—"

He was out in the open air again. The mountain was away from over his head, and the rock walls of Bartorstown no longer shut him in, and he could breathe and look at the sun. But the horror was still on him, and he thought of the destroyer crouched in a hole of the rock, and he knew he did not want ever to go back there. And at the same time he knew that he would have to go whether he wanted it or not.

Hostetter said, "I told you there'd be things you wouldn't like, things that would jar against your teachings no matter how much you said you didn't believe them."

"But you're not afraid of it," said Esau. He had been thinking hard, scuffing his boots against the stones of the road. Up above them on the east slope was the normal, comforting racket of the mine, and ahead the village of Fall Creek drowsed quietly in the late sun, and it was very much like Piper's Run if there had been a devil chained in the hills behind it. "You went right up and put your hands on it."

"I grew up with the idea of it," said Hostetter. "Nobody ever taught me that it was evil or forbidden, or that God had put a curse on it, and that's the difference. That's why we don't take strangers in but once in a coon's age. The conditioning is all wrong."

"I ain't worrying about curses," said Esau. "What I worry about is, will it hurt me?"

"Not unless you find some way to get inside the shield."

"It can't burn me."

"No."

"And it can't blow up."

"No. The steam plant might blow up, but not the reactor."

"Well, then," said Esau, and walked on awhile in silence, thinking. His eyes got bright, and he laughed and said, "I wonder what those old fools in Piper's Run, old Harkness and Clute and the rest, would think. They were going to birch us just for having a radio, and now we've got *that*. Jesus. I bet they'd kill us, Len."

"No," said Hostetter somberly, "*they* wouldn't. But all the same, you'd wind up, like Soames, at the bottom of a pile of stones."

"Well, I ain't going to give them a chance. Jesus! Atom power, the real thing, the biggest power in the world." His fingers curled with greedy excitement and then relaxed, and he asked again, "Are you *sure* it's safe?"

"It's safe," said Hostetter, getting impatient. "We've had it for nearly a century, and it hasn't hurt anybody yet."

"I guess," said Len slowly, leaning his head against the cool wind and letting it blow some of the darkness out of him, "we don't have any right to complain."

"You sure don't."

"And I guess the government knew what it was doing when it built

Bartorstown."

They were afraid too, whispered the cool wind. *They had a power too big for them to handle, and they were afraid, and well they should have been.*

"It did," said Hostetter, not hearing the wind.

"Jesus," said Esau, "just think if they had found that thing to stop the bomb."

"I've thought," said Hostetter. "We all have. I suppose every man in Bartorstown has a guilt complex a mile wide from thinking about it. But there just wasn't time."

Time? Or was there another reason?

"How long will it take?" asked Len. "It seems like in almost a hundred years they should have found it."

"My God," said Hostetter, "do you know how long it took to find atomic power in the first place? A Greek named Democritus got the basic idea of the atom centuries before Christ, so you can figure that out."

"But it ain't going to take them that long now!" cried Esau. "Sherman said with that machine—"

"It won't take them that long, no."

"But how long? Another hundred years?"

"How do I know how long?" said Hostetter angrily. "Another hundred years, or another year. How do I know?"

"But with the machine—"

"It's only a machine, it's not God. It can't pull an answer out of thin air just because we want it."

"How about that machine, though," said Esau, and once more his eyes were glistening. "I wanted to see it work. Does it really—" He hesitated, and then said the incredible word. "Does it really *think*?"

"No," said Hostetter. "Not in the way you mean the word. Get Erdmann to explain it to you sometime." Suddenly he said to Len, "You're thinking that only God has any business building brains."

Len flushed, feeling like what Sherman had called him, a conscience-ridden farm boy in the face of these men who knew so much, and yet he could not deny to Hostetter that he had been thinking something like that.

"I guess I'll get used to it."

Esau snorted. "He always was a doubtful-minded kind, taking forever to make up his mind."

"Why, God damn you, Esau," cried Len furiously, "if it hadn't been for me you'd still be shoveling dung in your father's barn!"

"All right," said Esau, glaring at him, "you remember that. You remember whose fault it is you're here and don't go whining around about it."

"I ain't whining."

"Yes, you are. And if you're worried about sinning, you ought to have minded your pa in the first place and stayed home in Piper's Run."

"He's got you there," said Hostetter.

Len grumbled, kicking pebbles angrily in the dust. "All right. It scared me. But it scared him, too, and I wasn't the one that tucked my tail and ran."

Esau said, "I'd run from a bear, too, till I knew it wouldn't kill me. I ain't running now. Listen, Len, this is important. Where else in the world could you find anything as important?" His chest puffed out and his face lit up as though the mantle of that importance had already fallen on him. "I want to know more about that machine."

"Important," said Len. "Yes, it is." That's true. There isn't any question about that. Oh God, you make the ones like Brother James who never question, and you make the ones like Esau who never believe, and why do you have to make the in-between ones like me?

But Esau is right. It's too late now to worry about the sinning. Pa always said the way of the transgressor was hard, and I guess this is part of the hardness.

So be it.

They left Esau at Sherman's to pick up his bride, and Len and Hostetter walked on together toward Wepplo's. The swift clear dusk was coming down, and the lanes were deserted, with a smell of smoke and cooking in them. When they came to Wepplo's Hostetter put his foot on the bottom step and turned around and spoke to Len in a strange quiet tone that he had never heard him use before.

"Here's something to remember, the way you remember that mob that killed Soames, and Burdette and his farmers, and the New Ishmaelites. It's this—we're fanatics too, Len. We have to be, or we'd drift away and live our own lives and let the whole business go hang. We've got a belief. Don't tangle with it. Because if you do, even I won't be able to save you."

He went up the steps and left Len standing there staring after him. There were voices inside, and lights, but out here it was still and almost dark. And then someone came around the corner of the house, walking softly. It was the girl Joan, and she nodded her head toward the house and said, "Was he trying to frighten you?"

"I don't think so," said Len. "I think he was just telling me the truth."

"I heard him." She had a white cloth in her hands, as though she might have been shaking it just before. Her face looked white, too, in the heavy dusk, blurred and indistinct. But her voice was sharp as a knife. "Fanatics, are we? Well, maybe he is, and maybe the others are, but I'm not. I'm sick of the whole business. What made you want to come here, Len Colter? Were you crazy or something?"

He looked at her, the shadowy outlines of her, not knowing what to say.

"I heard you talk this morning," she said.

Len said uncomfortably, "We didn't know—"

"They told you to say all those things, didn't they?"

"What things?"

"About what dreadful people they are out there, and what a hateful world it is."

"I don't know exactly what you mean," said Len, "but every word of what we said was true. You think it wasn't, you go out there and try it."

He started to push past her up the steps. She put a hand on his arm to stop him.

"I'm sorry. I guess it was all true. But that's why Sherman had you talk over the radio, so we'd all hear it. Propaganda." She added shrewdly, "I'll bet that's why they let you two in here, just to make us all see how lucky we are."

Len said, very quietly, "Aren't you?"

"Oh yes," said Joan, "we're very lucky. We have so much more than the people outside. Not in our everyday lives, of course. We don't even have as much, of things like food and freedom. But we have Clementine, and that makes up. Did you enjoy your trip to The Hole?"

"The Hole?"

"It's a name some of us have for Bartorstown."

Her manner and her tone were making him uneasy. He said, "I think I better go in," and started once more up the steps.

"I hope you did," she said. "I hope you like the canyon, and Fall Creek. Because they'll never let you leave."

He thought of what Sherman had said. He did not blame Sherman. He did not have any intention of going away. But he did not like it. "They'll learn to trust me," he said, "someday."

"Never."

He did not want to argue with her. "Well, I reckon to stay awhile, anyway. I've spent half my life getting here."

"Why?"

"You're a Bartorstown girl. You shouldn't have to ask."

"Because you wanted to learn. That's right, you said that this morning. You wanted to learn, and nobody would let you." She made a wide mocking gesture that took in the whole dark canyon. "Go. Learn. Be happy."

He got her by the shoulder and pulled her close, where he could see her face in the dim glow from the windows. "What's the matter with you?"

"I just think you're crazy, that's all. To have the whole wide world, and throw it all away for this."

"I'll be damned," said Len. He let her go and sat down on the steps and shook his head. "I'll be damned. Doesn't anybody like Bartorstown? Seems to me I've heard more griping since I got here than I ever heard in my lifetime before."

"When you've lived a lifetime here," she said bitterly, "you'll understand. Oh, some of the men get out, sure. But most of us don't. Most of us never see anything but these canyon walls. And even the men have to come back again. It's like your friend says. You have to be a fanatic to feel that it's all worth while."

"I've lived out there," said Len. "I think what it is now, and what it could be, if—"

"If Clementine ever gives them the right answer. Sure. It's been almost a century now, and they're no nearer than they ever were, but we've all got to be patient and devoted and dedicated—dedicated to what? To that goddamned mechanical brain that squats there under the mountain and has to be treated like it was God."

She leaned over him suddenly, in the faint glow of the lamplight.

"*I'm* no fanatic, Len Colter. If you want somebody to talk to, remember that."

Then she was gone around the corner of the house, running. Len heard a door open somewhere at the back. He got up, very slowly, and climbed the steps and went slowly into the house and ate his dinner at the Wepplos' table. And he did not hear hardly anything that was said to him.

TWENTY-FOUR

The next morning Len and Esau were called again to Sherman's place, and this time Hostetter was not with them. Sherman faced them over the table in the living room, balancing two keys back and forth between his hands.

"I said I wouldn't push you, and I won't. But in the meantime you have to work. Now if I let you work at something you could do in Fall Creek, like blacksmithing or taking care of the mules, you wouldn't learn anything more about Bartorstown than if you hadn't left home."

"Well, no," said Esau, and then he asked eagerly, "Can I learn about the big machine? Clementine?"

"Offhand, I'd say she's always going to be beyond you, unless you want to wait until you're an old man. But you can take it up with Frank Erdmann, he's the boss on that. And don't worry, you'll get all the machine you want. But whatever you pick will mean a lot of studying before you're ready, and until then—"

He hesitated for only the fraction of a second, perhaps he didn't really hesitate at all, and perhaps it was only by pure and unmeaning chance that his eyes happened to rest then on Len's face, but Len knew what he was going to say before he said it and he set himself hard so that nothing would show.

"Until then you've been assigned to the steam plant. You've had some experience with steam, and it shouldn't take you too long to master the differences. Jim Sidney, the man you were talking to yesterday, will give you all the help you need."

He got up and came around the table and handed them the keys. "To the safety gate. Take care of them. Jim will tell you your hours and all that. In free time you can go anywhere you want to in Bartorstown and ask any questions you want so long as you don't interfere with work in progress. You can make arrangements with Irv Rothstein in the library. And you don't need to look so stonyfaced, both of you. I can read your minds."

Len looked at him, startled, and he smiled.

"You're thinking that the steam plant is right next to the reactor and you would rather be anywhere else than there. And that is exactly why you're going to work on the steam plant. I want to get you so accustomed to the reactor that you'll forget to be afraid of it."

Is that the truth? thought Len. Or is it his way of testing us, to see if we can get over being afraid, to see if we can ever learn to live with it?

"Get along now," Sherman said. "Jim's expecting you."

So they went, walking in the early morning up the dusty road and across the slope between the rocks to Bartorstown. And at the safety gate they stopped and fidgeted, each one waiting for the other one to open it, and Len said, "I thought you weren't afraid."

"I ain't. It's just that—oh, hell, those other men work around it. It's all right. Come on."

He jabbed his key savagely in the lock and wrenched it open and went in. And Len closed it carefully, thinking, Now I am locked in with it, the fire that fell from the sky on Gran's world.

He walked after Esau down the tunnel and through that inner door, past the monitor room where young Jones nodded at them. And isn't he afraid? No, he's like Ed Hostetter, he's never been taught to be afraid. And he's alive, and healthy. God hasn't struck him down. God hasn't struck any of them down. He's let Bartorstown survive. Isn't that a proof right there that it's all right, that this answer they're trying to find is right?

But the ways of the Lord are past our understanding, and the wicked man is given his day upon the earth—

"What are you mooning about?" snapped Esau. "Come on."

There was a line of sweat across his upper lip, and his mouth was nervous. They went down the stairs again, the steel treads ringing hollow under their feet, past the level where the big computer was, down and down to the lowest step and then off that and out into the great wide cavern with the throb of power beating through it, past the generators and the turbines, and there it was, the concrete wall, the blank and staring face. And the sins of our fathers are still with us, or if not their sins their follies, and they should never, never have—

But they did.

Jim Sidney spoke to them. He spoke twice before they heard him, but this was their first time there and he was patient. And Len followed him toward the looming mass of the steam plant, feeling dwarfed and small and insignificant among all the tremendous power. He set his teeth and shouted silently inside himself, It's only because I'm afraid that I feel this way, and I'll get over it like Sherman said. The others aren't afraid. They're men, just like any other men, good men, men who believe they're doing right, doing what the government trusted them to do. I'll learn. Gran would want me to. She said Never be afraid of knowing, and I won't be.

I won't be. I'll be a part of it, helping to free the world of fear. I'll believe, because I am here now and there is nothing else I can do.

No. Not that way. I will believe because it is right. I will learn to see that it is right. And Ed Hostetter will help me, because I can trust him, and *he* says it's right.

And Len went to work beside Esau on the steam plant, and all the rest of that day he did not look at the wall of the reactor. But he could feel it. He could feel it in his flesh and his bones and the tingling of his blood, and he could still feel it when he was back in Fall Creek and in his own bed. And he dreamed about it when he fell asleep.

But there was no escape from it. He went back to it the next day, and the day after that, and regularly on the days that followed, except Sunday, when he went to church and walked in the afternoons with Joan Wepplo. It reassured him to go to church. It was comforting to hear from a pulpit that God was blessing their efforts, and all they had to do was remain patient and steadfast and not lose heart. It helped him to feel that they really were right. And Sherman's treatment did seem to be working. Every day the shock of being close beside that dreadful wall grew less, perhaps because a nerve continually pricked and rubbed will become too callused to react. He got so he could look at it calmly, and think calmly, too, about what was behind it. He could learn a little about the instruments set into its face that measured the flow of force inside, and he could learn a little more, of layman's knowledge, about what that force was and how it worked, and how in this form it was so easily controlled. He would get along like that sometimes for several days, laughing and talking with Esau about how the folks in Piper's Run would feel if they could see them now—Mr. Nordholt, the schoolmaster, who thought he knew so much and dealt his knowledge out so sparingly lest it should corrupt the young, and the other elders of the town, who would take off your hide with a birch rod for asking questions, and, yes, Pa and Uncle David, whose one answer was the harness strap. No, that wasn't true of Pa, and Len knew all too well what Pa would say, and he didn't like to think about that. So he would turn his thoughts to Judge Taylor, who got a man killed and a town burned up because he was afraid that it might sometime become a city, and he would think vindictively that he would like to tell Judge Taylor what was under the rock of Bartorstown and watch his face then. And I am not afraid, he would think. I was afraid, but now I am not. It is only a natural force like any other force. There is nothing evil in it, any more than there is evil in a knife, or in gunpowder. There is only evil in the way it is used, and we will see to it that no evil will ever be done with it again. We. We men of Bartorstown. And, oh Lord, the nights of cold and shivering along the misty creek beds, the days of heat and mosquitoes and hunger, the winters in strange towns, all the days and nights and years when we dreamed of being men of Bartorstown!

But the dream was different then. It was all bright and wonderful, like Gran used to tell about, and there was no darkness in it.

He would get along that way, and he would think, Now I really have got over it. And then he would wake up screaming in the night with Hostetter shaking his shoulder.

"What were you dreaming about?" Hostetter would ask.

"I don't know. A nightmare, that's all." He would get up and get a drink of water, and let the sweat on him dry. Then he would ask, casually, "Did I say anything?"

"No, not that I heard. You were just yelling."

But he would catch Hostetter looking at him with a brooding eye, and wonder if he did not know perfectly well what the nightmare was.

Esau's fear ran shallower than Len's. It was practically all physical, and once he was convinced that no unseen force was going to burn his bones to powder he got very casual and proprietory with the reactor, almost as though he had made it himself. Len would ask him sometimes, "Doesn't it ever worry you—I mean, don't you ever think that if this reactor thing hadn't been kept going here there wouldn't be any need to find an answer—"

"You heard what Sherman said. There could be other ones. Maybe enemy ones. Then where would you be?"

"But if it was the last one in the world?"

"Well, it ain't hurting anything. And anyway, Sherman said even if it was it wouldn't matter, somebody'd figure atoms out again."

Maybe not, maybe never. Maybe he's only saying that to justify himself. Hostetter had a word for it. Rationalizing. Anyway, it wouldn't be for a long time. A hundred years, two hundred, maybe longer. I'd never live to see it.

Esau laughed. "That woman of mine, she's sure a dandy."

Len didn't go around Amity much. There was a certain chill between them, a sort of mutual embarrassment that did not make for pleasant conversations. So he asked, "How's that?"

"Well, when she heard about this atom power being here she had a terrible fit. Swore she was going to lose the baby, it was so bad. And now do you know what? She's got it all fixed up in her mind that it's a big lie just to make her think everybody here is awfully important, and she can prove it."

"How?"

"Because everybody knows what atom power does, and if there'd ever been any here there wouldn't be any canyon left, but only a big crater like the judge used to tell about."

"Oh," said Len.

"Well, it makes her happy. So I don't argue. What's the use? She don't know anything about anything like that, anyway." He rubbed his hands together, grinning. "I sure hope that kid of mine's a boy. Maybe I can't learn enough to work that big machine, but he could. Hell, he might even be the one to find the answer."

Esau was fascinated by the big machine called Clementine. He hung around it every minute he could in his off hours, asking questions of Erdmann and the technicians who were working there until Erdmann began to talk up a tremendous enthusiasm for radio every time he even met Esau in the street. Often Len would go with him. He would stand looking at the dark face of the thing until a feeling of nervousness crept over him, as though he stood by the bed of a sleeper who was not really asleep but was watching him from under closed, deceitful lids. And he would think, It is not really a brain, it does not really think, it is only called a brain, and the things it knows and the mathematics it can do are only imitations of thought. But through the night hours a creature haunted him, a creature with a great throbbing heart of hell-fire and a brain as big as Pa's barn.

On the whole though, he was trying hard and adjusting pretty well. But there were other hours, waking hours, in which another creature haunted him and left him little peace. And this was a human creature and no nightmare. This was a girl named Joan.

TWENTY-FIVE

Three different groups of strangers came into Fall Creek before snow, stayed briefly to trade, and went away again. Two of them were little bands of dark hardy men who followed the wild herds, hunters, and horse tamers, offering half-broken colts in exchange for flour, sugar, and corn whiskey. The third and last were New Ishmaelites. There were about twenty-five of them, demanding powder and shot as a gift to the Lord's anointed. They would not stay the night in Fall Creek, nor come in past the edges of the town, as though they were afraid of contamination, but when Sherman sent them out what they wanted they began to sing and pray, waving their arms and crying hallelujah. Half the people in Fall Creek had come out to watch them, and Len was there too, with Joan Wepplo.

"One of 'em will preach pretty soon," she said. "That's what everybody's waiting for."

"I've seen enough preaching," muttered Len. But he stayed. The wind was icy, blowing down the canyon from snow fields on the high peaks. Everybody was wearing cowhide or horsehide coats against it, but the

New Ishmaelites had nothing but their shrouds and their goatskins to flap about their naked legs. They did not seem to mind it.

"They suffer terribly in the winters, just the same," said Joan. "Starve to death, and freeze. Our men find their bodies in the spring, sometimes a whole band of them, kids and all." She looked at them with cold contemptuous eyes. "You'd think they'd give the kids a chance, at least. Let them grow up enough to make up their own minds about freezing to death."

The children, bony and blue with the chill, stamped and shouted and tossed their tangled mops of hair. They would never be able to make up their own minds about anything, even if they did grow up. Habit would have got too big a start on them. Len said, "I guess they can't afford to, any more than your people or mine."

A man stepped out of the group and began to preach. His hair and beard were a dirty gray, but Len thought that he was not as old as he looked. New Ishmaelites did not seem to get very old. He wore a goatskin, greasy and foul, with the hair worn off it in big patches. The bones of his chest stood out like a bird cage. He shook his fists at the people of Fall Creek and cried:

"Repent, repent, for the Kingdom of God is at hand! You who live for the flesh and the sins of the flesh, your end is near. The Lord has spoken in flame and thunder, the earth has opened and swallowed the unrighteous, and some have said, This is all, He has punished us and now we are forgiven, now we can forget. But I tell you that God in His mercy only gave you a little more time, and that time is nearly gone, and you have not repented! And what will you say when the heavens open, and God comes to judge the world? How will you beg and plead and cry out for mercy, and what will your luxuries and your vanities buy you then? Nothing but hell-fire! Fire and brimstone and everlasting pain, unless you repent and do penance for your sins!"

The wind made his words thin and blew them far away, repent, repent, like a fading echo down the canyon, as though repentance was already a lost hope. And Len thought, What if he knew, what if I was to go and shout it at him, what's up the canyon there not half a mile away? Then what good would it all be to him, his dirty goatskin and the murders he's done in the name of faith?

Get out. Get out, crazy old man, and stop your shouting.

He did, at last, seeming to feel that he had made sufficient payment for the gift. He rejoined the group and they all moved off up the winding road, to the pass. The wind had got stronger, whistling cruelly past the rocks, and they bent a little under it and the steepness of the climb, their long hair blown out in front of them and their ragged garments lashing around their legs. Len shivered involuntarily.

"I used to feel sorry for them, too," Joan said, "until I realized that they'd kill us all in a minute if they could." She looked down at herself, at her coat of calfskin with the brown and white outside and her woolen skirt and her booted legs. "Vanity," she said. "Luxury." And she laughed, very short and hard. "The dirty old fool. He doesn't know the meaning of the words."

She lifted her eyes to Len. They were bright with some secret thought.

"I could show you, Len. What those words mean."

Her eyes disturbed him. They always did. They were so keen and sharp and she always seemed to be thinking so fast behind them, thoughts he could not follow. He knew now she was challenging him in some way, so he said, "All right, then, show me."

"You'll have to come to my house."

"I'm coming there for dinner anyhow. Remember?"

"I mean right now."

He shrugged. "Okay."

They walked back through the lanes of Fall Creek. When they reached the house he followed her inside. It was quiet, except for a couple of flies buzzing on a sunny windowpane, and it felt warm after the wind. Joan took off her coat.

"I guess my folks are still out," she said. "I guess they won't be back for a while. Do you mind?"

"No," said Len. "I don't mind." He took off his own coat and sat down.

Joan wandered over to the window, slapping vaguely at the flies. She had walked fast all the way, but now she did not seem in any hurry.

"Do you still like working in the Hole?"

"Sure," said Len warily. "It's fine."

Silence.

"Have they found the answer yet?"

"No, but as soon as Erdmann—Now why ask a question like that? You know they haven't."

"Has anybody told you how soon they will?"

"You know better than that, too."

Silence again, and one of the flies lay dead on the floor.

"Almost a hundred years," she said softly, looking out the window. "It seems such an awful long time. I just don't know if we can stand it for another hundred."

She turned around. "I don't know if I can stand it for another one."

Len got up, not looking straight at her. "Maybe I better go."

"Why?"

"Well, your folks aren't here, and—"

"They'll be back in time for dinner."

"But it's a long time till dinner."

"Well," she said, "don't you want to see what you came for?" She showed him the edges of her teeth, white and laughing. "You wait."

She ran into the next room and shut the door. Len sat down again. He kept twisting his hands together, and his temples felt hot. He knew the feeling. He had had it before, in the rose arbor, in the judge's dark garden with Amity. He could hear Joan rummaging around in the room. There was a sound like the lid of a trunk banging against the wall. A long time went by. He wondered what the devil she was doing and listened nervously for footsteps on the porch, knowing all the time that her folks would not be back because if they were going to come she would not be doing this, whatever it was.

The door opened and she came out.

She was wearing a red dress. It was faded a little, and there were streaks and creases in it from having been folded away for a long time, but those were unimportant things. It was red. It was made of some soft, shiny, slithery stuff that rustled when she moved, and it came clear down to the floor, hiding her feet, but that was about all it hid. It fitted tight around her waist and hips and outlined her thighs when she walked forward, and above the waist there wasn't very much at all. She held out her arms at the sides and turned around slowly. Her back and shoulders were bare, white and gleaming in the sunlight that fell through the window, and her breasts were sharply outlined in the red cloth, showing above it in two half-moon curves, and her black hair fell down, dark and glossy over her white skin.

"It belonged to my great-grandmother. Do you like it?"

Len said, "Christ." He stared and stared, and his face was almost as red as the dress. "It's the most indecent thing I ever saw."

"I know," she said, "but isn't it beautiful?" She ran her hands slowly down her front and out across the skirt, savoring the rustle, the softness. "This was real vanity, real luxury. Listen, how it whispers. What do you think that dirty old fool would say if he could see it?"

She was quite close to him now. He could see the fine white texture of her shoulders and the way her breasts rose and fell when she breathed, with the bright red cloth pressing them tight. She was smiling. He realized suddenly that she was handsome, not pretty like Amity had been, but dark-eyed handsome even if she wasn't very tall. He looked into her eyes and suddenly he realized that she was there, not just a girl, not just a Joan Wepplo, but *herself*, and something happened to him inside like when the electric lights came on in the dark tunnel that led to Bartorstown. And this feeling he had never had for Amity.

He reached out and took hold of her and she held up her mouth to him and laughed, a deep throaty little laugh, excited and pleased. A wave of heat swept over Len. The red cloth was silky, soft and rustling under his fingers, stretched right over the warmth of her body. He put his mouth down over hers and kissed her, and kissed her again, and all by themselves his hands came up onto her bare shoulders and dug hard into the white skin. And this too was not like it had ever been with Amity.

She pulled away from him. She was not laughing now, and her eyes were as hard and bright as two black stars burning at him.

"Someday," she said fiercely, "you'll want a way out of this place, and then you come to me, Len Colter. Then you come, but not before."

She ran away into the other room again and slammed the door and shot the bolt in its socket, and it was no use trying to get in after her. And when she came out again in her regular clothes, a long time later, her folks were coming up the path and it was as if nothing had been said or done.

But it was Joan, in another place, at another time, who told him about Solution Zero.

TWENTY-SIX

Winter came. Fall Creek became an isolated pocket of light and life in a vast emptiness of cold and rock and wind and blizzard snows. The pass was blocked. Nothing would move in or out of the canyon before spring. The snow piled high around the houses and drifted in the lanes, and the mountains were all white, magnificent on a clear day with the sun on them, ghostly in the dusk like the mountains of a dream, but too large and still to have in them any friendliness for man. And the air they breathed down across their icy slopes was bitter as the chill of death.

In Bartorstown there was neither winter nor summer, night nor day. The lights burned and the air went hushing through the rock rooms, never altering, never changing. The Power entrapped behind the concrete wall gave of its strength silently, untiring, the deathless heart beating and throbbing in the rock. Above in its chamber the brain slept, Clementine, the foolish name for the hope of the world, while men soothed and healed the frayed wires and the worn-out transistors of her being. And above that, in the monitor room, the eyes watched and the ears listened, on guard against the world. Len worked at his job, and sweated and struggled over the books he was advised to read, and thought how much he was learning and how few other people in the ignorant, fearful, guilt-ridden, sin-stricken world outside would have been able to do what he and Esau had done, and what they would do to make tomorrow different from the terrible yesterday. He wondered why the evil dreams still caught him unawares in the jungles of sleep, and he envied Esau his untroubled nights, but he did not say so. He hardly ever thought any more of the Bartorstown he had spent half his life to find, accepting the reality, and a little more of his youth slipped away from him. He thought about Joan, and tried to stay away from her, and couldn't. He was afraid of her, but he was even more afraid to admit that he was afraid of her, because then in some obscure way she would have beaten him, she would have proved that he did want to leave Fall Creek and run away from Bartorstown. She was a challenge that he didn't dare ignore. She was also a girl, and he was crazy about her.

Other people had work to do, too. Hostetter spent long hours with Sherman, doing what it seemed he had come home to do—giving the advice gained from his years of experience on how to make the system of outside trade work smoother and better. He was a different-looking Hostetter these days, with his beard trimmed short and his hair cropped, and the New Mennonite dress laid aside. Len had done this a long time ago, so he could not say why it seemed wrong, but it did. Perhaps it was only because he had grown up with one image of Hostetter firmly fixed in his mind, and it was hard to change it. They did not see very much of each other any more. They still shared the same room, but they each had their own work, and Hostetter had his own friends, and Len's spare time was pretty much taken up with Joan. After a while he got the feeling that the Wepplos figured they would probably get married any day. It made him feel guilty every time he went there, remembering what Joan had said, but not guilty enough to keep him away.

"Just girl talk," he would say to himself, "like Amity teasing me along when it was really Esau she wanted. They don't know what they're after. She's got an idea about outside just like I had about here, but she wouldn't like it."

And he told her over and over how she wouldn't like it, describing this and that about the great, quiet, sleeping country and the people and the life that was lived there. Over and over, trying to make her understand, until he got so homesick he would have to stop, and she would turn away to hide the satisfaction in her eyes.

Besides, that was crazy talk about a way out of the canyon. There wasn't any way. The cliffs were too steep to climb, the narrow gorge of the stream bed was too broken and treacherous with falls and rockslides, and beyond them was only more of the same. The site had been carefully picked, and it had not changed in a century. The eyes of Bartorstown watched, the ears listened, and the hidden death was always ready in that winding lower pass. There was a personal matter, too. Len knew, without having to be told, without having to see any overt signs of it, that every move he made was noted carefully by somebody and reported on to Sherman. The problem of finding Bartorstown would be easy compared with that of getting away from it again. And yet she sounded so sure, as if she had a way all planned. It kept nagging at him, wondering what it could be—just for curiosity. But he didn't ask her, and she didn't tell him, nor even hint at it again.

For everybody it was a dull and ingrown time, a time for peering too closely at your neighbors and getting too concerned with what they did, and talking about it too much. Before Christmas the whispers had started about Gutierrez. Poor Julio, he sure took that last disappointment hard. Well, his life's work—you know. Oh sure, but everybody gets disappointed, and they don't take to drink like that, couldn't he pull himself together and try again? I suppose a man gets tired, loses heart. After all, a lifetime—Did you hear they found him passed out in a drift by Sawyer's back fence, and it's a wonder he didn't freeze to death? His poor wife, it's her I feel sorry for, not him. A man his age ought to know this life isn't all cakes and roses for anybody. I hear he's hounding poor Frank Erdmann nearly out of his mind. I hear—

I hear. Everybody heard, and nearly everybody talked. They talked about other people and other things, of course, but Gutierrez was the winter's sensation and sooner or later any conversation got around to him. Len saw him a few times. Some of those times he was obviously drunk, an aging man staggering with stiff dignity down a snowy lane, his face dark with an inner darkness above the neat white beard. At other times he seemed to be less drunken than dreaming, as though his mind had wandered off along some shadowy byway in search of a lost hope. Len saw him only once to speak to, and then it was only Len who spoke. Gutierrez nodded and passed on, his eyes perfectly blank of recognition. At night there was nearly always a lamp burning in a certain room in Gutierrez' house, and Gutierrez sat beside it at a table covered with papers, and he would work at them and drink from a handy jug, work and drink, until he fell asleep and his wife came and helped him to the bed. People who happened to be passing by at night could see this through the window, and Len knew that it was true because he, too, had seen it; Gutierrez working at a vast tangle of papers, very patient, very intent, with the big jug at his elbow.

Christmas came, and after church there was a big dinner at the Wepplos'. The weather was clear and fine. At one in the afternoon the temperature topped zero, and everybody said how warm it was. There were parties all over Fall Creek, with people trudging back and forth in the dry crunching snow between the houses, and at night all the lamps were lit, shining yellow and merry out of the windows. Joan got very passionate with the excitement, and when they were on the way to somebody else's place she led him into the darkness behind a clump of trees, and they forgot the cold for a few minutes, standing with their arms around each other and their mingled breaths steaming in a frosty halo around their heads.

"Love me?"

He kissed her so hard it hurt, his hand bunched in her hair at the back of her neck, under her wool cap.

"What does that feel like?"

"Len. Oh, Len, if you love me, if you really love me—"

Suddenly she was tight against him, talking fast and wild.

"Take me out of here. I'll lose my mind if I have to stay here cooped up any longer. If I wasn't a girl I'd have gone alone, long ago, but I need you to take me. Len, I'd worship you all the rest of my life."

He withdrew from her, slowly, carefully, as a man draws from the edge of a quicksand.

"No."

"Why, Len? Why should you spend your whole life in this hole for something you never heard of before? Bartorstown isn't anything to you but a dream you had once when you were a kid."

"No," he said again. "I told you before. Leave me alone."

He started away, but she scuffled through the snow and stood in front of him.

"They filled you up on all that stuff about the future of the world, didn't they? I've heard it since I was born. The burden, the sacred debt." He could see her face in the frosty pale snow glimmer, all twisted up with anger she had saved and hidden for a long time and now was turning loose. "I didn't make the bomb and I didn't drop it, and I won't be here a hundred years from now to see if they do it again or not. So why have I got any debt? And why have you got any, Len Colter? You answer me that."

Words came stumbling to his tongue, but she looked so fiercely at him

177

that he never said them.

"You haven't," she said. "You're just scared. Scared to face reality and admit you've wasted all those years for nothing."

Reality, he thought. I've been facing it every day, reality you've never seen. Reality behind a concrete wall.

"Let me alone," he said. "I ain't going. I can't. So shut up about it."

She laughed at him. "They told you a lot of stuff up there in Bartorstown, but I bet there's one thing they never mentioned. I bet they never told you about Solution Zero."

There was such a note of triumph in her voice that Len knew he should not listen any more. But she jeered at him. "You wanted to learn, didn't you? And didn't they tell you up there always to look for the whole truth and never be satisfied with only part of it? You want the whole truth, don't you? Or are you afraid of that, too?"

"All right," he said. "What is Solution Zero?"

She told him, with swift, vindictive relish. "You know how they work, building theories and turning them into equations, and feeding the equations to Clementine to solve. If they work out, that's another step forward. If they don't, like the last time, that's a blind alley, a negative. But all the time they're piling these equations into Clementine, adding up these steps toward what they call the master solution. Well, suppose that one comes out negative? Suppose the final equations just don't work, and all they get is the mathematical proof that what they're looking for doesn't exist? That's Solution Zero."

"God," said Len, "is that possible? I thought—" He stared at her in the snowy night, feeling sick and miserable, feeling an utter fool, betrayed.

"You thought it was certain, and the only question was when. Well, you ask old Sherman if you don't believe me. Everybody knows about Solution Zero, but you don't hear them talk about it, any more than they talk about how they're going to die someday. You ask. And then you figure how much of your life that's worth!"

She left him. She had a genius for knowing when to leave him. He did not go on to the party. He went home and sat alone, brooding, until Hostetter came in, and by that time he was in such a mean, low mood that he didn't give him a chance to shut the door before he demanded, "What's this about Solution Zero?"

There was a cloud on Hostetter's brow, too. "Probably just what you heard," he said, taking off his coat and hat.

"Everybody's kept mighty quiet about it."

"I advise you to, too. It's a superstition we've got here."

He sat down and began to unlace his boots. Snow was melting from them in little puddles on the puncheon floor. Len said, "I don't wonder."

Hostetter methodically unlaced his boots.

"I thought they knew," Len said. "I thought they were sure of it."

"Research isn't done that way."

"But how can they spend all that time, and maybe that much more again, if they know it might be all for nothing?"

"Because how would they know if they didn't try? And because there isn't any other way to do it." Hostetter flung his boots in the corner by the potbellied stove. Usually he set them there, neatly, and not too close to the heat.

"But that's a crazy way," said Len.

"Is it? When your pa put seed in the ground, did he have a guarantee it was going to come up and yield him a harvest? Did he know every calf and shoat and lamb was going to stay healthy and pay back all the feed and care?"

He began to pull off his shirt and pants. Len sat scowling.

"All right, that's true. But if his crop failed or his cattle died there was always another season. What about this? What if it does come out—nothing?"

"Then they try again. If no such force-field is possible, then they think of other ways. And maybe some part of the work they did will give them a clue, so it isn't all lost." He slapped his clothes over the hide-seated chair and climbed into his bunk. "Hell, how do you think the human race ever learned anything, except by trial and error?"

"But it all takes such a long, long time," said Len.

"Everything takes a long time. Birthing takes nine months, and dying takes you all the rest of your life, and what are you complaining about, anyway? You just got here. Wait till you're as old as the rest of us. Then you might have some reason."

He turned his back and covered his head with the blanket. After a while Len blew out the lamp.

The next day it was all over Fall Creek that Julio Gutierrez had got drunk at Sherman's and knocked Frank Erdmann down, and Ed Hostetter had stepped in and practically carried Gutierrez home. A brawl between the senior physicist and the chief electronics engineer was scandal enough to keep the tongues all wagging, but it seemed to Len that there was a darker, sadder note in the gossip, a shadow of discouragement. Or maybe that was only because he had dreamed all night of rust in the wheat and new lambs dying.

TWENTY-SEVEN

Esau came banging at the door before it was light. It was the third morning in January, a Monday, and the snow was coming down in a solid desperate rush as though God had suddenly commanded it to bury the world before lunch. "Ain't you ready?" he asked Len. "Well, hurry up, this snow's going to slow us down enough as it is."

Hostetter stuck his head out of the bunk. "What's all the rush?"

"Clementine," said Esau. "The big machine. They're going to test her this morning, and Erdmann said we could watch before work. Hurry up, can't you?"

"Let me get my boots on," Len grumbled. "She won't run away."

Hostetter said to Esau, "Do you figure you can work with Clementine someday?"

"No," said Esau, shaking his head. "Too much math and stuff. I'm going to learn radio instead. After all, that's what got me here. But I sure do want to see that big brain do its thinking. Are you ready now? You sure? All right, let's go!"

The world was white, and blind. The snow fell straight down, with hardly a vagrant breath of air to set it swirling. They groped their way through the village, still able to follow the deep-trodden lanes, and conscious of the houses even if they could not really see them. Out on the road it was different. It was like being in the fields at home when it snowed like this, with no landmark, no direction, and the same old dizzy feeling came over Len. Everything was gone but up and down, and presently even that would go, and there was not even any sound left in the world.

"You're going off the road," said Esau, and he floundered back from the drifted ditch. Then it was Esau's turn. They walked close together, making the usual comments on the cursedness of fate and the weather, and Len said suddenly, "You're happy here, aren't you?"

"Sure," said Esau. "I wouldn't go back to Piper's Run if you gave me the place."

He meant it. Then he asked, "Aren't you?"

"Sure," said Len. "Sure."

They plowed on, the chill feathery flakes patting their faces, trying to fill up their noses and mouths and smother them quietly, whitely, because they disturbed the even blankness of the road.

"What do you think?" asked Len. "Will they ever find the answer? Or will it come out zero?"

"Hell," said Esau, "I don't care. I got enough of my own to do."

"Don't you care about anything?" Len growled.

"Sure I do. I care about doing what I want to do, and not having a lot of damn fool old men telling me I can't. That's what I care about. That's why I like it here."

"Yes," said Len. "Sure." And that's true, you can do what you want and say what you want and think what you want—except one thing. You can't say you don't believe in what they believe in, and that way it isn't much different from Piper's Run.

They stumbled and blundered up the slope, between the artfully tumbled boulders. About halfway up to the gate Esau started and swore, and Len shied too as he sensed a dark dim shape moving, in all that whiteness, furtively among the rocks.

The shape spoke to them, and it was Gutierrez. The snow was piled up thick across the top of his shoulders and on his cap, as though he had been standing still in it for some time, waiting. But he was sober, and his face was perfectly composed, and pleasant.

"I'm sorry if I startled you," he said. "I seem to have mislaid my own key to the gate. Do you mind if I go in with you?"

The question was purely rhetorical. The three of them walked on together up the slope. Len kept glancing uneasily at Gutierrez, thinking of the long night hours spent with the papers and the jug. He felt sorry for him. He was also afraid of him. He wanted desperately to question him about Solution Zero, and why they couldn't be sure a thing existed before they spent a couple of hundred years in hunting for it. He wanted to so much that he was certain Esau would blurt the question out, and then Gutierrez would knock them both down. But nobody said anything. Esau, too, must have been awed into wisdom.

Beyond the safety gate there was a drift of snow, and then only the darkness and the dank, freezing chill of a place shut off forever from the sun. Gutierrez went ahead. He had stumbled that first time, but now he did not stumble, walking steadily, his head held high and his back very straight. Len could hear him breathing, heavy breathing like that of a man who had been running, but Gutierrez had not been running. Where the passage bent and the light came on, far down over the inner door, he had left them far behind, and Len had a curious cold feeling that the man had forgotten them entirely.

They stood side by side again under the scanners. Gutierrez looked straight ahead at the steel door until it swung open, and then he strode away down the hall. Jones came out of the monitor room and looked after him, wondering out loud, "What's he doing here?"

Esau shook his head. "He came in with us. Said he lost his key. I suppose he's got some work to do."

Jones said, "Erdmann won't be happy. Oh well. Nobody told me to keep him out, so my conscience is clear." He grinned. "Let me know what happens, huh?"

"He was drunk the other night," said Len. "I don't reckon anything will happen."

"I hope not," said Esau. "I want to see that brain work."

They left their coats in a locker room and hurried on down to the next level, past the picture of Hiroshima, past the victims with their tragic impassive eyes. And the voices reached them from beyond the door.

"No, I am sorry, Frank. Please let me say it."

"Forget it, Julio. We all do things. Forget it."

"Thank you," said Gutierrez, with immense dignity, with great contrition.

Len hesitated outside, looking at Esau, whose face was a study in violent indecision.

"How does she go?" asked Gutierrez.

"Fine," said Erdmann. "Smooth as silk."

Their voices fell silent. Len's heart came up into his throat and stuck there, and a cold cord was knotted through his belly. Because there was now another voice audible in the room, a voice he had never heard before. A small, dry, busy whisper-and-click, the voice of Clementine.

Esau heard it, too. "I don't care," he whispered. "I'm going in."

He did, and Len followed him, walking softly. He looked at Clementine, and she was no longer sleeping. The many eyes on the panel board were bright and winking, and all through that mighty grid of wires there was a stir and a quiver, a subtle pulse of life.

The selfsame pulse, thought Len, that beats down there below. The heart and the brain.

"Oh," said Erdmann, almost with relief. "Hello."

The high-speed printer burst into a sudden chatter. Len started violently. The eyes on the panel board winked as though with laughter, and then it was all quiet, all dark again, with the exception of a steady light that burned as a signal that Clementine was awake.

Esau sucked in his breath. But he did not speak because Gutierrez beat him to it.

He had taken some papers out of his pocket. He did not seem to be aware that anyone was there but Erdmann. He held the papers in his hands and said, "My wife felt that I shouldn't come here and bother you today. She hid my key to the safety gate. But of course this was far too important to wait."

He looked down at the papers. "I've gone over this whole sequence of equations again. I found where the mistake was."

Something tightened and became wary behind Erdmann's face. "Yes?"

"It's perfectly plain, you can see for yourself. Here."

He shoved the papers into Erdmann's hand. Erdmann began to scan through them. And now there came into his face an acute discomfort, a sorrow, a dismay.

"You can see," said Gutierrez. "It's plain as day. She made a mistake, Frank. I told you. You said it wasn't possible, but she did."

"Julio, I—" And Erdmann shook his head from side to side and glanced in desperation at Len, and found no help there, and began to shuffle again through the papers in his hands.

"Don't you see it, Frank?"

"Well, Julio, you know I'm not mathematician enough—"

"Hell," said Gutierrez impatiently, "how did you get to be an electronics engineer? You know enough for that. It's all written out plain. Anybody should see it. Here." He fumbled at the papers in Erdmann's hands. "Here, and here, you see?"

Erdmann said, "What do you want me to do?"

"Why, run it through again. Correct it. Then we'll have the answer, Frank. The answer."

Erdmann moistened his lips. "But if she made a mistake once she might do it again, Julio. Why don't you get Wentz or Jacobs—"

"No. It would take them all winter, a year. She can do it right now. You've tested her. You said so. You said she was smooth as silk. That's why I wanted it to be today, while she's still fresh and unused. She can't possibly make the same mistake again. Run it through."

"I—well," said Erdmann. "Well, all right."

He went over to the input mechanism and began to transfer onto the tape. Gutierrez waited. He still had his heavy outdoor clothes on, but he did not seem to feel that he was hot or uncomfortable. He watched Erdmann, and from time to time he glanced at the computer and smiled and nodded, like a man who has caught someone else in an error and thereby vindicated himself. Len had withdrawn into the background. He did not like the look on Erdmann's face. He began to wonder if he should go, and then the lights on the panel began to glow and wink at him, and the dim voice hummed and murmured, and he was as fascinated as Esau and could not go.

He was startled when Erdmann spoke to them. "I'll be free in a bit. Then I'll answer your questions."

"Would you rather we'd come back later?" asked Len.

"No," said Erdmann, glancing at Gutierrez. "No, you stick around."

Clementine pondered, mumbling softly. Apart from that it was very still. Gutierrez was calm, standing with his hands folded in front of him, waiting. Erdmann fidgeted. There was sweat on his face and he kept wiping it off and running his hand over his mouth and looking at Gutierrez with an expression of utter agony.

"I think there were some circuits we missed on the overhaul, Julio. She hasn't been fully checked. She might still—"

"You sound like my wife," said Gutierrez. "Don't worry, it'll come out."

The output printer chattered. Erdmann started forward. Gutierrez knocked him out of the way. He snatched the paper out of the printer and looked at it. His face darkened, and then the color left it and it was gray and sick, and his hands trembled.

"What did you do?" he said to Erdmann. "What did you do to my equations?"

"Nothing, Julio."

"Look what she says. No solution, recheck your data for errors. No solution. No solution—"

"Julio. Julio, please. Listen to me. You've been working too long on this, you're tired. I put the equations just as they were, but they—"

"They what? Go on and say it, Frank. Go on."

"Julio, please," said Erdmann, with a terrible helplessness, and put out his hand to Gutierrez as one does to a child, asking him to come.

Gutierrez hit him. He hit him so suddenly and so hard that there was no way and no time to dodge the blow. Erdmann stepped back three or four paces and fell down, and Gutierrez said quietly, "You are against me, both of you. You had it arranged between you, so that no matter what I did she would never give me the right answer. I've thought of you all winter, Frank, in here talking with her, laughing, because she knows the answer and she won't tell. But I'm going to make her tell, Frank."

He had stones in his pockets. That was why he had kept his coat on, in the warmth of Bartorstown. He had a lot of stones, and he took them out and threw them one by one at Clementine, shouting with a wild joy, "I'll make you tell, you bitch, you lying bitch, deceitful bitch, I'll make you tell."

Glass on the panel board crashed and tinkled. Circuit wires twanged. One of the big glass tanks that held a part of Clementine's memory burst open. Frank Erdmann scrambled up unsteadily from the floor, yelling for Gutierrez to stop, yelling for help. And Gutierrez ran out of stones and began to beat on the panel with his fists and kick it with his boots, screaming, "Bitch, bitch, bitch, I'll make you tell, you've got my life, my mind, my work stored up in you, I'll make you tell!"

Erdmann was grappling with him. "Len. Esau, for God's sake, help me. Help me hold him."

Len went forward slowly, as a sleepwalker moves. He put his hands out and took hold of Gutierrez. Gutierrez was very strong, incredibly strong. It was hard to hold onto him, hard to drag him away from the ravaged panel, and now there were new lights winking and flashing on it, red lights saying I am wounded, help me. Len looked at them, and he looked into Gutierrez' eyes. Erdmann panted. There was blood coming out of the side of his mouth. "Julio, please. Take it easy. That's it, Len, back a little farther, now—It's all right, Julio, please be quiet."

And Julio was quiet, all at once. There was no transition. One second his wiry muscles were straining like steel bars against Len's grasp, and the next he was all gone, limp, sagging, a frail and hollow thing. He turned his face to Erdmann and he said with infinite resignation, "Somebody is against me, Frank. Somebody is against us all."

Tears ran down his cheeks. He hung like a dying man between Len and Erdmann, weeping, and Len looked at Clementine, blinking her bloody eyes for help.

Find your limit, Judge Taylor said. Find your limit before it is too late.

I have found my limit, Len thought. And it is already too late.

Men came and relieved him of his burden. He went down with Esau into the belly of the rock, and he worked all day with a face as blank as the concrete wall, and as deceitful, because behind it there was violence and terror, and astonishment of the heart.

In the afternoon the whisper came along the line of the great machines. They took him back home, did you hear, and the doctor says he's clear gone. They say he'll have to stay there locked up, with someone to watch him.

As we are all locked up here in this canyon, Len thought, serving this Moloch with the head of brass and the bowels of fire. This Moloch who has just destroyed a man.

But he knew the truth at last, and he spoke it to himself.

There will be no answer.

And Lord, deliver me from the bondage of mine enemies, for I repent. I have followed after false gods, and they have betrayed me. I have eaten of the fruit, and my soul is sickened.

The fiery heart beat on behind the wall, and overhead the brain was already being healed.

That night Len floundered through the deep new-fallen snow to Wepplo's. He said to Joan, quietly so that no one else should hear, "I want what you want. Show me the way."

Her eyes blazed. She kissed him on the lips and whispered, "Yes! But can you keep it secret, Len? It's a long time yet till spring."

"I can."

"Even from him."

"Even from Hostetter?"

Even from him. For a lamp is set to guide the footsteps of repentance.

TWENTY-EIGHT

February, March, April.

Time. A tight passivity, a waiting.

He worked. Every day he did what was expected of him, under the very shadow of that concrete wall. He did his work well. That was the ironic part of it. He could become interested now in the whole chain of great machines that harnessed and transmitted the Power, and he could admit the fascination, the sense of importance it gave a man to hold those mighty brutes in check and guidance as you held a team of horses. He could do this because now he recognized the fascination for what it was, and the fangs of the serpent were drawn. He could think what power like that would do for places like Refuge and Piper's Run, how it would bring back the bright and comfortable things of Gran's childhood, but he understood now why people were savagely determined to do without them. Because once you set your feet on the path you went on and on until you couldn't go back again, and suddenly there was a rain of fire from the sky. You had to get back to where it was safe and stay there.

Back to Piper's Run, to the woods and the fields, to the end of doubt, the end of fear. Back to the time before the preaching, before Soames, before you ever heard of Bartorstown. Back to peace. He used to pray at night that nothing should happen to Pa before he came, because part of the salvation would be in telling him that he was right.

Things happened in that time. Esau's son was born, and christened David Taylor Colter in some obscure gesture of defiance or affection to both grandfathers. Joan made careful, scheming arrangements for a separate house and planned a marriage date. And these things were important. But they were shadowed over and made small by the one great drive, the getting away.

Nothing else mattered now to him and Joan, not even marriage. They were already bonded as close as two people could be by their hunger to escape the canyon.

"I've planned this way for years," she would whisper. "Night after night, lying awake and feeling the mountains around holding me in, dreaming about it and never letting my folks know. And now I'm afraid. I'm afraid I haven't planned it right, or somebody will read my mind and make me give it all away."

She would cling to him, and he would say, "Don't worry. They're only men, they can't read minds. They can't keep us in."

"No," she would answer then. "It's a good plan. All it needed was you."

The snow began to soften and thunder in great avalanches down the high slopes. In another week the pass would be open. And Joan said it was time. They were married three days later, by the same little teetering minister who had married Esau and Amity, but in the Fall Creek church with the spring sun brightening the dust on the flagstones, and Hostetter to stand up with Len and Joan's father to give the bride away. There was a party afterward. Esau shook Len's hand and Amity gave Joan a kiss and a spiteful look, and the old man got out the jug and passed it around and told Len, "Boy, you've got the finest girl in the world. You treat her right, or I'll have to take her back again." He laughed and thumped Len on the back until his spine ached, and then a little bit after Hostetter found him alone on the back stoop, getting a breath of air.

He didn't say anything for a time, except that it looked like an early spring. Then he said, "I'm going to miss you, Len. But I'm glad. This was the right thing to do."

"I know it was."

"Well, sure. But I didn't mean that. I mean that you're really settled here now, really a part of it. I'm glad. Sherman's glad. We all are."

Then Len knew it had been the right thing to do, just like Joan said. But he could not quite look Hostetter in the face.

"Sherman wasn't sure of you," said Hostetter. "I wasn't either, for a while. I'm glad you've made peace with your conscience. I know better than any of them what a tough thing it must have been to do." He held out his hand. "Good luck."

Len took his hand and said, "Thanks." He smiled. But he thought, I am deceiving him just as I deceived Pa, and I don't want to, any more than I did then. But that was wrong, and this is right, this I have to do—

He was glad that he would not have to face Hostetter any more.

The new house was strange. It was little and old, on the edge of Fall Creek, swept and scrubbed and filled with woman-things provided by Joan's mother and her well-wishing friends, curtains and quilts and tablecloths and bits of rag carpeting. So much work and good will, all for the use of a few days. He had been given two weeks for his honeymoon. And now they were all ready. Now they could cling together and wait together with no one to watch them, with all suspicion set at rest and the path clear before them.

"Pray for Ishmaelites," she told him. "They always come as soon as the pass is open, begging. Pray they come now."

"They'll come," said Len. There was a calmness on him, a conviction that he would be delivered even as the children of Israel were delivered out of Egypt.

The Ishmaelites came. Whether they were the same ones that had come last fall or another band he did not know, but they were gaunter and more starved-looking, more ragged and suffering than he would have believed people could be and live. They begged powder and shot, and Sherman threw in a keg of salt beef, for the sake of the children. They took it. Joan watched them start their slow staggering march back up to the pass before evening, with her hand clasped tight in Len's, and she whispered, "Pray for a dark night."

"It's already answered," he said, looking at the sky. "We'll have rain. Maybe snow, if it keeps getting colder."

"Anything, just so it's dark."

And now the house fulfilled its purpose, giving up the things it had hidden for them safely, the food, the water bags, the blanket packs, the two coarse sheets rubbed with ashes and artfully torn. Len wrote some painful words to Hostetter. "I won't ever tell about Bartorstown, I owe you that. I am sorry. Forgive me, but I got to go back." He left the paper on the table in the front room. They blew out the candles early, knowing they would not be disturbed.

But now Joan's courage failed her and she sat shivering on the edge of the bed, thinking what would happen if they were seen and caught.

"Nobody'll see us," Len said. "Nobody."

He believed that. He was not afraid. It was as though some secret word had been given him that he was beyond harm until he got back to Piper's Run.

"We better go now, Len."

"Wait. They're weak and carrying the young ones. We can catch them easy. Wait till we're sure."

Dark, full night, and a drifting rain. Len's muscles drew tight and his heart pounded. Now it is time, he thought. Now I take her hand and we go.

The road to the pass is steep and winding. There is no one behind us. The rain pours down, and now it is sleet. Now the sleet has turned to snow. The Lord has stretched out his garment to hide us. Hurry. Hurry to the pass, over the steep road and the freezing mud.

"Len, I've got to rest."

"Not yet. Give me your hand again. Now—"

Into the black gut of the pass, with the snow falling and the winter's drifts still piled high where the sun can't reach. Now we can rest a minute, only a minute.

"Len, this looks like it might be a spring blizzard. It could close the pass again before morning."

"Good. Then they can't follow us."

"But we'll freeze to death. Hadn't we better turn back?"

"Haven't you any faith? Can't you see this is being done for us? Come on!"

On and up, across the saddleback and down the other side, going fast, much faster than the slow mule teams with the loaded wagons. Past the camping place, and onto the rocky slope beyond. There is a sound of singing on the wind.

"There. You hear that? Where's those sheets?"

I will put on the garment of repentance. The Ishmaelites have no wagons. They have no cattle to break their legs among the stones. They march all night, away from the haunts of iniquity and back to the clean desert where they do their lifelong penance for the sins of man. I have a penance too. I will do it when it is sent upon me.

Close now, but not too close, in the night and the falling snow. They sing and moan as they go along, into the lower pass, all straggled out in a ragged line. If they look back they will only see two Ishmaelites, two of their own band.

They do not look back. Their eyes are on God.

Down through the winding cut in the rock, and back there in Bartorstown in the monitor room someone is sitting. Not Jones, this isn't his time, but someone. Someone watching the little lights blinking on the board. Someone thinking, There go the crazy Ishmaelites back to the desert. Someone yawning, and lighting a pipe, waiting for Jones to come so he can go home.

Someone with a button close under his fingers, ready to use.

He does not use it.

It is dawn. The Ishmaelites have disappeared in the wind and the blowing snow.

Joan. Joan, get up. Joan look, we're out of the pass.

We're free.

Praise the Lord, who has delivered us from Bartorstown.

TWENTY-NINE

It was a spring blizzard. They survived it, crouched in a hole of the rock like two wild things sheltering together for warmth. It stopped the high pass and covered their tracks, and afterward they fled south along the broken line of the foothills, watchful, furtive, ready to hide at the slightest sign of human life other than their own.

"They'll hunt for us."

"I left a letter. I swore—"

"They'll hunt for us. You know that."

"I reckon they'd have to. Yes."

He remembered the radios, and how the Bartorstown men had kept track of two runaway boys, a long time ago.

"We'll have to be careful, Len. Awfully careful."

"Don't worry." His jaw thrust out, stubborn, bristling with a growing beard. "They ain't going to take us back. I told you, the hand of the Lord is over us. He'll keep us safe."

Piper's Run and the hand of God. Those were the burden of the first days. There was a mist over the world, obscuring everything but a vision of home and a straight path to it. He could see the fields very green with the sun on them, the crooked apple trees with their old black trunks drowned in blossom, the barn and the dooryard, still, waiting, in a warm and golden peace. And there was a path, and his feet were on it, and nothing could stop him.

But there were obstacles. There were mountains, gullies, rocks, cold, hunger, thirst, exhaustion, pain. And it came to him that before he could reach that haven of peace there was a penance to be done. He had to pay for the wrong he had done in leaving it. That was fair enough. He had expected it. He suffered gladly and never noticed the look of doubt and amazement that came into Joan's eyes, shading gradually toward contempt.

The ecstasy of abasement and repentance stayed with him until one day he fell and hurt his knee against a rock, and the pain was pain merely, with no holiness about it. The world rocked around him and fell sharply into place with all the mist cleared out of it. He was hungry and cold and tired. The mountains were high and the prairies wide. Piper's Run was a thousand miles away. His knee hurt like the very devil, and an old growling rebellion rose up in him to say, All right, I've done my penance. Now that's enough.

That was the end of the first phase. Joan began to look at him like she used to. "For a while there," she said, "you weren't much better than a New Ishmaelite, and I began to get scared."

He muttered something about repentance being good for the soul, and shut her up. But secretly her words stung him and made him feel ashamed. Because they were more than partly true.

But he still had to get back to Piper's Run. Only now he realized that the path to it was very long and hard just as the path away from it had been, and that no mystical power was going to get him there. He was going to have to walk it on his own two feet.

"But once we get there," he would say, "we'll be safe. The Bartorstown men can't touch us there. If they denounced us they'd denounce themselves. We'll be safe."

Safe in the fields and the seasons, safe in the not-thinking, not-wanting. A contented mind and a thankful heart. Pa said those were the greatest blessings. He was right. Piper's Run is where I lost them. Piper's Run is where I will find them again.

Only when I think now of Piper's Run I see it tiny and far off, and there is a lovely light on it like the light of a spring evening, but I can't bring it close. When I think of Ma and Pa and Brother James and Baby Esther I can't see them clearly, and their faces are all blurred.

I can see myself, all right, running with Esau across a pasture at night, kneeling in the barn straw with Pa's strap coming down hard on my shoulders. I can see myself as I was then. But when I try to see myself as I will be, a grown man but a part of it again, I can't.

I try to see Joan wearing the white cap and the humility, but I can't see that, either.

Yet I have to get back. I have to find what I had there that I've never had since I left it. I have to find certainty.

I have to find peace.

Then one evening just at sundown Len saw the man driving a trader's wagon with a team of big horses. He crossed a green swell of the prairie, showing briefly on the skyline, and was gone so quickly that Len was not sure he had really seen him. Joan was on her knees making a fire. He made her put it out, and that night they walked a long way by moonlight before he would stop again.

They fell in with a band of hunters—this was safe because the Bartorstown men did not go with the hunters, and Joan made doubly sure. They told a tale of New Ishmaelites to account for their condition, and the hunters shook their heads and spat.

"Them murdering devils," one of them said. "I'm a believing man myself"—and he looked warily at the sky—"but killing just ain't no way to serve the Lord."

And yet you would kill us if you knew, thought Len, to serve the Lord. And he nagged Joan, who had never needed to guard her tongue so rigidly, until she was afraid to speak her name.

"Is it all like this?" she whispered to him, in the privacy of their blankets at night. "Are they all like wolves ready to tear you?"

"About Bartorstown they are. Never tell where you came from, never give them a hint so they could even guess."

The hunters passed them on to some freighters, joining up at a rendezvous point to go south and east with a load of furs and smelted copper. Joan made sure there were no Bartorstown men among them. She kept her tongue tightly between her teeth, looking with doubtful eyes at the tiny sun-baked towns they stopped in, the lonely ranches they passed.

"It'll be different in Piper's Run, won't it, Len?"

"Yes, it'll be different."

Kinder, greener, more fruitful, yes. But in other ways, no, not different. Not different at all.

What is it that lies on the whole land, in the dusty streets and the slow beat of the horse hoofs, in the faces of the people?

But Piper's Run is home.

On a clear midnight he thought he saw a solitary wagon tilt far off, glimmering under the moon. He took Joan and they scurried eastward alone, over river beds drying white in the summer sun, working their way from ranch to ranch, settlement to settlement.

"What do people *do* in these places?" Joan asked, and he answered angrily, "They live."

The blazing days went by. The long hard miles unrolled. The vision of Piper's Run faded, little by little, no matter how he clung to it, until it was so faint he could hardly see it. He had been going a long time on momentum, and now that was running out. And the man on the wagon hounded him all through the summer days, plodding relentlessly out of the vast horizon, out of the wind and the prairie dust. Len's going became more of a running from than a running to. He never saw the face of the man. He could not even be sure it was the same wagon. But it followed him. And he knew.

In September, in a little glaring town lost in a gray-green sea of bear grass and shinnery on the Texas border, he sat down to wait.

"You fool," Joan told him despairingly, "it isn't him. It's only your guilty conscience makes you think so."

"It's him. You know it."

"Why should it be? Even if it is someone from there—"

"I can tell when you're lying, Joan. Don't."

"All right! It is him, of course it's him. He was responsible for you. He was sworn for you to Sherman. What did you think?"

She glared at him, her thin brown hands curled into fists, her eyes flashing.

"You going to let him take you back, Len Colter? Aren't you a man yet, for all that beard? Get on your feet. Let's go."

"No." Len shook his head. "I never realized he was sworn."

"He won't be alone. There'll be others with him."

"Maybe. Maybe not."

"You are going to let him take you." Her voice was shrill, breaking like a child's. "He's not going to take me. I'm going on."

He spoke to her in a tone he had never used before. "You'll stay by me, Joan."

She stared at him, startled, and then came a look of doubt, a stirring of some dark apprehension.

"What are you going to do?"

"I don't know yet. That's what I got to decide." His face had grown stony and hard, impassive as flint. "Two things I'm sure of. I ain't going to run. And I won't be taken."

She stayed by him, quiet, frightened of she knew not what.

Len waited.

193

Two days. He has not come yet, but he will. He was sworn for me.

Two days to think, to stand waiting on the battlefield. Esau never fought this battle, nor Brother James. They're the lucky ones. But Pa did, and Hostetter did, and now it is my time. The battle of decision, the time of choice.

I made a decision in Piper's Run. It was a child's decision, based on a child's dreams. I made a decision in Bartorstown, and it was still a childish decision, based on emotion. Now I am finished with dreams. I am finished with emotions. I have fasted my forty days in the wilderness and I am through with penance. I stand stripped and naked, but I stand as a man. What decision I make I will make as a man, and there will be no turning back from it after it is made.

Three days, to tear away the last sweet sunlit hopes.

I will not go back to Piper's Run. Whichever way I go, it will not be there. Piper's Run is a memory of childhood, and I am finished with memories, too. That door is closed behind me, long ago. Piper's Run was a memory of peace, but no matter which way I go I know now that I will never have peace.

For peace is certainty, and there is no certainty but death.

Four days, to set the stubborn feet firmly on the ground, teaching them not to run.

Because I am finished with running. Now I will stop and choose my way.

Sooner or later a man has to stop and choose his way, not out of the ways he would like there to be, or the ways there ought to be, but out of the ways there are.

Five days, in which to choose.

There were people in the town. It was the time of the fall trading, the hot dead time when the shinnery stands gray and stiff and the bear grass rustles in the wind and every plank of wood is as dry as a cracked bone. They came in from the outlying ranches to barter for their winter supplies, and the traders' wagons were lined up in a row at the end of the one short, dusty street.

All over the land, he thought, it is the time of the fall trading. All over the land there are fairs, and the wagons are pulled up, and the men trade cattle and the women chaffer over cloth and sugar. All over the land it is the same, unchanging. And after the trading and the fair there is the preaching, the fall revival to stock the soul against the winter too. This is the way it is.

He walked the street restlessly, up and down. He stood by the traders' wagons, looking into the faces of the people, listening to their talk.

They have found their truth. The New Ishmaelites have found theirs, and the New Mennonites, and the men of Bartorstown.

Now I must find mine.

Joan watched him from under the corners of her eyelids and was afraid to speak.

On the fifth night the trading was all done. Torches were set up around a platform in the trampled space at the end of the street. The stars blazed bright in the sky and the wind turned cool and the baked earth breathed out its heat. The people gathered.

Len sat on the crushed dry shinnery, holding Joan's hand. He did not notice after all when the wagon rolled in quietly at the other side of the crowd. But after a while he turned, and Hostetter was sitting there beside him.

THIRTY

The voice of the preacher rang out strong and strident. "A thousand years, my brethren. A thousand years. That's what we was promised. And I tell you we are already in that blessed time, a-heading toward the Glory that was planned for them that keeps the way of righteousness. I tell you—"

Hostetter looked at Len in the flickering light of the windblown torches, and Len looked at him, but neither of them spoke.

Joan whispered something that might have been Hostetter's name. She pulled her hand away from Len's and started to scramble around behind him as though she wanted to get to Hostetter. Len caught her and pulled her down.

"Stay by me."

"Let me go. Len—"

"Stay by me."

She whimpered and was still. Her eyes sought Hostetter's.

Len said to both of them, "Be quiet. I want to listen."

"—and except you go as little children, the Book says, you won't never get in. Because Heaven wasn't made for the unrighteous. It wasn't made for the scoffer and the unbeliever. No sir, my brothers and sisters! And you ain't in the clear yet. Just because the Lord has chose to save you out from the Destruction, don't you think for a minute—"

It was on another night, at another preaching, that I set my foot upon the path.

A man died that night. His name was Soames. He had a red beard, and they stoned him to death because he was from Bartorstown.

Let me listen. Let me think.

"—a thousand years!" cried the preacher, thumping on his dusty Book, stamping his boots on the dusty planks. "But you got to work for it! You can't just set down and pay no heed! You can't shirk your bounden duty to the Lord!"

Let it blow through me like a great wind. Let the words sound in my ears like trumpets.

I can speak. A power has been given me. I can kill another man as that boy killed Soames, and free myself.

I can speak again, and lead the way to Bartorstown as Burdette led his men to Refuge. Many will die, just as Dulinsky died. But Moloch will be thrown down.

Joan sits rigid beside me. The tears run on her cheeks. Hostetter sits on the other side. He must know what I am thinking. But he waits.

He was part of that other night. Part of Refuge. Part of Piper's Run and Bartorstown, the one end and the other and in the middle.

Can I wipe it all away with his blood?

Hallelujah!

Confess your sins! Let your soul be cleansed of its burden of black guilt, so the Lord won't burn you again with fire!

Hallelujah!

"Well, Len?" said Hostetter.

They are screaming as they screamed that night. And what if I rise and confess my sin, offering this man as a sacrifice? I will not be cleansed of knowledge. Knowledge is not like sin. There is no mystical escape from it.

And what if I throw down Moloch, with the bowels of fire and the head of brass?

The knowledge will still exist. Somewhere. In some book, some human brain under some other mountain. What men have found once they will find again.

Hostetter is rising to his feet.

"You're forgetting something I told you. You're forgetting we're fanatics too. You're forgetting I can't let you run loose."

"Go ahead," said Len. He stood up, too, dragging Joan with him by the hand. "Go ahead if you can."

They looked at each other in the torchlight, while the crowd stamped and raised the dust and shouted hallelujah.

I have let it blow through me, and it is just a wind. I have let the words sound in my ears, and they are nothing but words, spoken by an ignorant man with a dusty beard. They do not stir me, they do not touch me. I am done with them, too.

I know now what lies across the land, the slow and heavy weight. They call it faith, but it is not faith. It is fear. The people have clapped a shelter over their heads, a necessity of ignorance, a passion of retreat, and they have called it God, and worshiped it. And it is as false as any Moloch. So false that men like Soames, men like Dulinsky, men like Esau and myself will overthrow it. And it will betray its worshipers, leaving them defenseless in the face of a tomorrow that will surely come. It may be a slow coming, and a long one, but come it will, and all their desperation will not stop it. Nothing will stop it.

"I ain't going to speak, Ed. Now it's up to you."

Joan caught her breath and held it in a sob.

Hostetter looked at Len, his feet set wide apart, his big shoulders hunched, his face as grim and dark as iron under his broad hat. Now it was Len's turn to wait.

If I die as Soames died, it will not matter except to me. This is important only because I am I, and Hostetter is Hostetter, and Joan is Joan, and we're people and can't help it. But for today, yesterday, tomorrow, it is not important. Time goes on without any of us. Only a belief, a state of mind, endures, and even that changes constantly, but underneath there are two main kinds—the one that says, Here you must stop knowing, and the other which says, Learn.

Right or wrong, the fruit was eaten, and there can't ever be a going back.

I have made my choice.

"What are you waiting for, Ed? If you're going to do it, go on."

Some of the tightness went out of the line of Hostetter's shoulders. He said, "I guess neither one of us was built for murder."

He bent his head, scowling, and then he lifted it again and gave Len a hard and blazing look.

"Well?"

The people cried and shouted and fell on their knees and sobbed.

"I still think," said Len slowly, "that maybe it was the Devil let loose on the world a hundred years ago. And I still think maybe that's one of Satan's own limbs you've got there behind that wall."

The preacher tossed his arms to the sky and writhed in an ecstasy of salvation.

"But I guess you're right," said Len. "I guess it makes better sense to try and chain the devil up than to try keeping the whole land tied down in the hopes he won't notice it again."

He looked at Hostetter. "You didn't get me killed, so I guess you'll have to let me come back."

"The choice wasn't entirely mine," said Hostetter.

He turned and walked away toward the wagons. Len followed him, with Joan stumbling at his side. And two men came out of the shadows to join them. Men that Len did not know, with deer rifles held in the crooks of their arms.

"I had to do more than talk for you this time," said Hostetter. "If you had denounced me, these boys might not have been able to save me from the crowd, but you wouldn't have grown five minutes older."

"I see," said Len slowly. "You waited till now, till the preaching."

"Yes."

"And when you threatened me, you didn't mean it. It was part of the test."

Hostetter nodded. The men looked hard at Len, clicking the safeties back on their guns.

"I guess you were right, Ed," one of them said. "But I sure wouldn't have banked on it."

"I've known him a long time," said Hostetter. "I was a little worried, but not much."

"Well," said the man, he's all yours."

He did not sound as though he thought Hostetter had any prize. He nodded to the other man and they went away, Sherman's executioners vanishing quietly into the night.

"Why did you bother, Ed?" asked Len. He hung his head, ashamed for all that he had done to this man. "I never made you anything but trouble."

"I told you," said Hostetter. "I always felt kind of responsible for the time you ran away."

"I'll pay you back," said Len earnestly.

Hostetter said, "You just did."

198

They climbed up onto the high seat of the wagon.

"And you," Hostetter said to Joan. "Are you ready to come home?"

She was beginning to cry, in short fierce sobs. She looked at the torchlight and the people and the dust. "It's a hideous world," she said. "I hate it."

"No," said Hostetter, "not hideous, just imperfect. But that's nothing new."

He shook out the reins and clucked to the big horses. The wagon moved out across the dark prairie.

"When we get a ways out of town," said Hostetter, "I'll radio Sherman and tell him we've started back."

Printed in the USA
CPSIA information can be obtained
at www.ICGtesting.com
JSHW082205140824
68134JS00014B/439